THE CLAW

The Ceristen series
Book Three

Verity A. Buchanan

The Claw

The Ceristen Series, Book Three

ISBN: 978-1-64960-212-1
eISBN: 978-1-64960-320-3
Library of Congress Control Number: 2022937619

Cover Design by Hannah Linder Designs
Interior Typesetting by Dentelle Design
Edited by Susanna Maurer

AMBASSADOR INTERNATIONAL
Emerald House
411 University Ridge, Suite B14
Greenville, SC 29601, USA
www.ambassador-international.com

AMBASSADOR BOOKS
The Mount
2 Woodstock Link
Belfast, BT6 8DD, Northern Ireland, UK
www.ambassadormedia.co.uk

The colophon is a trademark of Ambassador, a Christian publishing company.

DEDICATION

To Melissa

whose constitution I have broken many times over the course of this book.

I hope it will stand for a reread.

Being a map of
Legea
The KNOWN WORLD, showing the lands north of the FALLEN CONTINENT as far as EDEL HARTHE and the HAVGEN MOUNTAINS
THE GREY LANDS
EDIVERNEL
EDEL HARTHE
FEARNISH MOUNTAINS
FEARNLAND
TO THE HEN
HAVGEN MOUNTAINS
THE GREAT WASTE
GALTHA RELDA
RIVER DALGANN
HARLAN
HARDTHA
MENEVACE
SEA OF PHERITRA
ERAHAR
CASCADE MOUNTAINS
RAESIR
GONTLAND
EDD RIVER
RODRON
DIRION
ORDEN
EVENA MOUNTAINS
ELERIAN MOUNTAINS
REHIRNE
MATTADON
Territory of the Northern Sunsters
Territory of the Southern Sunsters
RAESIR MOUNTAINS
SATHOEL ARON
MESOREMN
DIRION RIVER
WALK RIVER
RUNNICOR
GLUMINTOR
TERRAGERE
COASTAL SUNSTERS
BAY OF ARAHAD
ARAHAD
ENYDHWYN
HAELOR SEA
TO HAUSS
N
W
E
S

NOTE FROM THE AUTHOR

WHILE THE CONTENT OF MY writing remains clean, I think it is fair to alert my readers that *The Claw* is more emotionally intense than the preceding books in this series. *The Journey* and *The Village* depicted very little on-page violence; *The Claw*'s pages are a little more blood-splattered and tumultuous. *The Claw* is still quite mild by genre standards, and I do my best to under any circumstances avoid gratuity. Nevertheless, based on the reactions of my alpha and beta readers, I would rather provide a heads-up than give anyone whiplash.

But if you can enjoy an Agatha Christie whodunit, you'll find yourself at home in these pages.

VERITY A. BUCHANAN

PART ONE

The Honing of the Blade

CHAPTER I

"IT IS BURNT," DECLARED ISABELLE Thorne.

"I don't see that there is anything wrong with my porridge, Isabelle." Sandy tossed her long, fair plait defiantly over her shoulder and bent over the hearth again. "It may flavor of smoke, but that's naught to a real hungry stomach."

"Well, I should think I know the difference between my porridge and another's," retorted Isabelle.

Sandy glanced up, her cheeks red from both heat and temper. "Indeed? Well, if I've burned the porridge one day out of fifty others, I shouldn't think anyone has cause to complain about it!"

"Girls," said Daren mildly, but with audible rebuke.

Fred rose and beckoned to him. "Come, Daren; it is time we were making for the castle. Farewell, sisters, till this evening."

"Very well." Isabelle sprang up. "We must get the dishes cleared away. Sandy, don't forget you've got to mend that shawl of yours today. Cecelia, would you sweep the floor? It's quite filthy. And goodness, Gwenda, go see what's to do with the knocking at the door! And who'd be calling at this hour of the morning . . . "

Gwenda slid down from the bench and pulled the heavy door open, only to shrink back from the tall cloaked figure who stood on the threshold. The scarlet badge of a mail courier made a gleam of color in the sober study of the sunless morning.

"My land!" gasped Isabelle, paling. "No glad tidings ever came by letter."

The mail courier cast a contemptuous glance around the room. "I have heard this is the house of Frederick Thorne. Is he within?"

"I am Fred Thorne, sir," answered Fred, stepping forward, puzzlement and worry flickering over his face. The courier handed him a letter bound to a neatly tied parcel, whirled, and yanked the door ungraciously shut.

"Open it up, Fred," said Isabelle, coming anxiously to look over his shoulder. "Why, 'tis addressed to Brick Thorne, not Frederick! What can it *mean?*"

Fred broke the seal and unfolded the parchment.

My dearest brother,

How astonished was I to hear rumors of your presence in the east! Truly, I believed that my brother would never return from those wretched regions that he had so foolishly resolved to inhabit—but let us not dwell on the past.

No doubt you wonder how I heard tidings of you at all, but Berda the fur trader is a dealer in many places. Some time after a visit to Orden he came to my doorstep, where he passed the night, as we are old acquaintances. Then he told me that in a small hamlet called Ceristen, he had heard tidings of a family called Thorne! My dear brother, I could scarce believe my ears when I heard it.

But now to the point of the matter: I am delighted to have traced you, my brother, delighted beyond words. And as we are now so close to one another—for I still reside in Delgrass, in the same village of Cobren, so near our place of parting—you cannot object, dear brother, to journeying down the river Dirion for a joyous reunion between myself and your own family. Bring them all, for I long greatly to see your fair wife and all your offspring! I have included all that should be necessary for travel expenses, so your purse may not be inconvenienced by our happy meeting.

Your fond brother,

Robert Thorne

"But why did the mail courier ask for *Frederick* Thorne?" remarked Sandy as Fred scanned the lines of the letter again.

"Oh, that is easy," returned Isabelle. "When he asked about for the house of Brick Thorne, he would have been told the only Thorne here was Frederick. But gracious!" she continued, her eyes widening. "He doesn't even know that our mother is dead. And he thinks that Father is still with us!"

"Only natural," Sandy observed, "when he's heard nothing but a rumor of our existence."

Fred raised his head, a furrow of bewildered thought drawn between his eyes. "What do you think of it, Daren?" he asked.

"I do not know what to make of it," said Daren. "Surely I never knew that our father had a brother, much less where he lived. Do we truly know if this man is our uncle at all?"

"He did have a brother," Fred answered slowly, shaking his head. "I remember that he would speak of him at times. Only I do believe our family used to dwell in Mattadon, not Delgrass."

"It's fishy," was Sandy's succinct comment. She threw her heels up on the table and leaned back. "With Father a stranger and gone all these months anyway, what's any of it to us? Throw the letter in the hearth and go to work."

Isabelle's attention was busy with the attached parcel. "So he did send money after all! Why, this would buy a week's worth of meal."

"Well, we cannot use it for that," said Daren. "If our uncle has truly sent this money for passage down to his home country, it would be wrong to put it to another purpose."

"I suppose!" said Isabelle regretfully.

Cecelia, who stood with arms crossed and pale hair floating loose in the draft from the half-cracked window, had not spoken till now. Her low, clear voice carried over the conversation with a hint of severity. "We can hardly dare assume he is our uncle when we know nothing of him—save the letter."

"True," agreed Fred. "Yet if he is, to scorn his generosity would be rude, and at least we must either use the money he has sent or return it to him. Perhaps one of us alone should go, to see whether he is truly Robert Thorne, and see what may come afterwards."

"Now that is a good decision," said Daren thoughtfully. "As the eldest, you should go, Fred."

Fred nodded. "I will go."

~

Mordred stared after the disappearing rider.

"What is it?" asked Laufeia's voice behind him.

Mordred stirred and looked down at the letter in his hand. "A letter," he answered slowly.

"A letter? From whom?" Laufeia stepped up to his side, frowning.

"'Tis posted from Delgrass." Mordred ripped the missive open and scanned the close-set lines. A sharp cleft darkened his brow, and he read it again, aloud. "'Mordred Kenhelm, you have come to our attention as a suitable candidate for a partner in our—in our *clothier's* trade. We will be most gratified if you accept this offer.'"

"What?" Laufeia uttered.

He repeated the words, the frown deepening all the while.

"What does that mean?" she demanded.

He crumpled it in his fist. "*I* do not know! This is the most ridiculous thing I've ever heard of. How did a clothier's trade learn about me? My very name? How can they know that I am suitable for their 'partner'—I, a mere peasant, one out of a hundred thousand!"

"We did not always live in Orden," said Laufeia suddenly and softly. He looked down at her and saw the hint of worry in her eyes. "Do you think . . . "

"Hush," he said sharply, and turned to go into the house.

"Mordred, if someone wants to make trouble over—well—anything, we must put a stop to it."

"I cannot send them a letter in return, especially if I do not know what their real motives are. It would likely confuse matters rather than settle them."

"Then go to Delgrass. You can travel with Fred; he is going to see his uncle there already. Please, Mordred. Whatever this means, we ought to clear it up."

Mordred sighed. "All right, Laufeia. But you must promise not to worry about me."

Laufeia laughed, weakly. "Me, not worry?"

"Girls! You are so silly." Mordred patted her shoulder. "I can take care of myself. I'll be fine."

~

"Jared."

The wide, warm room hummed gently with morning sounds. Lia's spoon dug zestily against her dish and a cat that was not supposed to be inside sunned itself on the floorboards with a quiet *miaw.*

"Aye, Father?" answered Jared.

"Mordred Kenhelm and Fred are going down to Delgrass," said Arad Earle. "They must pass by way of Cobren, and I would have you accompany them, for your mother's family lives there, as you know. It would be good to hear from them again and know that they are well."

"Aye, Father." Jared did not lift his eyes from his plate.

Anger.

His whole reticent self was averse to the feeling of anger, yet it was in him now. It encompassed him and throbbed, a dull, pervasive raging in his veins. When it had first crept through his being, feeding on itself and mounting with the slow steadiness of the tide, he knew not, but now it burned like the edge of a white-hot blade.

Had it started with the castle work? He had begun to see more of Gallert then . . .

"Good morning, Jared."

It could be just those three words, but the loftiness in the address, the lazy dismissal, was great enough to rankle in Jared's mind for days afterwards. It had merely perplexed and bothered him at first. His cousin had no reason to feel better than him. They were of the same age, both employed in the same busy work at the castle, and their families were no better or worse off than one another. What could Gallert find to reproach?

Then, as the subtle taunts continued over the spring and summer, Jared noticed a certain pattern.

"You can't come down to Orden City?"

"I didn't say I couldn't." Jared bit his lips together imperceptibly. "But I'm working at present, if you didn't see."

"Oh, I see," said Gallert with a thoughtful air. "No, it's quite all right, I see. It's a pity, though, that your parents just think they can tell you everything to do. They keep you working all the time, it seems."

"I like work," retorted Jared, with an uncomfortable sensation that Gallert might be right.

Gallert sighed, as if at Jared's narrow-mindedness. "Well, how about when you're finished? That is, you will be finished at *some* point?"

"I'll have to ask my father. It's almost a day's trip there and back."

Gallert leaned back against the barn wall, his black eyes widening. "Your parents don't let you go where you please without asking permission? Can't you make any decisions of your own?"

Shut up, Jared longed to say to him. He kept his eyes on the pitchfork and thrust it viciously into the hay, the anger soaring higher.

Gallert was not finished. "Don't be angry, Jared. I'm not questioning your parents' judgment. After all, they probably do know best, and if they don't think you're man enough to make your own choices, then maybe you aren't."

"I don't want to go!" Jared had exploded, whirling to face him, the pent-up anger escaping loose for a moment. He realized how much like an excuse it sounded as it left his lips.

"Of course," Gallert agreed, his eyes saying otherwise. He turned with a pitying hitch of his shoulders and left the barn.

That was the first time Jared believed he hated his cousin. But over the six months since, it had hardly been the last. And as the hatred grew and flamed like a poisonous wound, it began to feed another growing anger.

Because, despite how spitefully Gallert made his accusations, he was right, and Jared hated how much he was right. He was tired of being told what to do. He was tired of others presuming his good will and submission. He did not want to feel disloyal to his father and mother, but a quiet, dark, resisting part of him refused to push the anger out. Someday, he resolved again and again, he was going to show Gallert that he was not a spineless puppet but a man.

Maybe now was the time to do it.

CHAPTER 2

FRED STOOD SILENTLY BY THE rail of the little boat as the riverbanks slid past. They had made good time, the captain of the craft told him, since hitting the Dirion River. Now, six days since their departure from Ceristen, he, Mordred, and Jared should be docking at Cobren by evening.

He did not quite know how he felt about the journey so far. It was odd to be idle all the time after so many weeks spent day after day in hard labor, dawn to dusk. It did not sit quite right in his mind to think that, left behind in Ceristen, his family continued to earn their bread with the same difficulty as before.

They were not the only passengers on the boat. There was a old man traveling to his son's house in Mattadon, just south of Delgrass; and two young men, who said that they were sailing as far as the south borders of Mattadon—the conclusion of the boat's journey—whence they would find passage on another down to the coast of the sea. Other than their destination, the latter two spoke very little about their travels or indeed anything at all. The older man was eager to talk, but only about the politics of Mattadon and Delgrass.

Thus, the three from Ceristen had kept mostly to themselves. But Fred, who longed ever for exercise of mind if not of body, had found the others poor companions as well. Jared answered his remarks obediently but briefly, without interest, and as for Mordred, something seemed to be disturbing him. Fred often saw him lost in thought, his brows drawn in a look of pensive worry that hardened into impassivity if he knew anyone was watching.

The noon sun soaked the deck in warm rays, heating the back of his neck. Fred turned and walked to Mordred, who stood nearby.

"Mordred," he said softly, "what is troubling you?"

Mordred's eyes jerked away from the white shoreline, fixating on Fred. He seemed about to deny any trouble, but simply stood, his lips tight. At last he spoke, so quietly that it was all Fred could do to hear him.

"Memories," he said. "That is all."

Maybe it was the truth, Fred thought, looking at him searchingly. Mordred sighed a little and whirled to walk down the deck.

But something rang awry in the younger man's words. It was not the whole truth.

~

"No, we don't want a carriage, thank you." Mordred snapped the words out, clearly losing patience with the wiry, unwashed man who had been pestering them for the past ten minutes, ever since they had disembarked onto the quiet docks.

A sailor came by, trundling a barrel toward the solid cobbles of the street. The carriage-driver hopped out of his way and towards their party of three, heedless of Mordred's spitting eyes. "But masters, I can take you wherever you desire to go. Not many a hired carriage as good as mine, and my horse can get you as far as the border of Rehirne by midnight."

"We are not going to Rehirne," Mordred said angrily; Fred could see that his temper was dangerously near cracking. "We are going to the nearest inn."

"And I can take you there, too, good masters."

"No." Fred stepped forward. "Thank you, but we do not want any carriage. We are well accustomed to walking, and that we shall do."

There was no leeway for argument in his direct, level tone. The man moved off in a huff to seek out less thrifty prey.

"You will be wanting to stay with your aunt?" Fred asked Jared. But the young man shook his head.

"They live outside the village three miles, and it is late already. I will share your room if you do not object."

"No indeed," Fred answered, and went aside to inquire directions to the inn.

~

Mordred woke before the sun had risen, and could not get to sleep again. Dark thoughts were crowding his mind. At last he rose, crossing the room as noiselessly as he could and turning the door-handle with a slight creak.

"Mordred?" Fred's voice sounded drowsily on his ear.

"Shh. 'Tis nothing. Can't sleep; I'm going out to clear my head." Mordred stepped out and shut the door.

~

Bulca was three days into the dratted thaw. It was all very well to have the pleasant sunshine and warmth in the unexpected time of early February, but all the man bent over the muddy flower beds could think about was how the crocuses were coming up too soon.

Wilhelm Dickson, Inspector of the Peace for Delgrass' northern riverside precinct, leaned back on his heels and rubbed a hand across his sweating forehead. "Don't come up, you silly bulbs," he muttered. "This isn't spring."

"Fretting about your flower plants, Dickson?" came a lazy voice behind him.

"No concern of yours," returned Inspector Dickson shortly, rising and turning to face his fellow inspector James Harris. "I like to see them bloom, that's all."

"For an inspector, you are one softie." James Harris chuckled and walked back into the small house.

Inspector Dickson swiped an annoyed hand across his brow again, wiping away the smear of dirt that he suspected was there. Some days Harris was bearable, and other days Inspector Dickson wished they had been assigned fifty miles apart.

"I am not a softie," he muttered, following his partner into the house. "My life is not bound up in flowers, either."

He sighed. Harris thought it was funny, that was all. He had no idea he was being annoying. And for that reason, Inspector Dickson endeavored to put up with it.

Harris was puttering in the kitchen area, banging pots in a pile as he tried to find a clean one. "Fried eggs, Dickson?"

"Where on earth did you get eggs?"

"Picked 'em up off a lass in the market yesterday."

Inspector Dickson slapped his forehead. "Throw them out, Harris. They're bound to be rotten. Nobody goes selling eggs in the slowest part of laying season."

"She said they were laying extra because of the thaw . . . " Harris mumbled grumpily.

"For an Inspector, you are one gull," Dickson muttered, unable to resist. He snatched up the eggs and set them in a cloth, to bury outside later.

The door shuddered under the impact of a knock, and Inspector Dickson looked up. "Harris, that thing is about to burst off its hinges.

Have you—never mind." He stalked over to the door and yanked it open.

"What is it, sir?" he asked, seeing the short man waiting outside, a grimy apron over his tunic and pudgy arms folded over a paunch.

The man chewed his lip a moment. "I'm from Cobren. Just some miles south of 'ere."

"Yes," Inspector Dickson assented. "I know where Cobren is."

The visitor nodded again. "I'm the innkeeper; 'ave a hostel by name of the *Fisherman*. We need the Inspector there," he pursued, creased eyes darting up under the brows in a kind of confidential, almost ghoulish grimness. "It's murder."

"Murder?" Inspector Dickson stared past him at the sunshine that suddenly seemed less bright.

He looked down at the other man. "Are you sure?"

He wouldn't be pulled out all the way down to Cobren for a tavern brawl gone bad or someone taken ill in bed.

"Fellow stabbed through the heart," answered the innkeeper. "Nasty scratches all over his face, too. Don't know who did it, but nobody's left the inn since the night before."

Inspector Dickson turned back into the house and swept up his long knife, buckling it around his waist. He picked up a satchel and slung it on his shoulder. "You are sure?"

"No one passed the door anyhows," said the man. "The dog barks like a mad thing if they do, and it wakes me up. An' if they climbed out a window, they sure didn't leave no footprints in the snow."

Inspector Dickson walked into the kitchen. "I've no idea how long I'll be gone," he said to Harris. "It might be the morning, it might be three days. You handle things."

"Right," said Harris casually, giving his porridge a flailing stir.

Inspector Dickson followed the innkeeper out the door.

~

The coppery scent of blood hung in the common room. It was the first thing Inspector Dickson noticed as he stepped under the lintel.

"Stinks, don't it?" grunted the innkeeper. He stomped over to the far wall and threw open a pair of shutters. Light streamed in, and Inspector Dickson saw the body on the floor.

He was no stranger to sickening sights, not after eleven years in the law enforcement. But he had never seen one quite like this.

"Scratches, you said," he muttered, striding across the room.

"Aye, quite the scratches, ain't they?" agreed the innkeeper.

"It looks like someone ripped his face open!" Inspector Dickson studied the bloody tears, three of them, ripping sideways across the dead face. "Who was he?"

"Don' know." The man shrugged. "He took a room last night, didn't give me his name though."

Not good. With the man's face disfigured like that, there had better be someone who recognized him here or there was no way he'd be finding out.

"Look here." The innkeeper had left the room and was returning now, prodding someone in front of him. "I caught this lad and his friend prowling round earlier. Thought you might want to—"

"I'll talk to all the guests, later," said Inspector Dickson, giving barely a glance up as he walked around the common room. "Just see that no one leaves." *It shouldn't be difficult to determine the culprit here. Most likely a fight. Someone will have heard the noise going on.*

He hoped.

~

"Send them in, please." Inspector Dickson slid a chair across the rattling floorboards, in front of the small writing table, and stepped around it to seat himself in the one already placed opposite. "One at a time."

The innkeeper, who gave his name as Galesper, had proposed Inspector Dickson summon all the tenants to the common room as a body and hector them for the truth, with the grisly atmosphere of the corpse hanging over their heads to presumably incentivize confession. This Inspector Dickson had adamantly turned down. All he wanted, he maintained, was to talk to people. If Galesper could simply send them to him—

"Will you be wanting a room of your own, sir?"

Inspector Dickson glanced up, stifling impatience at the delay. "I should hope not. But you may prepare one for me, if you want, in case of need. Now, if you would see to the guests?"

The back room, warm with the diffused heat from the kitchen fire, offered no light beyond a musty, ill-kept window, but it was enough to write by. Alone with the sound of the innkeeper's retreating footsteps, Inspector Dickson withdrew pen and parchment from his satchel, arranged them neatly, and tapped his fingers thoughtfully against the parchment's edge.

When the innkeeper reentered, he was leading a man who seemed slightly familiar.

"This here's the one who was slinking round," said Galesper, pushing him forward. The young man, tall and cold-faced, jerked away at the touch.

"Thank you," said Inspector Dickson tiredly. It was apparent the innkeeper had found his suspicion and was not going to let Inspector Dickson ignore it.

"But see here," persisted the man, edging forward and pointing down. "See that?"

Inspector Dickson saw it. There was a dark stain imprinted on the young man's boots, traveling up to the knees of his trousers. "I will attend to it," he said with barely concealed annoyance.

"He had him a friend, too," said Galesper.

"Send him in later," said Inspector Dickson between his teeth.

Reluctantly, the innkeeper trailed out.

"What do you want to know?"

The young man had spoken, his voice cold and arrogant as his face.

"Little enough," said Inspector Dickson with equanimity. "Your name, if you will give it."

"I am—" He hesitated. "Mordred Kenhelm."

"You are young. Twenty, maybe?" Perhaps some simple conversation would put him more at ease.

"Eighteen." His chin tilted up in aloof withdrawal.

So be it, thought Inspector Dickson resignedly. "Now, considering that you appear to have a bloodstain on your clothing, perhaps you might explain to me what you've been doing this morning."

"I did not kill him," Mordred snapped.

"I said nothing of the kind," said Inspector Dickson, trying to remain patient. "However, if you don't want people to say you did, you had better tell me everything you *did* do."

"Very well." If possible, Mordred's chin lifted higher still. The disdain in his voice could have frozen molten metal.

Inspector Dickson's pessimism increased by the second. He had talked to enough men who believed that the law wanted to see every soul behind bars to know what he was facing. The fact that the young man's resentful attitude came with less outright resistance and more civilized antagonism provided no encouragement whatever.

Mordred continued, his voice clipped, his gray eyes hard. "I woke this morning; I could not sleep. So I left my room and wandered around. I came down to the common room and tripped over . . . over that."

He broke off sharply, and Inspector Dickson scrutinized his expression in that moment of hesitation.

"How long were you roaming around?"

"I do not know." His tone suggested that it was a stupid question. "Half an hour?"

"And how long has it been since you found this body?"

"That was near sunrise, and it must be noon now."

Inspector Dickson reviewed it in his head. *The blood was still wet.* "Did you hear anything like a scuffle? Weapons, crashes?"

"Naught like that," returned Mordred coolly.

"And that is all to your story?" He dropped the question simply enough, but the thrust of intent lay behind it. For he knew there was more; the innkeeper must have found Mordred at or near the body, and had also spoken of a "friend."

Mordred shrugged. "All that needs to be told."

Inspector Dickson twitched one eyebrow up and shook his head.

Mordred's jaw clenched. "As I was getting up, I saw a friend of mine entering behind me. He—he came to me and we spoke a while, discussing what to do. Then that innkeeper came up behind us like a sneaking fox, pulled us apart, and ordered us out of 'his common room'."

Inspector Dickson considered. It could have been this young man. 'Twould be, in fact, convenient if it was. His story was full of gaps in all the right—or wrong—places, and had been told in a haughty way that almost suggested he was lying. Some inspectors would probably arrest him now, particularly considering the telling bloodstain on his breeches.

Unfortunately, Inspector Dickson had too much respect for the law for that. So far he had nothing to contradict Mordred's story, and given it were true, it was nigh impossible to trip over a wounded body and not taint oneself with blood. And in such a case, it was no wonder if one should grow defensive about it.

"What is your friend's name?" he asked, deciding it was time he got another perspective on the morning, if an equally biased one.

Mordred's statue-stiff face cracked with an unambiguously threatening look. "Frederick Thorne."

Quick to change his moods as a summer sky, thought Inspector Dickson, rising. *A hot head under that cold look, maybe.* "Would you stay here a moment?" he asked, and walked to the door where he called for Galesper, who appeared almost instantly.

"Bring Frederick Thorne here," he said.

A short while later the door opened to admit a second man, older and quieter in bearing than the first. His gaze was steady and direct, but a tenseness flitted through it as he glanced at Mordred. "You asked for me, sir?" he asked.

"Aye, thank you. Please, sit down." He gestured to a slatted chair near Mordred's. "I am Wilhelm Dickson, Inspector of the Peace in this region. You are Frederick Thorne?"

"You may call me Fred," responded the other with a nod.

"Well, then, Fred, I am inquiring about the murder this morning. You rose early yourself, I understand. Did you hear any sounds of brawling?"

"No, sir. I did not rise as early as Mordred, in any case. I came down to the common room but a moment after he found the man."

"Ah, yes. About that. What happened there?"

"I . . . sir, what is there to tell? I woke and left to see where Mordred might be, and when I came into the common room he was getting up from the floor."

"You see," Mordred cut in. "I had nothing to do with it, but he certainly had even less than I did."

Inspector Dickson turned to face him. "Your desire to protect your friend is admirable," he said. "However, I would appreciate no interruptions while I am trying to talk to him."

A slight flush came to Mordred's high cheekbones. He shifted away. "As you please."

"Now, Fred. Mordred says you spoke for some time after finding one another?"

"Aye."

Inspector Dickson had expected more elaboration. "About what . . . ?"

"I—truly, it was naught. Naught to concern anyone."

He allowed his eyebrow to twitch up again. "No?"

Fred looked at Mordred. "Truly, sir."

"Nonetheless, I am afraid I can't know that myself. If you would please tell me what you discussed?"

Mordred stood up, knocking his chair over with the sharp movement. "He was calming me," he said, and strode across the room to stare out the window.

Fred met Inspector Dickson's eyes pleadingly, and though Inspector Dickson could not read his unspoken message, one thing was clear.

I am getting nothing out of him while Mordred remains in here at least.

He looked over to the window. "Mordred Kenhelm, you may go. I have nothing else to ask you."

Mordred whirled and stormed out.

"It was as he said," Fred explained in his quiet voice, looking at Inspector Dickson. "He was distraught, so I sought to comfort him; that was all. Yet his pride would not stand for me to say it in his hearing."

"No matter," Inspector Dickson muttered. "You may go as well, Fred Thorne. I suppose you did not recognize this dead man?"

"I do not think I ever saw him. Or at least, never well enough to recognize him under those slashes."

"Ask your friend the same for me, if you will. If this is not to prove an easy matter, someone must identify him or I'll have to abandon the business altogether. But it seems I may be able to deal with it quickly."

"Sir," Fred exclaimed, hesitating as he moved towards the door. "You cannot mean that you suspect him—us?"

Inspector Dickson shrugged. "I do not suspect you any more than the others so far. What I mean is that the man was killed by one of the people in this inn, and there are only a few of you to choose among. It cannot be hard to determine the killer."

~

Inspector Dickson uncurled his aching fingers from around the pen, pressed them to his aching forehead, and leaned back in the chair where he had been sitting for the past hour.

He had assumed he would get more help in talking to the other inn guests. He had not.

Not that there had been a great many to ask. One maid, poor terrified lass, a sea captain's bride who was going down to join him in Pheth-Pirr on the coast of Arahad. A grave young lad who had accompanied Fred Thorne and Mordred Kenhelm, named Jared Earle. They had both given him the same information: a sound night's sleep and no recognition of the body.

The gruff man of about forty, on the other hand, told Inspector Dickson bluntly that he hadn't slept all night, nor heard a single sound but the creaking house. So no one had heard a brawl of any kind, not to mention that no one bore any indication of injury. And so, while simple manslaughter was not yet written off the list, it was far less likely.

Murder. Not pleasant to think about, and much harder to pin down.

He turned back to the man in front of him, the last one in the inn. "Excuse me, I was lost in thought. You said you woke early, Mr. Wilson?"

"Yes, sir," said the other. His brown hair and beard jiggled with his nod. "I always wake up early, at least a few hours before dawn this time of year. So I sat down to write a letter to my sister, and I was but half through when I heard footsteps and the servant lad poked in to say that someone had been killed and we weren't to leave."

"Nothing disturbed you?" Inspector Dickson asked tiredly. "No scuffling or clashes?"

"No, sir. I thought something might have woken me, for it was a bit sudden, the waking, but it couldn't have been a loud or long sound."

Inspector Dickson noted it down. Not helpful for now, but who knew?

"Do you sicken at the sight of blood, man?"

"No, sir."

"Good. Come on into the common room. I would like you to see the corpse."

Gregory Wilson followed him under the low lintel, out into the room now shot with long beams of afternoon sun.

"Do you recognize him?" he asked.

There was a moment of silence.

"N-no," Gregory Wilson stuttered. His face was pale, his hands shaking.

"Are you sure?" Inspector Dickson asked, jerking him away so that they faced.

Gregory looked everywhere but his eyes. "Y-yes, no, I mean yes. Yes! I am sure. I've never seen him, never."

Inspector Dickson let go of him, shaking his head slightly. "Mr. Wilson, you are lying."

"I'm not!" cried Gregory, his voice rising shrilly.

Inspector Dickson half-turned, and then spun on his heel to face him squarely. "Mr. Wilson, you are lying to me. You've obviously seen the man before. You are at present under more suspicion than anyone in this hostel. I give you one day to tell me everything you know, and then I will arrest you."

So saying, he left a stricken Gregory Wilson and strode off to see the innkeeper about his promised room.

CHAPTER 3

INSPECTOR DICKSON TRIMMED THE TRAILING wick and relit the candle, seating himself once again at the small table, which Galesper had obligingly transferred to his new quarters upon request. He scratched a piece of wax free of the stack of papers in front of him and smoothed them out.

It was so much easier to think through things when he had noted them down and reread them half a dozen times. Odd things jumped out at one, things he would have forgotten and never considered again . . .

He stared thoughtfully at the name written at the top of one sheet. That was curious. Perplexing. Maybe it had nothing to do with the murder, but still!

Slowly, Inspector Dickson got up and walked down the hall.

The room he entered was empty except for one person, who sat with a candle burning on the window beside him and a pen in his hand. He looked up as the door opened.

"Yes?" The tone, cool and insolent, sheared through Inspector Dickson's guard and he bit back a cutting retort with difficulty.

"Mordred Kenhelm. Where are your companions?"

"Dining below. I am finished already."

"Well, 'tis no matter. I was here to speak to you."

"Speak away," said Mordred distantly.

"Your last name . . . Kenhelm . . . that is not a common one."

He knew he had touched something, for Mordred's shoulders suddenly stiffened and he stood up, turning his back to look at the dark windowpanes.

"I have heard of it as a noble's surname—"

"Be quiet," said Mordred harshly, not turning around.

"You do not have call to be so rude."

"Is this your concern? No, it is not. Kindly leave."

"I was merely curious! It is a peculiar point, for you do not seem wealthy."

"A man of better sense would have kept your prying questions to himself."

"Maybe. All the same, Mordred Kenhelm, I would give a good deal to know who you are and what you are up to."

"Up to!" Mordred cried angrily, whirling. "I am up to nothing. All I wish to do is journey on, conclude my business, and return home. I would give a good deal to know why *you* cannot determine the culprit and let the rest of us be."

Inspector Dickson's jaw tightened at the obvious insult to his competency. "My apologies for such painful questions, and I will take my leave now."

"Thank you," said Mordred with a mocking inflection and a slight bow.

How is it possible for a man to be so infuriating? Inspector Dickson slammed the door shut, but that did little to release his pent-up anger.

Even after the sting of the conversation had faded away and he was in his own room again, he could not shake the sense of dissatisfaction, of unease. He leafed through the scrawled notes, letting his finger rest on Gregory's name.

"Either I'll see him tomorrow or I won't," he murmured aloud. "If he's guilty, he may come with a false explanation or he may not; but if he's innocent, he won't sit for an unjust accusation." He sighed heavily.

"I don't think he is guilty," he admitted to the room. "Or do I? I don't know what to think any more. None of this is working out the way it should, so tangled, so confusing . . . I need to sleep. Things will look better in the morning."

~

"Up you get, Dickson."

Someone was prodding his shoulder. Inspector Dickson groaned and sat up. "Don't you know how to leave a man alone—Murcod!"

The man standing over him grinned. "Thought I'd come see what my childhood friend was up to."

Inspector Dickson reached up to rub the back of his neck disbelievingly. "You came all the way down from the north of Rehirne to see your childhood friend on a whim?"

"Of course, Dickson. No! My father sent me down here three days gone to a smith he knows, says it's time I was out earning my own way in the world and not putting a strain on his purse any longer. Well"—he shrugged—"what's the first thing I hear this morning but that Inspector Wilhelm Dickson is down this way looking into a gory murder."

Inspector Dickson's shoulders slumped. "That's right."

"Come on now," said Murcod cheerfully, slapping his back. "It can't be that bad."

"Oh, but it is." Inspector Dickson got up and pulled his boots on. "You see, Murcod, I came here and I thought this was simple. But it's not. Instead of a quick drunken fight heard by the whole inn, I've got a sly fellow who goes around murdering people with less noise than a mouse, who could be one of six different people, one of them so maddening I could happily throw him in the river."

"You'll solve it, Dickson." Murcod patted his shoulder reassuringly. "You've solved everything that ever came your way. Come, I have an hour before I need to report to the smithy. Tell me about it all."

Inspector Dickson consented reluctantly, but as he told it aloud to Murcod's eager and sympathetic ears, he felt some of the anxiety ebb away.

"This Mordred Kenhelm," Murcod interrupted at one juncture. "That sounds like a Rehirnish name to me."

"What, Kenhelm?" asked Inspector Dickson in surprise.

"No, Mordred. It's Rehirnish all right."

"But Kenhelm, that's Dirionian." Inspector Dickson shook his head. "Besides being maddening, he's maddeningly curious. What is a poor lad with a Rehirnish name doing with the surname of a nobleman?"

"He is a nobleman!" said Murcod, getting excited. "A nobleman's son, and his father disowned him so he wanders around, penniless—"

"Eight," said Inspector Dickson suddenly.

"What?"

"It's eight people, not six. I didn't think of the innkeeper and the servant boy. Drat it! And the innkeeper could have lied about no one leaving the inn . . . oh, drat."

"Why would he?" asked Murcod. "If he murdered him, then he'd hardly have a reason to hide that someone left the inn. It'd be someone new for you to chase after. If he didn't, he still wouldn't have a reason."

"None we know of," said Inspector Dickson pessimistically.

"You're too cynical, Dickson. That's your problem. You won't trust anybody or anything."

"You try finding a murderer sometime!" retorted Inspector Dickson.

"If he's Rehirnish," said Murcod, returning to Mordred again, "maybe I've met him before. Do you suppose I could see him?"

"Of course you could see him! Not that he'll be happy about it, I daresay. Whatever you do, don't mention my name or he'll likely throw you out."

Murcod disappeared; Inspector Dickson transferred his attention to his notes.

~

Murcod came in whistling.

"It went . . . well, I take it?" said Inspector Dickson, looking up dubiously.

"Oh yes," said Murcod, sitting down. "He was quite pleasant, really."

"I daresay we all needed a good night's sleep." Inspector Dickson was relieved that Murcod had not been insulted, and the slightest bit jealous.

"I came in," Murcod went on, "breezily saying, 'Hello!' And they all looked up like—like I'd come from the moon.

"'Who are you?' asked the handsome young man in the corner, not sounding like he was sure he wanted to know anyone like me.

"So I stammered and fumbled, because I really couldn't tell them who I was, at least not to explain what I was doing here. But he got up as kind as you please, saying, 'It's all right; perfectly natural to make a mistake like that.' They'd decided I was a guest who had mistaken my room, and, well, I let them think that. We had a friendly chat. He was writing to his sister and brother, he told me. Apparently, they all hail from a little hamlet near Orden City."

"Orden! But, impossible. That doesn't fit with anything!" Inspector Dickson scratched his head. "Murcod, this is beginning to bother me.

How does someone with the names of a Dirionian lord and a Rehirnish man end up in a hamlet near *Orden City*?"

"If I could tell you that, Dickson, I'd be a seer—or a dreamer."

"Maybe he said something else, something that would explain it."

"I feel like a real snoop now," Murcod muttered, a sheepish smile poking at the corners of his mouth. "Well, let me see. I tried to avoid the subject of the murder, but he, that is, the young fellow, Mordred, got us on it anyway. We talked about you a little."

"Oh? What did he say?" Inspector Dickson braced for the worst.

"Not much. He seemed dismissive of you overall. Said rather lightly that you didn't see eye to eye."

"I should say . . . "

"Let me see. I asked what he was down here for, and that was when he clammed up. 'Nothing,' he said, and stared most forbiddingly into space.

"Naturally, I dropped that. He mentioned that his friend Fred Thorne had just been engaged to be married . . . "

"I did not need to know that."

Murcod looked mildly hurt. "You wanted me to tell you."

"Not utterly irrelevant details, and that was about Fred Thorne, not Mordred. You've told me enough that he'll be more than furious if he ever finds out."

"He will not," Murcod promised. "To be honest," he went on after a moment of silence, "if he is Rehirnish, then . . . you know what, Dickson?"

"What?"

"Dickson, I think he's an orphan."

Inspector Dickson's eyebrows arched. "Indeed."

"He didn't speak of parents at all; the only family he mentioned were the younger brother and sister. And I happened to mention that I'd lived in Rehirne for the past ten years, and he—he looked at me rather queerly. A startled, you might say nervous look. Then he changed the subject pointedly. So . . . "

"You may well be right," Inspector Dickson mused. "But it is no use to know, at any rate not now. If I could but know who the dead man was!"

"But you will—soon."

"Yes, soon." Inspector Dickson twirled the quill pen pensively between his fingers. "I hope. Till then, I honestly don't know of anything else I can do."

~

Inspector Dickson shut his eyes. Hours of poring over the close-written sheets of parchment had developed a fierce headache and no answers. Evening was closing in. Where was Gregory Wilson?

He was tense, the palms of his hands damp. *'Tis only the waiting,* he told himself. *It is not as though the fate of Legea rests upon this one question.*

No, he answered reluctantly. *But I want the waiting to be over all the same.*

Why are there three people from a little village in Orden coming down to Delgrass?

It is not your business. Look what happened when you got curious about the name.

He sighed, got up, and paced around the room. Dark shadows veiled the corners and pushed against the little candle-flame burning valiantly on the table. Out the window, a wavy sickle moon gleamed over the snow.

He undid the window latch and let the panes swing apart with a click. Cold air flooded the stuffy room, and the keen scent of an oncoming storm filled his nostrils. The thaw was over, winter blowing back home to claim its own.

"Inspector Dickson."

The voice came like a stuttering breath behind him. Inspector Dickson whirled.

"Mr. Wilson?"

"I will—I will tell you."

"Very well." Inspector Dickson waited.

"Not now," the man stammered. "May I have the night to think about things? It . . . it is a long story, and I am not certain what I remember."

What? Inspector Dickson cried inwardly. "Yes," he said. "Think on it, write down what you remember. Bring it to me by noon tomorrow; I will not wait longer than that."

"Aye, then, sir." The door creaked on its hinges as Gregory Wilson hauled it slowly closed.

Inspector Dickson sat down. Then he slammed his fist down as hard as he could on the table top.

CHAPTER 4

INSPECTOR DICKSON WOKE TO PALE light glinting off the snow. The storm had come; the window was white with frost and frozen shut, and the room chilled. He hurried shivering across the room to light the fire, which had died away to embers sometime during the night, and left to seek out some breakfast.

And, hopefully, Mr. Wilson.

Yesterday the servant boy had brought him his noon meal after he failed to show up for breakfast at all. He had come down late for dinner as well. As he entered this morning, however, the other guests were seated at the tables, eating and talking to one another. Mordred Kenhelm, notably sitting alone, looked up, and met his eyes briefly. Then, with the merest of shrugs, Mordred's eyes narrowed, and he looked away.

Inspector Dickson spun around forcefully and found an empty corner to sit in.

"Some storm last night, sir," said Galesper, hurrying to supply him with a plate and mug.

"Was it? I slept through it all, I suppose," replied Inspector Dickson absently.

"Aye, started around moonset it did, and didn't let up till dawn this morn. Howling wind like a pack of wolves. See them drifts? They're up higher than the houses in some places. Anybody had cattle out last night, they're dead."

"We may hope that no person was out in it then, either," muttered Inspector Dickson.

He noticed that Fred Thorne and Jared Earle were not far from Mordred, and also Houk, the older man. The sea captain's wife and Gregory Wilson, however, were not to be found. Inspector Dickson satisfied his hunger and leaned back, rolling his empty cup between his hands and half-listening to the conversation between Fred and Jared Earle.

" . . . no, you are right, Jared. I do not want to wait much longer myself. Perhaps the inspector might be persuaded to let you leave for a short time."

"It is not as if I am days away from them either," Jared said, uncharacteristic frustration coloring his level voice. "They are not expecting me, true, but I am tired of being held here like a prisoner."

"Aye." Fred laid a calming hand on Jared's arm. "In truth, I am already missing my own family. Perhaps I should have remained at home and ignored the letter."

Inspector Dickson got up and walked over to them. "I am sorry," he said, and they turned to look startled at him, "that I could not help but hear your conversation just now. And I am still more sorry to be hindering you from your travels. As you know, there are no guards blocking you from fleeing these walls. I could fetch some, but I have not seen the need to do so, as none of you have tried to flee at all. If you have business to carry out in this town, you have my leave to take care of it. Only be back before the sun sets today, if you please. If you have not returned then, I have men at my disposal whom I *will* send out after you."

Fred Thorne bent his head in respect. "Thank you for your trust, sir. With your leave, then, I will depart, and Jared as well—and Mordred?" He ended in a question.

Mordred looked up, and rested his palms carefully on the table in front of him. "You may take this letter and post it," he said, shrugging towards a folded paper beside him. "It explains where I am and why. If they want to come talk to me, let them."

Fred picked up the letter, and Jared followed him out the door. Inspector Dickson watched them leave, wondering idly where they were going, and stood still there for some time, lost in thought.

Recollecting himself, he glanced down at Mordred, studying the face that had so antagonized him two days before—the curiously thin but sensitive mouth, the gray eyes cold and closed, and the unruly lock of hair licking at his forehead. Such a proud face, he thought. Outwardly impassive, yet so impetuous and unpredictable the disposition that burned behind it . . .

Mordred looked up.

"You wanted something?" he asked.

"I, ah, no." Annoyed to be caught staring, Inspector Dickson brushed hurriedly by, when the thought suddenly came to him.

He turned and strode past Mordred again to the innkeeper, who was leaning against the doorframe and polishing a spoon on his sleeve. "Gregory Wilson has been down, hasn't he?"

"Nay."

"But he usually rises early."

"That he has these past few days," assented Galesper, his eyes opening widely. "Suppose he's—"

But Inspector Dickson was already running back toward the stairs.

I am so stupid. Of course he would run away the first opportunity I give him. Angrily he turned the handle and flung the door open.

There he stopped. A sickening feeling washed through him, heavy with the bitterness of failure and the dread of unknown consequences.

He walked again slowly forward and lifted the blood-soaked coverlets away from Gregory Wilson's still body. The red gashes across his face twisted the pleasant, puzzled features into a nearly unrecognizable grimace.

"I was wrong," he whispered, laying a hand over the dark, oozing patches that marred the doublet. "Forgive me."

A medley of emotions smote him with cruel force, and he sank shuddering to his knees by the bed. Anger at his rash assumption, grief for the man who would never stir and breathe again, despair over the words that he did not and never could know. The words that might have stopped this killer already . . .

It was there that Murcod found him, kneeling by the dead man's side, the tears running unchecked down his face.

"Dickson," he said quietly, laying a hand on his shoulders, "what on earth is it?"

"I don't know," answered Inspector Dickson huskily, standing to his feet. "He is dead, dead without reason. Alive and whole yesterday, and because of my failing he is dead.

"I should have pressed him. I should have made him tell me. Now he cannot, and there is no one else. I don't know what he knew, but it was something that might have helped, something to go upon. I've nothing now, Murcod. I should give up on it now, go back to Bulca. I simply can't find out."

Murcod said nothing; he gave him no platitudes, none of his usual cheery sentiments. He seemed to understand that this was not the time for optimism, and Inspector Dickson took comfort from his silence.

But then he spoke. "Dickson, you can't give up. Not yet. Did he write anything down? Maybe the murderer left something behind him. It's not time for you to drop hope yet."

Inspector Dickson stared ahead, the weight of loss and despair subsiding into something grimmer and resolved. Lifting a hand, he dashed the dampness from his cheeks. "You are right, Murcod." He walked to the door. "Have a look around."

He caught Galesper in the kitchen, jerked him about. "When Fred Thorne and Jared Earle return," he said, "send them to me at once." Then he turned and mounted the stairs.

~

"Gregory Wilson is dead."

Mordred set his pen down and looked up. "Who?"

"One of the boarders here."

"Oh." Mordred took out his knife and began to methodically trim the edge of the quill. "I am sorry to hear it." The dismissal was evident in his attitude.

It took all Inspector Dickson had not to snatch the pen out of the man's hand. "May I speak to you about last night?"

"I had nothing to do with it," said Mordred without looking up.

Inspector Dickson strode angrily across the room and halted in front of him, his voice hard and compelling. "I do not care whether you had nothing to do with it. What you should care about is that there is a man lying in the room next to yours who will never speak or laugh again, whose family will never see their father, son or brother; and that the man who killed him is still walking around free without any qualms to kill again! It is your concern, Mordred Kenhelm, whether you like it or not, and I must have your help if I am to do my own duty."

Mordred flinched. “I see,” he said softly, in acquiescence if not apology. “Well, all I can tell you is I slept soundly last night. I heard nothing peculiar and certainly did not prowl the halls trying to kill anyone.”

Inspector Dickson let out a sigh, the sense of hopelessness dragging on his heart again. Even the dart in Mordred’s last words did not prick him. Were they all to be like this?

Someone is lying. Why can I not find out who?

He left silently, hesitated in front of Houk’s door, lacking the will to open it and be disappointed yet again.

“Dickson!” Murcod called, emerging from Gregory Wilson’s room. “Nay, you’re busy. But when you have done, come in here. I found something—I think.”

~

Murcod was delving into the cobwebbed corner behind the bed when Inspector Dickson came in. “Hullo,” he said, scrambling up. “How did it all go?”

“I don’t know,” said Inspector Dickson honestly. “Mordred was no help, not that I suppose I could have expected him to be. Mistress Syrinna told me that she woke up in the middle of the night and saw a huge man walking past her door, eyes like fire and the face of a mountain troll. I told her that was definitely a nightmare.”

Murcod laughed.

“As for Houk, he was sleeping when I came in, and none too happy to be woken. It seems he has trouble sleeping at night often, so I asked him if he had heard anything.” Inspector Dickson snorted bitterly. “Of course not. The wind was high, the storm was battering his window, there was naught possible for him to hear!”

He dropped down on the chair in the middle of the room. "Oh, Murcod. One of them is a murderer. One of them is lying to me. How long is this going to go on? Until everyone in this hostel is dead?"

Murcod dropped his gaze, silent. "Dickson, do you know what bothers me?" he asked at last.

"Hm?"

"None of them have tried to leave. You said it had to be someone in the inn who did it. Well, everyone in the inn has just stayed here. I know you ordered them to, but if I'd done a murder I wouldn't wait for the Inspector of the Peace to find out it was me! I'd hightail it out of the country and run away to Arahad or something." He hesitated. "Am I making sense? What I mean, Dickson, is they're not inhabitants of Cobren. Not as far as you or I know, right? Naught is keeping them here."

"Aye." Inspector Dickson tapped the arm of the chair distractedly. "The innkeeper is the only one who—"

He leaped up. "Fred Thorne! He and Jared. I let them leave this morning. What was I thinking? I'll never see them again, will I!"

"Dickson, slow down. What are you talking about?"

Inspector Dickson lowered himself again. "I don't know. I was leaping for the worst, I suppose; I let them leave, really. They hadn't asked me yet, although they were going to do so. Still, they did go, and if they don't return, I'll send out men to search for them directly."

"If they do return?"

"Then—I don't know. Murcod, even if I were mistaken about the first night, and someone had left the inn, no one could have done it in the storm! Not unless he had a wish to die. Maybe it is the innkeeper; though whatever reason he could have is beyond me . . . "

"Maybe," suggested Murcod, "this murderer had several victims, and he got them all in one place so he could kill them together. That's why he didn't leave, because he had to kill them all first."

Inspector Dickson groaned. "Fanciful, but possible. In that case, how many victims do you propose he had? I suppose I should start asking who has received a letter requesting that they come spend a night at this inn. No, Murcod, that won't wash. He would try to kill them all at once, like you said, not wait two days in between.

"Murcod, good grief, what did you want me in here for anyway? I thought you said you found something!"

"Oh! I did!" Murcod bolted up in comical discomfiture. "Oh, and I'm sorry, Dickson, but I should have been at the smithy a quarter of an hour ago. Here, I found it under the bed. Looked like it caught on the frame and rolled down." He handed him a small object and rushed out.

Inspector Dickson studied the polished, dark green-black circle, obsidian, maybe: a button thick in the middle with a raised design on the top, used either to hold a garment closed or sewn on as a memento of a relation. "I don't know what he was thinking," he muttered. "This could be Mr. Wilson's for all we know."

He turned it over in his hands, running his fingertips over the smooth surface. Threads of wool were still trapped in the hole at the back, remainder of the cloth that had held it. The symbol engraved on the top was a mountain, no, three mountains, and small indentations like a crown surmounting their feet. The emblem of Orden.

He frowned and unconsciously lifted it closer to his eyes. Had Gregory Wilson been Ordenian? He could have, but all the same—

He slipped the button into his pocket and left the room.

CHAPTER 5

"DID IT HELP?"

Inspector Dickson dropped a stick into the fire and looked up at Murcod, frowning. "You can't keep coming here, Murcod. I do not want you getting bad repute about your work because you're always here instead of at the smithy. You are a man now; you have responsibilities."

"It didn't help, did it?" asked Murcod.

"Not to speak of." Inspector Dickson poked at the stick, watching it disintegrate into black, ashy rubble. "Fred and Jared returned in mid-afternoon; so that's all right, though I wish they had disappeared, and then I would have known something. Then I asked everyone if they had buttons like that. I—" He laughed sheepishly. "I even demanded to see all their spare garments. And for what? I found nothing certain, and only established myself in everyone's mind as a prying busybody of the worst sort."

"Something tells me you mean Mordred," said Murcod wryly.

Inspector Dickson groaned and did not bother to reply.

"Still, Dickson, the thing was of Ordenian make. You have that to go on."

"I know it. But I still have nothing certain, and that is what I want. Something certain," he repeated, feeling very useless and very tired. "Murcod, please leave. You are enjoyable to have here and encouraging, but I won't have you shouted at for wasting your time here."

"Dickson, you keep saying the blacksmith was angry. He was not! No one shouted at me. They hardly noticed I'd been gone."

"You think I will let you push him till he does notice? Murcod, please go."

The door shut behind Murcod with a faint squeak; and while Inspector Dickson was glad he had gone, he did not attempt to deny that he felt lonely without him. The darkened sky outside, whirling with bursts of snowflakes, seemed to mirror his gloomy mood.

Pull yourself together, Dickson. After eleven years of this, will you let one wretched problem get you down so?

"Sir."

The voice was not one he recognized. It was well-enunciated and carrying even in the one brief syllable, but composed and almost dismissive. "I have been told I may find Inspector Wilhelm Dickson here," it went on, so steady it was almost a drone, but in a peculiarly captivating way.

Inspector Dickson raised his head to the shadow in the doorway. "Sir, you have found him. What do you need?"

"I have been following a certain man this past fortnight; I traced him to this village, and heard that he was staying at this inn. But now, I hear, he is dead. Four days since, by the report."

"Can you know it was he you were seeking? I did not think any in Cobren knew his name."

"They did not," returned the other, "but the description is incontestable."

"Then you know this man!" exclaimed Inspector Dickson.

"Claude, Simon's son, of Croth Dale." He nodded. "I knew him."

Inspector Dickson collected himself. "I am sorry for you," he acknowledged to the stranger.

The man shrugged. "It does not matter."

"You wished, sir—"

"To know the manner of his death, and who killed him." The man came forward into the light, and Inspector Dickson saw a man of ordinary height and slender build, whose face was neither handsome nor ugly and yet carried a very potent calm. "You may call me Sam," he continued.

"And are you of Croth Dale as well?"

"No. It matters not where I am from."

"As you will," Inspector Dickson yielded, somewhat reluctantly. "I fear we do not know who killed your—friend, Sam. That is what I am now trying to determine. As to how he died, it appears that someone stabbed him in the heart."

"That was all?"

"All that killed him, I would guess. But he left slashes on his face as well, three of them, maybe out of—" About to say *anger,* he stopped. They had been left on Gregory Wilson's face, too. He had no idea what they were meant to represent.

Sam stood, his gaze turned inward, seeming to contemplate deeply what Inspector Dickson had said. He said nothing.

"Sir," said Inspector Dickson at last, with a flash of sudden desperation. "Do you know anything you can tell me? Who might have wanted this man dead? Why? You knew him, you say—for how long?"

"Fifteen years," answered Sam simply. "Maybe nearer sixteen."

"Please—"

"You wish to find the murderer, that is so? Well, I care nothing for his murderer. I will tell you some things, but I will not tell you all. Make of them what you will."

Inspector Dickson listened silently and waited, feeling half bemused, half expectant. Sam paced the room briefly with a graceful motion, alert but relaxed.

"I met Claude, and our acquaintance progressed without incident for several years. Then he invited me to make a journey with him to Mattadon, as he had business there with one Warwick Cunningham, and thither I accompanied him.

"We did not travel alone; two other men went with us, one named Gregory Wilson and the other Grimshaw."

Sam paused, watching as Inspector Dickson bolted to the table, dropped into his chair, and seized the pen.

"Our journey was hindered with a peculiar number of bandit sorties. Pitiful attempts which we easily avoided, but they delayed us greatly and I began to suspect that Grimshaw was behind them. But I said nothing of this to the others."

"Why not?" Inspector Dickson demanded.

"The reasons are mine," said Sam calmly. "When we were nearing Mattadon, Grimshaw disappeared altogether and I have not seen him since. Gregory Wilson was much disturbed by his departure, but Claude seemed pleased rather. I think that he expected it."

"Why would he expect it?" Inspector Dickson asked, feeling more bewildered by the second.

Sam shot him a look that would have been annoyed if his implacable features had been capable of expressing such a petty emotion. "Please, sir, refrain from interrupting with all these questions whose answers I am not going to provide."

Inspector Dickson wanted to protest but had no leeway to do so. No matter what this Sam knew, he was only going to tell what he chose, and there was no bluff for Inspector Dickson to hold over his head.

"We journeyed on for several days after that, and then Gregory Wilson, still upset because of Grimshaw's disappearance, vented his anger on Claude and accused him of leaving Grimshaw in the wilderness to die. Claude endeavored to persuade him to a more settled state of mind, but in the end he turned back, and we parted at enmity with one another.

"This affair left Claude most put out. The next day, I found him gone as well. I could not have this for sundry purposes, and I tracked him westward for three days until I caught up with him. We argued for another day, but in the end I convinced him to go on to Mattadon, and go on we did. Having reached Mattadon, he concluded his business with Warwick very swiftly, and we were soon traveling home again. After we returned, he forbade me to visit or speak with him again.

"And that, sir, is the end of all remarkable dealings I have had with Claude of Croth Dale."

"Remarkable they were," agreed Inspector Dickson, laying down his pen unwillingly. *Is this all I am to get from him? It is interesting, certainly. But helpful, how am I to tell if I cannot even understand it?*

"I can see you are dissatisfied," said Sam, turning towards the door. "If you wish to learn more, you may travel to Mattadon and speak to King Andra there."

"What?" asked Inspector Dickson, startled.

"Need I repeat myself?" asked Sam patiently.

"Nay, but—but what does the king of Mattadon have to do with this?" His one-time visit to the south side of the Mattadonish border had been years and years ago, during a session of diplomatic training.

He and his instructing officer had seen much of prudish nobility and stratified social structure, but certainly nothing of King Andra himself.

Sam sighed. “Your questions grow very tiresome.”

“Had I not better go see this Warwick Cunningham, or Grimshaw? The king is hardly likely to even see me.”

“I am not ordering you to do anything,” said Sam simply. “However, even if I could direct you to Grimshaw, which I cannot, I really should not advise you to try either of them. I really should not.”

And with a peculiar, dry smile, he turned and the door shut behind him.

~

“What came of your departure, Fred and Jared?” Mordred looked questioningly at the other two. “I scarcely saw you last night, particularly as the Inspector dragged you off to interrogate you at once. Did you find your uncle well, Fred?”

Fred hesitated, and looked up. “I did not find him. I was told he died nearly a fortnight ago.”

“Cobren is a burying ground, it seems,” Mordred muttered, rising angrily to pace the room. “Doubtless we shall be next.”

“It is not like that, Mordred,” Fred remonstrated gently. “He was not killed; he ailed of a wetland sickness and died peacefully enough in his bed.”

Mordred twitched his shoulders in irritation. “Still, I would that this Inspector could do his job, instead of hindering innocent travelers from returning home.”

Fred sighed, and was silent. It troubled him that Mordred and the Inspector were so at odds with one another, but there was naught he could say to ease his friend’s high-strung temper.

He might only hope that it was resolved soon. Then they could return to Orden in peace.

"You, Jared?" Mordred demanded with a clear change of subject.

"Aye, my family was well," answered Jared laconically. His thoughts seemed elsewhere.

Fred left the room, feeling a need to walk in quiet a little. In the corridor, a door opened abruptly and Inspector Dickson strode rapidly past him, purpose in his gait and countenance. He did not spare a greeting or acknowledgement for Fred, but hurried on down the stairs; Fred heard the front door creak open, and shut.

~

Inspector Dickson reined in by the dull stone walls of the prison. "Find me Selwyn," he ordered the door-ward at the gate.

The burly, gray-haired man appeared shortly. "Inspector Dickson? What's the need?"

"I am departing for Mattadon, and shall be gone for doubtless a se'ennight or more. Send several trustworthy men to the hostel in Cobren; have them ensure that none of the present inhabitants depart the inn during my absence."

"It shall be done," answered Selwyn promptly.

"Selwyn? Be sure that there is no imposition or rough treatment. They are guarding men under suspicion, not accused criminals. 'Tis but a safety measure, and I do not expect any of them to be causing trouble."

"Can't speak for a lot of them," returned the gaoler stolidly. "But I'll send my lad along as captain; he should keep them in line."

"Good. My thanks, and farewell."

"Good speed to ye on your travels," grunted Selwyn, and shut the gate.

CHAPTER 6

INSPECTOR DICKSON HAD ALWAYS HATED travel. His urgent inner wish was to have things *done,* and travel was an insurmountable block in the road to doing them. Desperate for some sense of control over his progress, he preferred riding anywhere rather than taking a boat or carriage. And when he traveled, he went alone.

Now, three days into the unrelenting ride south, he saw the square watchtowers protruding up from the city's dark line into the red of the setting sun, and released a grateful sigh.

"We shall be in Balhorde soon," he said to his mare, patting her neck. "And then, the castle . . . "

He fell silent, doubt welling up. "Will they admit me? I still do not know what the king of Mattadon's part is in all this. Will he be disposed to speak where this Sam would not? Will he not as likely send me away when he knows why I have come?"

The questions hung dark and forbidding in the still evening air.

"No matter," he said at last. "There is one way only to find out. After all"—he laughed rather grimly—"the worst they could do is execute me for bringing up a painful subject."

The mare whickered, shifted restlessly under him.

"Aye," Inspector Dickson answered her wordless signal. "We'll move on."

~

"I am here to see the king," Inspector Dickson stated in answer to the challenge of halberds and spears thrust his way.

"He is likely retired for the evening," returned one of the guards coolly.

"If he is not, may I see him?" Inspector Dickson persisted.

Their eyes locked, but at last the guard looked away, seeming to decide that this was a visitor who would not be put off easily. "I shall ask whether he will see you or not. And if he will not," he added with a trace of warning, "I expect you to leave at once."

Inspector Dickson nodded. "Fear not; I will leave."

Pacified by Inspector Dickson's courteous words and tone, the man exchanged words with his companions and turned back into the dark portcullis. He returned shortly, and beckoned Inspector Dickson to follow him. Through a straight, dank hall they went, up a cold flight of stairs with torches high on either side, and across an expanse of gloomy, empty stone that stretched to the right and the left beyond the reach of the lantern the man carried. He halted in front of an aged wood door and heaved his shoulder against it to shove it open.

"King Andra the Twenty-first of Mattadon. Wilhelm Dickson, Inspector of the Peace from Delgrass."

"Why are you here?" demanded the man seated on the throne some yards away. "Go, Getta," he added to the guard. He rose and paced carelessly in and out of the shadows vibrating through the hall. "Well?" he repeated after a moment, striding towards Inspector Dickson. "What do you want here?"

Inspector Dickson stared at him. How could a man be king, he wondered, and not possess any sort of imposing presence? Andra the Twenty-first of Mattadon might rule a country, but there was naught to inspire awe or alarm in his air.

Yet there was no bashfulness or humility either. He walked with a confident, lordly swing to his shoulders; the dark, close-clipped beard did not hide his obstinately jutting chin. He was not a timid man, but one used to his way, assured in it.

Aye, Inspector Dickson realized, so assured that he had never felt the need to assert his own authority. He owned a birthright which he relied on without ever stepping forward to claim it; he had no dignity, no poise. And Inspector Dickson felt briefly annoyed that he had feared this meeting, this king, for so long, only to find that he was not worthy of any fear at all.

The king was still waiting for an answer to his question, and Inspector Dickson did not know what to answer. At last he said slowly, "I was sent to you by a man who calls himself Sam."

The easy pacing faltered for a moment in a fleeting look of uncertainty, before King Andra gave a light chuckle. "Sam? Who is this Sam?"

Inspector Dickson wondered momentarily whether this had been all a cruel jest of Sam's, to send him to a man who must have met a hundred Sams in his lifetime and had probably never met this one. He shook off the cold feeling and drew upon all he could remember.

"By his dress he is well off but not rich. His bearing is courtly, his diction careful and refined; his manner of speech is educated and deliberate, as one accustomed to politics. He shows little to no emotion, save for a bare touch of sardonic humor. He is reticent concerning his own identity and connections, and indeed would give me no name or city concerning himself, besides Sam."

King Andra had stopped pacing; he shifted, as though uneasy. "Why did this . . . Sam send you to me, then?"

"I—my lord, I do not quite know myself. Only that it concerns the life of one Claude of Croth Dale."

King Andra gasped, his face paling. “Claude—Claude of—” He whirled on Inspector Dickson. “Why did he send you to me? Why? Have I not suffered enough already? Yes, I daresay he *would* find a sadistic pleasure in causing me pain!”

“My lord, are you speaking of Sam, or Claude?” asked Inspector Dickson, bewildered.

“Sam, of course!” the king snapped. His jaw worked. “After ten years of peace, I am to be dragged through it all again, thanks to Sam—”

“My lord! Dragged through what? I am not at the pleasure of knowing what you are talking about.”

“Are you supposed to be?” King Andra cut back disagreeably.

“Yes.” Inspector Dickson folded his arms and stared the king in the face. “Your Majesty, if this Claude has done you any harm, you need fear nothing from him, for he is dead. He died six days ago.”

“Dead!” sighed King Andra. He wiped a hand across his sweating brow. “So much for that then. You may go now.”

Inspector Dickson could barely believe what he had heard. “Go? But my lord, you do not understand.”

“What do I not understand?” barked the king.

“That I have not yet heard anything from you concerning Claude, and that is why I came. I am seeking his killer, my lord, and I was given to understand that you might have information to help me in that search.”

King Andra’s nose wrinkled. “The world,” he said pompously, “is better off without that rat. In fact, if I met his killer, I’d shake his hand. And it is certainly not worth the disclosure of all my private matters to you, a puny little Inspector playing at law enforcement.”

“I have been playing at it for many years now, your Majesty,” said Inspector Dickson, disregarding the sorry insult. “I should think I have mastered it well. As for his deserving death, I did not know him and cannot speak to that. But let me tell you, he is not the only one who has been murdered. For all I know, there may be more deaths to come." He met the king's pale, shifting gaze unflinchingly. "For all I know, he may want to kill you now."

King Andra's lips pulled into a nervous grimace. He whirled and stalked to the right-hand wall and the set of narrow windows that lined it.

Inspector Dickson waited tensely. Surely the threat, uncertain though it was, would be enough.

King Andra came back towards him, his shoulders slumped in admission of defeat. "I will tell you what I know of the vile brute," he said coldly. "But you must swear that you will not reveal to anyone what I tell you."

"I swear that I will pass on nothing that can injure your good name and repute, King Andra."

He appeared satisfied. "So be it. Well, as to that stupid, donkey-brained son—"

"Your Majesty, will you draw back on the insults? It is wasting both our time."

King Andra shrugged huffily. "When I was young, I once accompanied my father to Rehirne on a diplomatic mission. While there, I slipped away with a young Rehirnish man into the room of a most eminent noble, in fact the second to Rehirne's king. We may have been slightly, er, not—we had . . . " King Andra fell silent, apparently unable to think of a favorable way to phrase his sentence.

"Were you drunk?" demanded Inspector Dickson.

"Ah, yes. At any rate, we made a great wreck of the room, and wrote insulting things on his walls and ripped up his bedding and . . . and we were not discovered. No one ever knew who did it. When I came to kingship, however, Claude, the Rehirnish dog—" King Andra ground his teeth. "He instantly began to extort money from me, threatening to tell everyone of my misconduct if I did not give him what he asked."

"Did he not fear that you would tell his part?"

"Oh, it did not matter." The king spat. "He is a good liar, and I would only seem like I was trying to save face. He needed the money, too. He was willing to risk much."

"Go on."

"I gave him what he wanted, of course, and he went away back to Rehirne. He came back after a year, and asked for more. It went on in this way for five or six years. During this interval I also learned that he had tried his blackmailing ways on others besides me; in fact, I became acquainted with one of his victims, Warwick Cunningham."

Inspector Dickson leaned forward, his eyes bright.

"Claude returned to Mattadon after a longer absence of about three years, and Warwick Cunningham and I made plans in secret to kill him."

Inspector Dickson studied the king's face at this alarming reveal, but he appeared unconcerned by the confession of murderous intent to a man bent on finding a murderer. "Yet you did not kill him then."

"No." King Andra's face puckered in distaste. "That . . . that Sam. He interfered in our plans, and refused to let us do it. After Claude departed Mattadon, he never returned again. I suppose he must have forgotten about me. I did not hear of him until today."

"Thank you, your Majesty," said Inspector Dickson, bowing. "You have given me much to consider."

"You are welcome to it," said the king magnanimously. "Oh—what was it like, may I ask?"

"What was *what* like?"

"The death." King Andra smiled gruesomely. "How was he killed?"

Inspector Dickson struggled to keep the disgust off his face. "Stabbed in the heart," he said briefly. "And three slashes along his face, like a claw's mark."

Even in the candlelight he saw the color leach from King Andra's face. The man's eyes were round with mute terror. " . . . m . . . ha . . . " he uttered faintly, the words lost in the breathy gasp.

"What?" asked Inspector Dickson, taking a concerned step forward.

The king drew himself up shakily and composed his features. "That is strange." His voice cracked. "Most strange," he added, gaining further control. "What a peculiar thing to do."

"Indeed." Inspector Dickson scanned the king's still-quivering features. "Have you heard of such a thing before?"

"No," said King Andra with a bland smile.

Inspector Dickson narrowed his eyes in plain disbelief. "Your Majesty cannot expect me to accept that."

"I do," replied the king coldly. "Go away. Out of this castle. I do not want to see you here again."

"What did you say?" persisted Inspector Dickson, desperate to know what information was hiding behind those pale brown eyes. "Grimshaw?"

"No!" shrieked the king. "No! Get out of here! Guards!"

"I am going," said Inspector Dickson hastily. He turned and fled the hall, finding his horse at the gate, and rode out into the city, where he secured an inn-room for the night.

~

The rhythmic bangs would not stop. They grew louder and more violent, pulling him slowly away from the clutches of a heavy sleep.

He blinked at last in the cool air of the early morning and stared at the shuddering door.

"Come in," he called, still too sleepy to raise his voice much above the noise. But whether by his invitation or simple impatience, the door slammed open.

"Found you." Several grim-faced palace soldiers surrounded him, one of them with the tall helmet of a captain.

"Up you get, Inspector."

"What do you want?" Inspector Dickson asked, perplexed and not a little frightened.

"We've spent the night looking for you. King Andra's orders. Get up."

"What does he want?" Inspector Dickson got reluctantly up. He remembered the conversation of last night, the king's frantic attitude and calling for the guards. *Does he want me imprisoned then?*

"How should we know?" retorted the captain. "Maybe kill you. You made him angry."

The men at the castle gates admitted them without question. "So you have returned," said Getta.

"Aye," answered the captain. "We have our quarry as well."

Getta surveyed them, the yawning gate an ominous frame behind him. "Perhaps you should not take him before the king now; I do not know whether he will receive you. He has acted strangely this morning."

"He asked for this man, and I will not wait an hour because you tell me to," said the captain rudely.

"It is but advice," returned Getta. "And advice that maybe you should heed. There was a strange wind in the air last night, a dread hanging over us as we stood watch. All the torches were darkened, as though something was suppressing their light. I would wait."

"Maybe you should be keeping yourself from the bottle on duty," sneered the captain. "If you thought that there was danger in the air, why did you do nothing?"

"The thing, whatever it were, clouded our minds as well," answered Getta earnestly. "It seemed that we perceived evil, but could not withstand it."

The captain's brows lifted in scorn. "Indeed! And what does this supposed hypnotism have to do with the king's wishes this morning? I will not be dissuaded by the dreams of drunkards." He turned and marched into the castle, and Inspector Dickson could not hear Getta's answer, if indeed he had any.

As he had the night before, Inspector Dickson mounted the long staircase, the soldiers all around him. But rather than going on to the throne room, they steered him to the right and through a series of narrow corridors, up to a broad door overlaid with silver and gold. The captain raised his fist and struck the door with a harsh blow, a sound that echoed strangely down the corridor.

"Aye?" King Andra's voice shouted within.

"We have caught the Delgrass Inspector, sire, as you bade us."

"I do not want to see him! Take him away!"

"Where, sire? The dungeons?"

"Of course not!" A fearsome howl made the captain take a step back from the door. "Set him free outside the gates. I never want to see you again, Inspector! You are forbidden to set foot in Balhorde from this day forth!"

The captain stared at the door. Finally he turned to Inspector Dickson. "You heard him," he said gruffly. "Get out of this place."

And so, free in body yet confused in mind, Inspector Dickson left the castle and rode back over the hills of Mattadon towards Delgrass.

Have I learnt anything by this?

Aye, he answered himself. *Of course you have. If nothing else, that this Claude dealt in blackmail, and that could have well been the reason for his death.*

What about Gregory then?

To silence him and whatever knowledge he carried, of course. But it is still theorizing. I know nothing for certain.

And what of the claw mark?

Inspector Dickson released a heavy breath, his gaze circling from the watery lowlands ahead of him to the pale gray sky above. "I do not know what that meant," he said aloud. "Whatever it was, it terrified the king unspeakably . . . but I only used it as an—an example!" He threw up his hands to the silent earth and sky. "I did not mean to say that it *was* a claw mark. Maybe, most likely, it was not!"

He rode on a little longer. "I still do not know who made the mark, however," he said quietly at last. "And *who* is what I want to know the most."

CHAPTER 7

THE GLOOMY WEATHER HAD FOLLOWED him all the way back to Delgrass. The air was moist, the sky very dark, and the clouds looking as though they were not sure whether to drop rain or snow. Inspector Dickson sighed as he guided the mare down the churned, muddy snow of the street.

She, as though in answer to his mood, blew out her breath in a huff and shook her head in disapproval. Inspector Dickson smiled and patted her neck, tilting his head back to watch the rude, haphazard buildings pass by. "Well, we're almost back, my girl, and whether or not you hate traveling as much as I do, you'll be glad to have a stable roof over your head again and your nose in a bag of oats, I daresay."

He swung off in front of the inn's dangling sign and handed the horse's reins to the servant boy who was already running out to meet him.

"Back again, sir?" the lad remarked.

"Aye," answered Inspector Dickson curtly. He strode in the door, returning the innkeeper's nod. There were a few regulars sitting at the tables, and he glimpsed Houk and Jared Earle, as well as young Will, Selwyn's son. He would speak to Will later about how matters had gone. Not waiting for the questions he knew would come from many quarters, he hurried to the back of the room and mounted the creaking stairs.

As he neared the top, he heard voices faintly; a conversation was going on in the room of the Ceristen group. He would have passed on with little notice. But even as he drew abreast of the door the words lit on his ear—half-distinct, muffled—*"killed him . . ."*

Inspector Dickson stiffened, pulled up short, and without a second thought flung the door open.

Mordred spun around, meeting his gaze with eyes like daggers. He tore his hand loose from Fred's. "What is this, Inspector? Is there no more privacy in a man's room?"

"What were you speaking of?" Inspector Dickson's voice was hard and unrelenting.

"Is it business of yours?"

Inspector Dickson was so very tired of that question. "Considering that I heard the words 'killed him' as I passed your door, yes!"

"I see. My words that you heard were, in fact, 'old age and disease killed him'. Now would you please go?"

"Of whom were you speaking?" The grimness of Inspector Dickson's tone did not lessen. He faced Mordred, his own jaw set as obdurately as the young man's.

"It matters not, I tell you." Mordred's mouth worked as he struggled to hold in some emotion—anger, or was it fear? "Go! I was speaking of private matters, which can be of no concern to you and which I certainly will not disclose to your overeager ears."

"You will tell me what you were speaking of, at once." Inspector Dickson braced his arm against the door, in case Mordred should attempt to hurl it shut in his face. "The fact that you are withholding the truth from me is, let me assure you, a most black suspicion on you. How do I know you were not just conversing about either of those two murdered men?"

"I will not tell you." Mordred's breath was coming quickly through flared nostrils.

"You shall!"

"You will not believe me!" Mordred cried hotly. "You will laugh me to scorn, and what use will it be? I will not make myself a mockery for you!"

"I will know!" Inspector Dickson took a swift pace into the room and made as if to grasp Mordred's shoulder, but the young man whipped away and tossed his head up with an angry flush and curling lip of scorn.

"So you will know, will you? Then know you shall. I have another brother."

Inspector Dickson blinked. "So?"

"He is the king of Dirion."

"What?"

Inspector Dickson uttered it as though the intensity of the word might make the statement more believable. He stared at Mordred speechlessly for a second, before recovering his wits.

"What do you mean, 'he is the king of Dirion'?"

"What do I mean?" Mordred laughed, high and mocking. "I mean he sits on the throne of Ederan and wears a gold crown and has servants at his beck and call, and all the country bows to him. What else? Now that you have discredited me as a madman, will you go your way and let me finish explaining to my friend?"

Inspector Dickson rubbed his forehead. "You do not mean that the old king Hiartho of Dirion is your brother—" He caught himself, just in time. Of course, Hiartho had died near two months past. He was no longer on the throne of Dirion, nor was his distant cousin Fingan, whose ascension to power Dirion had so dreaded. They had found another relation—rumors had reached even the little villages in Delgrass—a nearer kinsman to Hiartho than the infamous young

Fingan. Where they had found him, that had not been heard here, nor his actual lineage, but the name had come through . . .

"Ahearn?" he said, posing the question to Mordred's cold, proud face. "Ahearn, lately crowned king of Dirion, is your brother?"

"As you say." Mordred's look of disdain did not soften.

"Then, may I ask, how did such a thing come about? You claim you are Ordenians . . . " He hinted delicately at the question, for he knew with near certainty that Mordred must have lived in Rehirne for some years of his life at least.

"How do such things ever come about?" Mordred shrugged one taut shoulder. "People search for another heir; he is found."

"You will pardon me if I find it extremely difficult to credit your story. Why are you not then in Dirion with him? You are a prince, according to your own admission."

There passed over Mordred's face such a look as though he might have struck Inspector Dickson, and indeed Inspector Dickson flinched back from him.

"I am not a prince," said Mordred in a deadly quiet voice, chilling in its utter fury. "I tell you this, and it is the truth: Ahearn is my brother. As for why I am cut off from him, that is mine and mine alone to know and I will not tell it to *you*."

The oddest thing was that Inspector Dickson was quite certain, in that moment, not all the anger in Mordred was directed at him. In his eyes was a strange hurt, a bitterness or an almost-regret. But it hardened into nothing and Mordred turned sharply away.

Inspector Dickson lifted his eyes and unwittingly met Fred's steady brown gaze. They held there for a second before Fred looked away and Inspector Dickson, more perplexed than ever, turned on his heel to leave.

He had no idea what to make of anything he had just heard. His steps took him to his room, where he sat down and wrote it all out, examining and re-examining Mordred's words. Could they—

No. It was impossible. A more ridiculous and unfounded story he had never heard. It would . . . it would explain his surname, he admitted. But—so would other explanations far more reasonable than that! Brother to the king of Dirion, indeed! No, Mordred must have been trying to distract him, to lead him astray—to throw him off of the initial purpose for his interruption. He had been trying to hide whatever he and Fred had really been talking about. Which had been what?

~

The open, peaceful atmosphere of the common room was welcome after the oppressive silence in the dark of his own chamber. Inspector Dickson stood in the doorway, surveying the meandering activity and savoring the sense of relaxation that meant he was no longer alone with his gnawing thoughts.

It was those thoughts, those dark thoughts chasing one another in circles, frantic, worried, trying fruitlessly to find an answer, that had driven him out here. In the presence of other, oblivious people, he found, he was able to ignore them.

"Huh."

The grunt snapped him out of aimless muse. A heavy-set figure was standing in front of him. Inspector Dickson realized he was blocking Houk's path up the stairs and moved to the side with a quick apology.

Mordred and Fred were not to be seen. Still talking in their own room, he supposed, and felt an unhealthy urge to go right back up the stairs and listen at the door, which he quelled firmly. In extreme cases, he would condone eavesdropping, but this was not extreme . . . yet.

The captain's wife, Syrinna, was not present either, but that was usual; she often kept to herself. Inspector Dickson felt true pity for her, such a young, nervous, helpless thing she was, and he would hate to think she had done it. Professionally, however, he knew that until he had found the culprit she was a possibility, and he could not let her go on her way.

But Jared Earle was there, seated on a bench in the back, his arms folded on the table in front of him and the somber shadows masking his taciturn young face.

Inspector Dickson had a sudden, sure thought flash into his head, and the next instant he was making his way across the room. If he wanted to find anything out about Mordred, Jared was the person to ask.

He almost wished he had thought of this before, and berated himself for not doing so. The solution was obvious: Mordred himself was like a clam with jaws of steel, and Fred, though he did not share Mordred's antipathy of police, nonetheless always held himself with a certain wariness around Inspector Dickson. Besides, courteous attitude notwithstanding, he seemed to consider Mordred a topic that was not to be discussed. Jared, on the other hand, had never shown any discomfort or unease in speaking to him; he seemed to regard Inspector Dickson as someone to be answered respectfully, truthfully, and trustfully. Aye, Jared would not think of concealing anything from him.

Inspector Dickson reached Jared and took a seat beside him on the long wooden bench. "Good day to you, Jared Earle."

"And to you, sir," responded Jared quietly, not giving Inspector Dickson more than a glance.

"How are you finding Delgrass, lad?"

"Well enough, sir, though I have seen little of it." He paused, and added, "Mordred says the countryside is much like Rehirne, if something less marshy."

Inspector Dickson frowned, his mind shooting back to the fortnight-old discussion of the young Kenhelm's given name. "Mordred is from Rehirne, then?" He maintained an easy, conversational manner.

"As I understand it, sir."

Inspector Dickson let a placid moment elapse before he posed his next question. "This Mordred, have you known him long?"

Jared turned his head and looked at him as though wondering what gave rise to such an inquiry, but answered willingly enough. "Only since he arrived, sir."

"Arrived at your Ordenian village?"

"Aye, sir. That was in the first days of January."

Not long ago, that! Scarcely more than a month and a half. "And you say he came from Rehirne to begin with?"

Jared gave a shrug. "I am not sure; I never asked him. I have only heard someone say he came with his family from Rehirne."

Rehirne, not Dirion. Murcod had been right. But he must still ask. "Not Dirion, then?"

"No; no indeed." Jared looked puzzled. "Why, sir?"

"Oh—naught. I heard some odd, farfetched tales."

"Farfetched tales are best not listened to," said Jared, rather as though he were quoting a word from someone else.

"True, that." Inspector Dickson smiled and gave Jared a familiar clap on the shoulder. "But what brought Mordred to Orden, do you suppose?"

But the young man shook his head. "I could not say. I have never heard his reason, if ever he gave one." He hesitated, and looked keenly at Inspector Dickson. "If you do not mind me asking, sir, why are you so interested in Mordred?"

Inspector Dickson paused in his turn. After all, he decided, why not tell Jared? He was all but convinced that Jared had nothing to do with the matter anyway—more so, if possible, than pretty young Syrinna. He was a laconic young man, yes, even a withdrawn one. But there was a certain innocence about him which could not be feigned. He knew little of the world and the darkness in the world, unlike either of his two companions. No, Jared was not the man he sought, and Jared might as well be warned.

"I want to know if Mordred is all he claims to be," he said deliberately.

"What do you mean?"

"He has declared peculiar things to me, most notably being the brother of Ahearn, king of Dirion. Either he is mad, or he is trying to cover up other designs and purposes from my eyes."

"What designs?" Jared stared at Inspector Dickson, alarm growing behind those level eyes.

Inspector Dickson rose. "I do not know yet, Jared."

~

"Selwyn?" Inspector Dickson caught the gaoler's son by the shoulder.

Will Selwyn turned quickly, dipping his head in a bow. "Sir?"

Inspector Dickson smiled. He liked young Selwyn, and was glad to have him here for the time being. Only nineteen, he was nonetheless a reliable and intelligent man, and having grown up in the shadow of the prison possessed a certain rough-hewn wisdom concerning the world and human nature, along with a knowledge of how to handle difficult or unruly men. "How has it been here, Selwyn? No one gave any trouble?"

"No, sir. That Mordred Kenhelm, he balked a bit when he found out he was supposed to be 'under guard'—that was how he put it, begging your pardon—but he was quick enough to see the sense of things, and he's not so bad company after all. We've had some pleasant conversations, Mordred and I."

The annoyance that flickered up in Inspector Dickson at Selwyn's ease in making friends with that impossible young man was balanced instantly by the sensible consideration that it was not often the lad had a companion his own age. Inspector Dickson had no need to begrudge him that happiness.

"I'm glad for you then, Selwyn," he said. "I find him unbearable, I must admit. Don't find yourself too attached to him, of course—but I needn't tell you that."

"Are we finished here, now that you have returned, sir? Or do you want us to stay on?"

Inspector Dickson did not need to think on that long. He had already threshed it out on the journey back to Delgrass. "Stay on for a while, Selwyn. So far there's been no mishap, but I don't want to take the chance that one of them will slip out from my watch in a heedless moment. This is a dark business, and it doesn't seem like it's getting any lighter as time goes on."

Selwyn nodded, his brown eyes dark with worry and sympathy. "It'll be all right, sir."

"I hope so, Selwyn."

Inspector Dickson turned to go up the stairs, the picture of Mordred's tight, angry face pestering his thoughts. An unpleasant nagging feeling persisted in his stomach that he had missed something important.

What had Mordred and Fred been discussing?

CHAPTER 8

THE CAPRICIOUS WEATHER CHOSE RAIN that night. Inspector Dickson woke to find it sheeting down out the window, incessant walls of shimmering, dark, blue-tinged grayness. He lit a candle and leaned his shoulder against the damp wooden bracings sloping up the roof.

While his fingers warmed over the small flame, his head ticked off the events of yesterday and flitted for the thousandth time over the six guests—nay, the five guests now. His mouth tightened bitterly with the memory of Gregory Wilson.

Breakfast was gloomy and awkwardly quiet, sullen skies without and subdued people within. Miss Syrinna picked at her food in the corner, petting at her eyes with her white headkerchief. Jared ate silently and stolidly, never lifting his eyes to anyone. Fred rested his cheek on his hand, a look of uncertainty or unease in his face. Mordred seemed restless in his chair; he touched scarcely any of his meal, his gaze constantly lifting to flick absently over the room. At one point it met Inspector Dickson's, and held there for just a moment before the younger man tilted his chin with thinning lips and looked away.

Alone in his room again, Inspector Dickson stood before the window and watched the deluge make its way down the tiny panes, blurring the outside world to a haze of paleness. The voice in the door startled him.

"*Dickson*! So you are back!"

Inspector Dickson swung around to face Murcod's familiar homely, grinning features. "Just yesterday," he answered. "How goes it for you, Murcod?"

"Well enough," Murcod said with a casual twitch of his shoulders. "Smithying is a fascinating task when I put my mind to it, at least the theoretical part. But I've been wondering about you, Dickson, worrying about you. You never told anyone where you were going!"

"I was in a hurry." Inspector Dickson felt himself relaxing, returning Murcod's grin with his own.

"Or when you might be back either!" Murcod gave him a disapproving clap on the shoulder. "Dickson, what were you doing?"

"I was in Mattadon." Inspector Dickson's brow knit in a pondering frown, and he pulled the chair away from the wall and gestured to it. "Here. Sit down—unless you must be on your way."

"Quite the opposite, in fact," said Murcod. "That's why I'm here, Dickson. I turned out such nice soldering a few days ago that the smith offered me a free day, but I didn't take it then; asked if I could wait until you returned. So here I am." He dropped grandly down in the chair and fixed expectant eyes upon Inspector Dickson.

Inspector Dickson sat himself down on the bed and told Murcod the tale from beginning to end: Sam's visit, his parting words, the king of Mattadon, and the peculiar things he had learned there.

"Blackmail!" exclaimed Murcod when he reached King Andra's account of Claude. "It seems your victim, Dickson, wasn't so innocent himself. Do you think the person who killed him was one whom he was extorting?"

"Nothing's certain," answered Inspector Dickson. "Yet so far, it is the only reason we have, and I'll have to go on it." He sighed.

"What do you look so unhappy about? You have something to follow now!"

"I have something to follow, but I don't feel that it's going to get me anywhere. Every time I talk to anyone, Murcod, it's been the same: no one knows anything. Why should this be different? They'll all look blankly at me, tell me that they never heard of this Claude Simon's son, and they certainly weren't blackmailed by him, and one of those blank faces will be lying. How do I know who?" He groaned in frustration. "And that Mordred Kenhelm will just stick his nose in the air and give off his princely airs, exuding the outrage that I would dare to think him capable of any crime at all—" He snorted. "You know, he claimed to me yesterday to be the Prince of Dirion."

"Maybe," began Murcod in a pondering sort of way—and then, "*What* did you say?"

He laughed for the better part of a minute. At last, wiping his eyes, he said, "I think I had a thought in my head earlier. What were you talking about?"

"Nothing important. I was bewailing my inability to worm the truth from people." He had let something out with the words; suddenly a sense of failure, of helplessness, struck heavily on him. He rose to his feet and began to pace across the floor.

"Yes! Dickson, listen. They're wary of you by now, they know what you are. But maybe I could help find out what you want from them! Nobody suspects gangly, wide-eyed young Murcod—look at what happened with Mordred Kenhelm, he was softer than pear pudding to me." He shrugged at Inspector Dickson. "Well?"

Inspector Dickson heard him out in silence with folded arms. "I don't like the idea of it," he said finally. "It sounds like shirking my own duties. Besides, you are not experienced in subtly leading conversation to your own advantage. And furthermore, it will involve you in things you would probably be better not involved in. Your life is in the smith work, and by prying secrets from people here you're endangering yourself. I am serious, Murcod," he persisted, overriding Murcod's attempt to speak. "If by any chance you did discover something important, you could well get killed."

Murcod stood up, his mouth thin and firm set. "Dickson, it is just one day. I am not intending to spend my life doing this. But you are my friend, and I can see you need help. If you're too proud to accept the help I want to give, that is a sorry thing."

Inspector Dickson sat down, and flicked his finger along the bedstead. "Let me talk to everyone first, Murcod. If they are all closemouthed, then I shall stand back, and you do what you like."

"Only about the name, Dickson."

"What?"

"Ask after the name, Claude or whatever it was. But don't mention anything of the blackmail. How else am I supposed to ask questions without gaining their suspicion?"

Inspector Dickson stared at him, wanting to protest. But he threw up his hands in surrender. "All right! Have it your way."

~

Will Selwyn entered the room.

He liked the air about it. Liked how Mordred, often gazing absently out the small window, turned his head and flashed a welcoming smile at him. How Jared accepted his presence with a nod, and how Fred rose and greeted him with honest civility. Will was an acknowledged presence in the room, one that came and went but was never unwelcome.

"Will Selwyn," said Mordred, bringing his chair legs to the floor with a thud. "How goes it?"

"Dull," answered Selwyn with a grin. "That's why I came here."

"No good company in your men?"

"Not much. Cander is a fair conversant on occasion, when he isn't stringing oaths through his words like feathers on a roast goose. As for the rest of them—they were Da's choice, not mine. They'd take to drink, the lot of them, if I let them for an instant."

A swift, laughing grin lighted Mordred's lips and whisked away, the traces of it lingering bright in his eyes. "So, has your father always been the gaoler?"

"And his before him. I don't know where it began."

"So it goes; 'tis the way of things for sons to follow their fathers. Have you ever thought of being something different?"

"Na." Selwyn shook his head, shrugged. "'Tis what I was raised to. I never longed for aught much."

"Well, I am not following mine; that is certain. I suppose my sons—if I have any—will be farmers on the soil of the mountain."

"You live on a mountain?"

"A little one, yes."

"I've never seen a mountain," said Selwyn thoughtfully. "'Twould be a wondrous sight, I think. But I'm not like to."

"There's a-many things that one longs to see," said Mordred pensively, almost dreamily, his eyes looking on some distant thing. "And most will never see them. But that's good, I think. It's good for a man to have something to hold to, to dream about . . . "

"I wonder if you're right," murmured Selwyn. Mordred had a trick of catching one up in his visions that he spun out of the air, thoughts and abstractions which Selwyn was sometimes not quite sure he grasped, but sensed that there was truth behind them all the same.

He did not like to think that any of them could be a murderer. In fact, he had all but made up his mind that it was none of them. How could it be Fred, so openly gentle and loving? There was not a trace of malice in his being. Or Mordred, quick-thinking, alert, and friendly, with an odd vivacity that could light his whole person, who seemed to understand and sympathize with Selwyn himself so deeply?

Jared, well, Jared was so quiet. He could not speak for Jared. But the other two—there was nothing of a cold killer in them. Selwyn, as he left the room at last with a call of farewell, was in his heart quite sure.

~

Murcod was always heartening, somehow. Inspector Dickson found himself going to question the guests with a certain impetuous confidence in his heart and bearing. He struck a knock on the first door and swept it open with an elegant audacity that surprised himself.

Mordred, who appeared to have been pacing the room, checked instantly and dipped his head in a very restrained bow. He withdrew to the corner and let Fred come forward and ask Inspector Dickson courteously what he wanted.

Inspector Dickson's eyes went from him, to Jared who was sitting leisurely with a leg crossed over his knee, to Mordred's tall, cold figure in the corner. "Do any of you know of a man called Claude, Simon's son, of Croth Dale?"

Fred stared at him with eyes that were full only of a questioning vacancy. "I know not the name, sir," he answered.

Jared merely shook his head, looking quite disinterested.

But it was Mordred's reaction, the thin, expressive brows coming together in a mulling, uncertain look, that Inspector Dickson caught and watched with an almost feverish tensity.

"Do you know him?" he asked in clipped, quick words.

Mordred lifted his head and met Inspector Dickson's eyes squarely. "I think I have heard the name somewhere," he admitted, his tone even. "I can hardly recall where; it was a long time ago. I think—I think I may have seen a man with that name."

"When?" The question fired from his lips, a black, angry dart that sprang out before Mordred's words had quite closed.

The stubborn jaw stiffened a little. "You need not put your questions so forbiddingly. I said, it was a long time ago; I could not have been more than seven years old. I think he was a traveler, passing through the village, no more. The name sticks in my memory as Claude of Croth Dale."

Inspector Dickson tilted his head a little to the side, holding the other's gaze narrowly. "Would one traveler's name retain itself so strongly in a boy's mind?"

"This one did," returned Mordred. "Maybe there were reasons I cannot recall. And 'strongly' is hardly the word for it when I barely recognized the name."

"Perhaps," said Inspector Dickson softly, "the reason that you recognize it at all is that the man who died in this hostel was Claude of Croth Dale."

Mordred made a starting movement forward and said in a voice hard like steel, "I did not know that. I swear to you, I did not know it."

"Maybe," said Inspector Dickson, refusing to drop his hard stare from Mordred's. "You are the only one who has admitted to knowing of him before he was found dead. Maybe you knew him before."

"I tell you I did *not*." Mordred's voice was rigid with a harsh control, as though he were fighting not to let it shake.

Inspector Dickson said no more, either to concur or argue, but turned on his heel and left the room.

~

"So," said Murcod expectantly.

Inspector Dickson gave him a shove half in jest. "Go, talk to them all you like."

"Did it go so badly?"

"No, not so badly. Out of all of them, only Mordred claimed to have heard the name, but that is quite a discovery in itself."

"The other Ordenians did not know it, then?"

"Fred did not claim to."

"And the other, who again—Jared?"

"It isn't Jared." Inspector Dickson hesitated and looked sideways at Murcod.

As he expected, his friend looked at him as though he had said he was the Man in the Moon. "Dickson, what do you mean, 'It isn't Jared'?"

"I do not think Jared Earle is the man who murdered them."

"Why?"

"He does not . . . he does not know the darkness of the world. It is in his whole being somehow. He is still a boy."

"Dickson, you are the most cynical, proof-mongering man on the face of the earth and then you turn around and declare this!" Murcod shook his head, snorting with laughter. "Well, since you're refusing to consider Jared Earle, I think I shall have to keep an eye on him for you. I daresay he is the culprit—I think he has hypnotized you."

"Murcod, now you are being nothing less than absurd."

"Someone has to suspect him," said Murcod pleasantly. "I can see it'll have to be me."

"Oh"—Inspector Dickson made a shooing motion at him—"go out and do your spy work."

Murcod got up and made for the door. "I'll be sure to pay close attention to Jared," he shot over his shoulder. The door shut with a resounding thud.

~

"Have you ever . . . been threatened?" *You're doing a bad job of this, Murcod.*

"Threatened?" Syrinna Nehr-Sazin squeaked.

Murcod attempted to mend his words lamely. "I worry that, er, that a pretty young woman, you being a pretty young woman—what I mean to say is that I hope you have not been threatened on your journey downriver."

The appeal to her vanity was successful and she simpered at him. "Unless you call the way that horrid Inspector detains me a threat."

"Now, now, is he all that bad?" Murcod could not sit in silence while she demeaned poor Dickson like that.

"Well, you know . . . " She glanced down with a sad flutter of lashes. "He is so big and frightening! Such a short way he has of talking—very menacing to nervous, delicate women."

Murcod could not answer her for a short moment, for he was trying to contain his hilarity at "big." Inspector Dickson was of a square-shouldered but not stocky build, and Murcod was in fact three inches taller than him. "Cool" and "authoritative" were words that might come to mind in describing Wilhelm Dickson, but not "frightening."

"Ma'am," he suggested at length, resolving that it was time to attend to his real purpose again, "there are many wicked people in the world, aren't there?"

"Oh? Yes."

"I'm sure, being the wife of a sea captain, you have seen more dreadful things than any poor young woman should have to."

"Many dreadful things," Syrinna assured him with an abominably sweet smile.

"Perhaps you've even seen murder, or even blackmail." He watched her critically.

Syrinna yawned, distorting her pretty features into a most ugly expression, and put a languid hand to her head. "All this horrid talk is really upsetting me, dear sir. I can say happily that I've never encountered any blackmailers, or murderers for that matter."

Murcod wanted to press her further, but recognized that he was dismissed. With a bow as graceful as he could manage, he left for Houk's room.

"Aye?" Houk growled as he entered, rising up like a bear disturbed in its winter's sleep.

It was an unpromising beginning.

The business ended with Murcod backing ignominiously out of the room while Houk bellowed after him that if young brats wanted to play at snooping they should begin with less snooping questions.

"I feel," said Murcod to himself as he strode unhappily towards the last room, "that this whole inn is biting itself to pieces."

He gave a polite few raps to the door and cracked it open.

"Who—" someone began angrily, starting up.

Mordred Kenhelm's sharp question broke off as Murcod pushed the door wide, revealing himself. "Oh." He frowned at Murcod. "Have I not seen you before?"

"I—er—mistook your room once," said Murcod with a hopeful grin.

"Yes; I remember you." Mordred looked not much appeased.

"I've a job at the smithy, but they gave me a holiday; I thought I'd come by again. Still stuck here, I see?"

"Thank the Inspector," said Mordred curtly, sitting down, and Murcod saw that he had—grudgingly—been granted admittance.

He shut the door and took another seat by Mordred. "It's a pity that he can't find the criminal," he observed to the room in general. "Is he still convinced it was one of you guests?"

"Aye," said Mordred, snappishly.

"Pity. You know, I've heard rumors that there was blackmail involved." Having dropped his bait, he eyed them all, but there was no guilty intentness or startlement on any of the three faces. Jared looked even bored.

"Where did you hear that?" Mordred asked in a tone that suggested Murcod should not be listening to gossip.

"Somewhere," said Murcod vaguely.

Dickson was right; he was not made for this kind of work. He forged on nevertheless. "It seems this Claude might have been blackmailing someone who had enough and killed him."

Mordred shot him an odd glance. "You are aware," he said coldly, "that you are speaking to people who would be highly suspected of this thing?"

"Well, yes," stammered Murcod. "I suppose—"

"Then you are either very stupid or trying to get information out of us," Mordred spat. He sprang to his feet. "If that Inspector Dickson sent you here to spy on us, then you can take yourself out of here this instant. Tell him to come himself next time!"

Murcod felt the color building in his face, and his fighting blood was up. For an instant he wanted to punch the other in the face. They stood face to face, staring at each other like two strange dogs, and then Murcod turned quickly and left the room.

CHAPTER 9

INSPECTOR DICKSON WOKE IN A black mood. In spite of all he had found out yesterday, the truth seemed to be still very far off. And time was passing; how was Harris managing alone back in Bulca?

Was it really possible that he could find this evil-minded person? What if he had been wrong? Suppose that the murderer had left the inn that night, and he had been burrowing down a false trail all this time?

He went down and questioned the innkeeper closely again on the events of that first morning.

Galesper was busy, distracted, but when Inspector Dickson finally held his attention long enough for him to cast his memory back, he shook his head.

"No, sir."

"Are you sure? Think back."

Galesper obediently ruminated for some time, his balding forehead wrinkled in a frown. But he shook his head obstinately again. "They never went out by the door, sir. I know, for I've had far too many a customer slip out without paying him due. So I put the dog beside the door at nights, an' he's trained to bark if ever someone passes by. But I never heard no barking that night. An' when I found that body, I remember thinking that the fellow might've climbed out a window, so I walked all round but there was nothing in the snow."

"And you are sure that no one left while you came to fetch me?"

"I counted all of 'em up, before I left. In partica'ler that lad that was slinkin' round and him friend. And none of 'em were gone when I came back." Galesper folded his arms.

Inspector Dickson had no more questions to ask. It was very clear that the man he sought was still among them.

Besides, he realized as he wandered to an empty table and sat slowly down, if the murderer had killed Claude and fled instantly, he would never have known his danger from Gregory Wilson. He would not have come back to kill again. Even if he had not been someone in the hostel, he had to be living in the town.

But which of them could it be? The truth was so tantalizingly near, and yet he was no closer to it than he had been that first day.

Except—except that Mordred had known Claude's name . . .

That was nothing certain in itself, but it was the most certain thing so far. The lines were dangerously black against the young man—and, Inspector Dickson thought, Mordred was aware of it.

He found himself treading the stairs and entering his room again, and realized in vexation that he had not got his breakfast, which he had meant to do while down there. He turned muttering around and descended the rickety steps yet again.

There was a newcomer in the common room, he noticed when he returned—a traveler, for he was familiar with the inn's regulars by now and this man was not one of them. A stout, round-shouldered man, who looked like he had spent most of his life on a scribe's stool or accountant's bench.

"When did he come in?" he murmured to the innkeeper, jerking his shoulder in the direction of the stranger.

"Just now," came the reply. "Name's Warwick."

Inspector Dickson could not suppress a start. "Warwick?"

Galesper stared blankly back at him.

"Warwick who? Did he give another name?"

"Nay."

Nonsense, Inspector Dickson told himself. It was just a name, a name anyone might have—but Warwick was not such a common name.

Inspector Dickson, with a slow, determined step, walked over to the squat figure in the corner.

The man lifted his head as Inspector Dickson stopped beside him, disclosing a wide face sunken in middle age, a fat nose, and two shrewd, even sly eyes.

Inspector Dickson bent a little closer to him and asked in a low voice, "Are you Warwick Cunningham?"

The man blinked at him, those sly black eyes sharpening. "Aye," he answered in an equally quiet tone; his voice was gravelly as though from phlegm in the throat. The tilt of his head at Inspector Dickson seemed to ask, *And what is it to you?*

Inspector Dickson sat beside him. "I believe," he murmured, "I may have met a friend of yours—King Andra of Mattadon?"

Warwick's face screwed itself into a squint. He hemmed for a moment, grinning in a curiously unnerving way, still with his head perched to one side as he regarded Inspector Dickson.

"Ah, I see," he said finally, his rattling tone sinking to a whisper. "You're one of Grimshaw's folk, ain't you?"

Inspector Dickson suddenly felt a dizzying sensation, as though he were on the deck of a tilting ship; he knew, beyond a shade of doubt, that he was on the edge of something desperately important. There was an instant for him to say "No"; an instant to draw his foot back.

Very deliberately, he said, "Yes."

Warwick let out his breath in a small, almost satisfied sigh. He winked at Inspector Dickson, but in the same movement he drew away, the breadth of a hair or less. It was a movement so small that Inspector Dickson felt rather than saw it. "So," Warwick said. "He sent you after me, did Grimshaw?"

"Yes," said Inspector Dickson carefully. He must be so careful; he was playing a game now, and he did not even know how dangerous it might be.

"Ah-h; he was scared, wasn't he? Well, you tell him I don't know nothing."

"What do you know?" Inspector Dickson asked softly.

Again that faint edging away. "I don't know none of what he does. Just that it ain't quite"—he made another meaningful, squinting wink—"within the law. And that ain't leaving my lips. I got my own reasons for staying on the blind side of sheriffs and that ilk. So Grimshaw can just let me alone, see? I don't do him no harm, and he don't do me none. 'Course," he added, rising casually and distorting his face in that horrible wink, "we don't know but what's the truth that they say, do we? Who's to know what's the truth? Maybe t'were a claw, eh?"

Inspector Dickson cast his mind frantically back for what had just jogged at it. King Andra. King Andra paling in the fire-glow at the word "claw," gasping out, "*. . . m . . . ha . . .*"

Grimshaw?

"What did King Andra tell you?" he questioned quietly, rising to his feet as well. That was a gamble—the biggest gamble he had taken yet. But if it proved false, it should do no harm, and if it were true . . .

Warwick started and glared at him, the black eyes glittering like a snake. "Hsst!" he growled. "Who told you? Ah, Grimshaw has his spies, don't he? Him and his men!"

"Soft," said Inspector Dickson coolly; "this is a public place. Perhaps we ought to talk more in secret."

Warwick shot him one wild glance and whirled about, his bowed legs carrying him at a run across the room and out the door. It banged loudly shut behind him, and startled heads raised.

Inspector Dickson stood with his arms clasped about one another, staring after him, still half in the mind of the character he had been playing on Warwick. A calm, menacing character with a sinister message from Grimshaw—*why*? What had Warwick done? What had King Andra told him?

What did he mean by speaking of "a claw"?

~

He went for a walk to clear his head. He could not think in the noisy, dark inn, with his heart still beating quick in his breast from the encounter with that man who had told him of so much, and yet so little.

A claw.

He had told King Andra of a mark like a claw, which the king had instantly connected with something. Inspector Dickson had not been able to guess at what until now. And now? Half-guessed, half-formed ideas flitted through his mind. The rippings across Claude's face, and Gregory Wilson's. Claude, a blackmailer . . . a troublemaker . . .

He remembered with a quick, blinding flash, almost out of nowhere, something Sam had said: how Grimshaw had been behind the bandit attacks.

And Warwick had seemed to believe that Grimshaw had men outside the law.

It all fit together in an odd picture, but what exactly was the picture? He needed something more.

A cur came slinking out of the shadows, whining and yipping at his heels. He aimed an irritated kick at it and it fled.

What did he know? He knew at least that Grimshaw was involved in illegal business; what sort of illegal business, that he did not know. He knew that Claude had been acquainted with Grimshaw—had he been blackmailing the mysterious stranger? But that, too, he did not know.

Inspector Dickson's thoughts wandered over the same path until he was weary of it, and he found himself staring at the sky and the wide, fallow fields. The sky was very blue. Perhaps spring was coming early this year, he thought, looking over the soaked, brown earth that the rain had left behind.

With a sigh, he turned back toward the inn.

The road seemed full of an irksome bustle after the quiet of the countryside. He pushed his way down towards the swinging sign of the *Fisherman*, getting himself spattered in the filth cast up by cartwheels and boots, and entered the dimness of the inn.

It, too, was humming with the noon rush. Laughter and loud talk filled his ears, smoky odors his nose, while his vision acclimated itself to the lack of sunlight. He started across the floor, nudging elbows and backs aside, but a hand snatched at his arm and he turned to see Galesper's boy.

"What is it?" he asked.

"'E wants you," replied the boy, jerking a thumb at Galesper, who was beckoning rapidly in the doorway of the kitchen.

Inspector Dickson shoved his way to the man's side. "Aye?"

“There’s someone wants you,” Galesper said with a worried scowl as Inspector Dickson approached him. “Waiting up in your room, he is.”

“Who is it?” He had a guilty fear that it might be Harris, come to berate him on his lengthy time away—or worse, Murcod’s smith.

The man’s scowl deepened. “Funny fellow he is. Says his name is Sam.”

CHAPTER 10

HE TOOK THE STAIRS TWO and three at a time, nearly tripping in his haste. Why had Sam come back—why on earth? He could have nothing more that he wanted to know from Inspector Dickson. Could it be that he wanted to release further information that he had previously held back?

Eagerness pounded hotly in Inspector Dickson's veins as he approached his room and entered.

Sam was standing with head bowed beside the hissing fire, a look of intent thought transforming his placid, unremarkable features. The sense of absolute control that Inspector Dickson remembered radiated from him even in his posture of reflection.

Has anything touched him? Inspector Dickson wondered. *Has he ever been angered? Has he ever loved?*

Sam raised his head and inclined it towards Inspector Dickson politely. "You have seen Warwick."

"Aye." Inspector Dickson shut the door behind himself with a sense of receding power. In this space, Sam was the master.

Sam looked ever so slightly displeased.

"Is it amiss, sir, that I should have seen him?"

"What did he say to you?" Sam countered.

"Little enough," retorted Inspector Dickson, irked that Sam seemed to resent Warwick's coming when it had been more helpful than anything else so far. "He mistook me for 'one of Grimshaw's men'. What did he mean by that?"

Sam was silent. "Would you mind telling me what you said that elicited such words from him?" he asked at last.

"I cannot remember—I think I said that I had met his friend King Andra. Yes, that was it. Now, sir, will you explain to me what Grimshaw and these men of his are?"

Sam sighed. "Must you know?"

"I must. I am trying to find a murderer, sir, and it begins to look as if the matter of Claude's death may be related to Grimshaw and this claw."

It almost seemed that Sam grew a shade more intent. "What did you hear about a claw?"

"Warwick mentioned it, and King Andra," answered Inspector Dickson, his heart quickening. Sam seemed willing to speak. "Or—King Andra connected the idea of a claw with Grimshaw's name, at any rate. Certainly Warwick did."

Sam gave a little assenting grunt and stared thoughtfully into the fire.

"Sir."

"Yes?" There was an irritating patience in his tone.

"Grimshaw?"

Sam lifted his eyes. "You must understand, sir, I can and will have my secrets. As it happens, Grimshaw is a subject that I am not willing to disclose for the present time."

"But what am I to do? I may as well search for Warwick, since I can get nothing out of *you*! I do not know why you are so angered at the idea of him speaking to me, when you will not." Inspector Dickson folded his arms, returning Sam's serene brown gaze with a glare.

"In all seriousness, sir, if you value your life where it is within your body, do not seek out Warwick Cunningham. As you desire to find out more about Grimshaw, I would suggest seeking out the brother of Claude. His name is Corian."

Inspector Dickson blinked in sudden bewilderment, like a man who has been hitting another and suddenly finds that his opponent is nowhere to be found. "And—and you can tell me where to find this Corian?"

Sam gave a calm, secretive smile. "He is on his way here."

~

Inspector Dickson was in a state of feverish impatience the remainder of the day. Sam had not said when Corian would arrive here, and Inspector Dickson in his own confusion had not thought to ask him until long after the strange man had gone his way to whatever place he haunted.

So Inspector Dickson paced around his room and the whole inn that day, and even Selwyn, who did not consider it 'proper' to pry into the doings of those over him, asked him at the blue fall of evening, "Has something gone very wrong, sir?" But he looked perplexed, for Inspector Dickson's manner was hardly one of alarm and distrait.

"Nay, Selwyn, nay. It is rather that something has gone very right—or I hope it to. I am waiting, Selwyn, for someone."

Understanding lit Selwyn's features. "Who, sir?"

"One Corian. Tell me if he arrives."

"That I'll do, sir."

But it was the following evening before the man called Corian of Croth Dale crossed the threshold of the *Fisherman* and asked for Inspector Dickson.

~

Corian was a little man, not stout like Warwick, but the soft, scrupulously shaven chin looked like it might tend to fat if left to itself too long. His blue eyes roved often, and he had a quick, breathy way of prattling on distractedly. However, when Inspector Dickson spoke of Claude, he became quite sober and attentive.

"Aye, sir, I knew of the blackmailing, and I never liked nor approved of it. Claude wasn't much of a kind fellow any of his life, though, and he didn't listen if any man told him to stop, even when it was for his own good. But a brother's a brother, and when I heard he was killed of course I wanted to come straight here and see how it all was, and if there was anything I could do."

It occurred to Inspector Dickson that Sam had a shrewd way of using people. He did not think that this flighty, well-off man would have left the comforts of his home to supply an Inspector with information on a brother two weeks dead—a brother he had had little liking for. But Sam had come, and whatever persuasions he had applied, they had proved effectual; for here the man stood.

"Thank you, Corian. I shall gladly hear anything you have to give me concerning enemies of Claude, or other words of value, but I am particularly seeking what you may know of a certain acquaintance of his: one Grimshaw."

Corian's eyes grew very round. "Sir! You mean—oh, that's a bad business, it is." He shook his head. "A bad business, that claw thing. A very, very bad business."

Inspector Dickson leaned forward. His hands were shaking, in spite of himself, out of excitement, not fear. "A *claw*?"

Corian gave a sudden, nervous glance around the room. His naturally pale face paled further, and he sucked on his lower lip. "I don't know that I ought to speak more about this, sir. Claude always assured me I was safe, but if they killed Claude, perhaps they are coming after me."

"There is no one listening to us here," said Inspector Dickson reassuringly. "We will see to it you are safe, at least for now; but it is desperately important that you tell me all you know of Grimshaw."

Corian shivered, but he nodded. "I know not when Claude became friends with Grimshaw, nor how," he said at length. "If friends I can call them; maybe Claude regarded them as such, but Grimshaw seemed to hold him in contempt. But over the years of their acquaintance I gathered bits of information, this, that, and I daresay I know as much now as perhaps any outsider does except Claude.

"There's this band of people, sir. They call themselves the Claw and brand themselves with it like a sign. 'Tis said they mark the ones they kill in like manner."

Inspector Dickson's breath caught, and Corian marked it. "You've seen such a thing, sir?"

He gave a nod for answer.

Corian wet his lips. "On—on my brother?"

Again he nodded silently.

Corian shivered again. "Well, as to Grimshaw's men, a shady lot they were. All the ones I ever saw, at least, not the kind you'd ever want to sleep under the same roof as. Glumintorians, thieves, slavers—the like."

"But what did they do under Grimshaw?"

"I don't know rightly *what* they do, sir. They seem to be a mercenary assassin band, you might say, or that's the nearest I ever got to it. They did killing for a living, or robbery—though more often it was killing. But Claude, he always felt there was more behind that Grimshaw was hiding."

"What?"

"He never said what. But he said he knew there was something more, and he was always prying for it in his clever, underhanded way."

"And do you think there was more?"

"Well, sir, I never quite knew what to think. But if so . . . if so, I'd warrant ten to one that's what got him killed."

"So perhaps Grimshaw thought he knew too much and murdered him?"

"He had the claw mark on him, sir, you say. I can think of nothing else."

Inspector Dickson nodded. Yes; that was how a man like Claude would meet his end. A man who delighted in the power he could hang over another's head, a man who stepped in too deep with one who was not afraid to strike back. Claude had been silenced, and marked. Gregory after him, who had known Claude, who had accompanied him and Grimshaw on the journey related by Sam, who had been strangely terrified at the sight of the body in the common room . . . Gregory had known something, too. Or guessed.

His hands, folded together in front of him on the table, no longer shook, but the pulse still pounded in his veins. "What is his appearance, this Grimshaw?"

"He's a hefty fellow, sir, taller than you, I should say. He had a wild hair and beard, and nasty pale eyes that would follow you about. Terrible uncanny, it was."

If Grimshaw were in this inn, he could only be Houk. But Houk's eyes were dark; and Grimshaw had men at his command, any of whom he might send to dispatch a threat who was growing too troublesome. Inspector Dickson's mind rapidly skimmed the inn guests again.

"And Grimshaw is the ringleader of this group," he said aloud.

"Yes, sir, but . . . but I hope you're not thinking of going after them! It would be madness—worse than that—suicide!"

In that moment, Inspector Dickson was afraid. "All I can say," he answered quietly, driving the cold dread far down into himself, "is that my duty is the apprehension of this murderer. If that lies in ferreting out Grimshaw and his men, so be it."

Corian shook his head slowly. "It's not my business, sir. But don't you see what happened to Claude?"

"I saw what happened to him," answered Inspector Dickson. "And I saw what happened to another man two days later. And I'd be a liar to say you don't make me fear. But my job is the keeping of the peace, as it has been for eleven years, and this will not be the first time I have courted death. If I do not, then others will die."

Corian got up, his eyes speaking doubt and disbelief. "You're mad," he said.

"Maybe so." Inspector Dickson was a little amused.

"Or else you still don't understand the peril."

"Peril or no peril, I am bound to do what I must. I chose this work, knowing full well it would bring me into peril." Inspector Dickson too rose and bowed courteously. "Will you be staying here long?"

"A few days, perhaps."

"Tell me at once, please, if you remember or discover anything more of importance."

"I shall, sir."

Corian left the room, still slowly shaking his head.

And Inspector Dickson sat long in his chair, staring out the window, sensing at last what darkness he had been chasing all this time. And, though he did not show it in his face, he quailed at that darkness.

Corian was right, in a way. Who would think less of him if he dropped the matter now? He was trying to embroil himself in the affairs of the immensely powerful and evil, things outside his control—men whose crafty minds had webbed out nets of rot for years. The sane, the respectable, did not interfere. Why not draw back now?

Let it go. Let someone else take care of the problem.

And it will never be taken care of.

His own words came back to him. "If I do not, then others will die."

He rose and stretched with an oddly grim sense of freedom. "However it turns," he murmured, "I'll see it through to the end."

~

Some forty miles to the north, in a drowsy little Rehirnish village, the traveler on a brown, stubby-legged mare drew rein in front of the low-roofed inn. He gave his mount into the hand of the stable boy with a cautionary word, "She spooks easily," and went inside, where he paid for a meal and night's lodging and took immediately to his room.

He was down for dinner, which he ate in a cool, collected manner, sitting alone in the corner; and the only peculiar thing the innkeeper observed was that he sniffed his ale before he drank it.

The innkeeper found himself watching the stranger repeatedly as the evening progressed, as though looking for possible trouble, but there was nothing about the man to indict him as a trouble maker. He was quiet, polite. But something kept drawing his glance all the same, perhaps the quietness itself; for it was eerie, that quietness.

The last light was still in the sky when a sturdy, bearded courier entered the inn and asked after a quiet-faced man—about so tall, nothing remarkable in his dress, plain in feature, a certain noble bearing and an iron control in his manner? When told that he had retired to bed, he gave the innkeeper two folded parchments and bade him deliver them to the aforementioned man directly.

The boy was sent upstairs with the missives, and the stranger took them, shut the door, and examined them both. One cool, humorous eyebrow lifted as he studied them, and taking a small knife out of his boot he slit the first open and read it through without a change of expression. In the same manner he perused the second, that calm, almost cynical look never altering—except that once a swift flicker of something like comprehension passed through his brown eyes.

After he was done, he refolded the two letters and fed them deliberately to the fire until black curling shreds were all that remained, stirring the telltale leavings into the ashes with the poker.

When morning came, the stubby-legged mare was still in the stables, and the tiny knife was still lying on the table, but the stranger was gone.

CHAPTER II

A LIGHT TAP ECHOED IN the white early-morning stillness.

Inspector Dickson squinted into the fuzzy reflection of the small, polished copper mirror and pulled the razor carefully along his jawline. "Aye?" he mumbled.

Whoever it was repeated the knock louder. Inspector Dickson sighed and set down the razor, giving his face a swipe with the damp rag beside him. "Come in," he called, turning toward the door.

"Hullo, Dickson." Murcod's lanky form poked itself into the room. He was grinning. "Thought at first I'd caught you still napping."

"I answered you," Inspector Dickson retorted, "but you didn't hear." He set himself back to the task of shaving, while Murcod lounged cheerfully against the wall and made the occasional comment—"Get it a little more up by your ear. Cut yourself yet? Am I talking too much?"

"You always do," Inspector Dickson tossed back at him, hanging hone and cloth on a small nail. "What are you here for again?"

"I have an unhealthy interest in crime," said Murcod with a slight snicker. "Besides, it's your birthday."

"It is not."

"Isn't it?"

"My birthday is the twenty-first. You are two days early."

"No!" Murcod smacked his head. "I was sure I had it. Well, anyway, I wanted to see what's been doing here over the last few days."

The memories of last night nudged Inspector Dickson unpleasantly. He had an odd feeling that he was living in two worlds, two planes: one full of color and life, with the everyday tasks and Murcod's banter—the other very dark, with only foreboding and uncertainty lying in its dense shrouds.

"Sam returned, for one," he said aloud.

"Who? Oh yes, Sam. That fellow you talked about, the peculiar all-knowing one. What did he come back for?"

"Why Sam does what he does, I think only the man himself knows, if that! But I believe his main purpose was to tell me that he had sent Claude's brother here." Inspector Dickson frowned, the words striking oddly on his ear. "I wonder—why *did* he come? Surely he did not need to tell me that he had sent Corian, not when the man was arriving the very next day. And yet that is the only thing he did tell me!"

With a shrug he went on. "Corian arrived last night. And at last I understand what this claw is." He went on to outline all Corian had said to him, and Murcod listened silently. He was still silent for a long time after Inspector Dickson had finished.

At last he stirred and said, "That's bad."

Inspector Dickson nodded.

Murcod squared his shoulders and said briskly, "But as long as you tread this road, you have me beside you. Now, what do we know?"

Inspector Dickson smiled, and then the smile faded. That instant, wholehearted promise was not something that one could answer lightly. "Thank you, Murcod," he said soberly. "What do we know? We know that Grimshaw ordered the death of Claude, most likely because he was snooping into matters where he was not wanted. And that he himself, or a subordinate sent to do his bidding, is among us now." He dropped into a brooding silence.

Murcod broke it. "What is next?"

"Next? To ask Mordred, Fred, and the others what they might know of the Claw band."

"But Jared, I suppose, will be left out of this asking?" Murcod looked wisely at him.

"I will question Jared, since you are so insistent on it, Murcod! I would ask him most likely anyway. But I know Jared is not the man I seek."

"I won't let you ask him," Murcod declared. "You probably will ruin it, because he has befuddled your mind already. Leave all the interrogation to Murcod."

They walked down to the common room arguing in a half-serious way.

"I insist, Dickson," Murcod muttered as Inspector Dickson found a seat for the two of them. "And look at that," he added. "Fred and Mordred are down here, but I don't see Jared anywhere."

"That could mean anything." Inspector Dickson rolled his eyes fervently.

"Anything?" Murcod lowered his voice ominously. "It means danger, I'm sure of it. Jared is up to something sly and nefarious. I doubt he's even in his room."

"Then go look." Inspector Dickson shoved Murcod. "And let me eat my breakfast in peace."

~

Murcod grinned as he headed for the stairs. Dickson had needed cheering up, all right. Who wouldn't, after hearing what he had repeated to Murcod just now?

But although he had exaggerated his concern to Inspector Dickson, he was convinced that there was more to Jared than his friend was willing to admit. Someone had to be keeping an eye on the young man, and Murcod was clearly the only one prepared to do it!

He pushed the door open after a quick knock and peered inside. Jared was, disappointingly, there, sitting before the small writing table afforded to the chamber.

Murcod resolved that at least he would get his due and question Jared a little about the Claw. Inspector Dickson could hardly object to that, since he was already here in the room, he reasoned smugly to himself.

Something about Jared's bent posture checked Murcod as he was coming forward, however. He sat with his back to Murcod, his expression hidden, but another step revealed that the young man's face was buried in his hands.

Murcod had seen despair before, and he knew it now. Instantly all his glamorous suspicions fell crumbling and meaningless like husks before the wind. The pretense became cruel in the face of reality.

He took a soft step backwards, meaning to leave at once and never look back, never speak or worry about Jared Earle again. *Let be what is, Murcod,* he thought, *and never think you know more than you have been told.*

But Jared Earle suddenly stirred and turned, lifting his head to meet Murcod's eyes. And Murcod could not retreat without looking foolish.

He opened his mouth, half a dozen foolish excuses quivering on the tip of his tongue. What came out was none of them, but it did not surprise him somehow. "Is anything wrong?"

Jared's pale gray eyes held Murcod's in a kind of desperation, trembling with a nameless torment. And suddenly, like a chain being loosed, he spoke, and Murcod heard the whole tale of Gallert Boccin, his superiority, his taunts, and Jared's growing anger.

"It would not—could not—stop growing. Even after I came here. All I wanted was to prove somehow that I was not my family's tool, that I was a man in my own right. Last night, something came to a head in me, and I did not care what I did, but I had to do something—anything—and so I went down to the wineshop past the carpenter's."

Murcod said nothing. By day the wineshop was a place of respectability and a cordial rival to the *Fisherman* where travelers could rest their feet a little and treat themselves to finer liquor than the inn offered. By night it was a haven of drunkenness, fights, and all manner of licentious.

Jared inhaled an awkward, catching breath. "The moment I walked out the door I felt foolish, senseless, *frightened*—like I had cut a hawser and there was no way to get back to shore. 'Twas a naked sort of feeling. It worsened the further along I went, but I didn't stop; I had to prove it to him. And I came there, and opened the door, and I stood looking in, and I saw how it was.

"Men and women, as foolish as I felt; a fearful uproar and filthiness; the noise was frightening, the sights worse. They did not care—they were past caring, I think." Jared drew in a heavy, shivering breath. "But that was not the worst of it. The worst was that I . . . I wanted that. I had gone desiring to share in all of that degradation and more, if it would prove my case to anyone. I saw the distortion of my own mind, and it made me sick."

"Did you still go in?" Murcod asked quietly.

Jared shuddered. "No! I would never touch the threshold of that place again. I was still there, watching, when one saw me and gestured for me to come, but that signal—it was like my wits came to me, and I turned about and ran."

His shoulders were shaking. He spoke jerkily. "I believed Gallert in everything he said. I thought my parents did not give me the trust I deserved; I hated them for it. And at the—the very moment I was despising him so, my father trusted me to send me three hundred miles from his side. Without a word of rebuke or caution. And I scorned his trust."

Jared's head fell forward onto his arms again, and he was weeping, silently; there was no sound in the room but his harsh, ragged breaths.

Murcod knew of nothing he could say. To most people, it would not seem that Jared had done anything so very bad; he had not even stepped inside the place of debauchery, much less joined in it himself. But he could not say such things now, for to Jared it was not a question of the actuality, but of motive. Not a question of what he had done, but what he had been willing to do. To the young man bent over the table, it made no difference that he had stopped himself at the door; he had in his eyes wholly betrayed his father's trust, and this was no time for words of empty praise.

Instead, Murcod spoke haltingly aloud other thoughts that came, after a while, into his mind. "But you have learned," he said. "You know now. Do they not say, 'The burned hand will not touch the fire again'? I think you will never doubt your father's wisdom or love for you after this."

"Will he trust me when he knows?" Jared's voice choked away.

Murcod hesitated, and then he spoke again with conviction. "I do not know your father. But a man who can raise his son with such a tender, pure conscience will not, I think, fail to forgive. You will tell him, of course. You must tell him. But far better he hears it from you—from your repentant lips—than from another, later, because you concealed it from him. A confession is like the cleaning of a wound. It hurts, but the thing is better afterwards—for both of you."

Jared nodded silently. His head still rested on his arms, but it was a weary droop now, and his shoulders no longer shook with those silent sobs.

Murcod got up; somewhere in that long while he had taken a second chair beside Jared. "As far as I am concerned, Jared," he said, "this thing is between you and me. I'll not speak of it to any man, and it's to your discretion whom you disclose it to after this. But there was no harm done, and no one will ever hear of it from my mouth." He touched Jared lightly on the shoulder. "Good day, Jared Earle."

He departed, and found Inspector Dickson busy over the notes in his room. He watched him, feeling oddly old and weary of the world.

Inspector Dickson glanced up, noticing his presence. "I thought you'd have left for the smithy by now," he said. "Everything all right?"

Murcod gave a heavy sigh, wandering over to sit with a thump on the bed. "It isn't Jared," he remarked abruptly.

Inspector Dickson blinked at him. "I knew that."

~

Murcod had been quite closemouthed about what had happened over the past half hour. Inspector Dickson had not pressed him, but he had observed with amusement and slight concern that Murcod was highly preoccupied, even absentminded, which was hardly a usual state of affairs with him. He packed him off at last to the smithy with a good natured clap on the back and the half-laughing remark, "I hope you manage to walk in the right direction!"

Now he strode rapidly down the hall, whistling between his teeth. 'Twas high time to speak to the inhabitants of the *Fisherman* about the Claw.

He waited on the Ceristen folk till last. In the first place, they would take the longest, because there were three of them. Second, he did not want his good mood ruined any sooner than it had to be. And third, there was a certain anticipation stirring in him, if he dared admit it to himself. Mordred Kenhelm had known Claude. Might he, also . . .

Houk and Syrinna both flatly denied any recognition of the Claw organization. Houk, he was sure, might have been lying; but Madame Syrinna, with her dainty ways and nervous twittering, was increasingly difficult to reconcile with Corian's depiction of a rough and ruthless criminal band.

Inspector Dickson gave a rap with his knuckles and entered the last room.

Mordred rose at once, his proud face scornfully polite. "Good morning, Inspector," he said with a slight, affected bow.

Inspector Dickson bit the inside of his cheek, struggling to stifle a reply in kind. Was Mordred trying to gain his ill favor today? He gave a short nod in answer to Fred's usual greeting.

"Well?" asked Mordred. "Are we to know the happy reason that you have solicited our presence today? It must have inconvenienced you greatly to come here, so be sure to make your speech concise, for all our sakes."

The man *was* trying to infuriate him, deliberately, and in the keenest way possible. "My business," he said between his teeth, "is not of a particularly immediate nature. I would suggest you resign yourself to several minutes in my company."

"What a pity," said Mordred with a delicate toss of his head. "I hope the strain will not affect you too greatly."

Inspector Dickson checked himself from yet another angry retort. The only way, he realized, to effectively counter Mordred's distant sarcasm was with more of the same. "I hardly expect so," he returned coolly.

Mordred lifted one eyebrow. "'Tis gratifying to hear."

Inspector Dickson seated himself and motioned to Mordred to do likewise. The young man looked as though he might refuse, but after an instant he lowered himself gracefully to the chair, his chin in the air, as if it had been all his own idea.

Inspector Dickson leaned forward and commanded his gaze. "I have learned something of the reason behind Claude's death."

That thin eyebrow lifted again. "At last?" Mordred said sardonically.

Inspector Dickson knew he should not have been horrified at the audacious insult, but he had really not expected Mordred to go so far. Drawing in a slow, taut breath, he continued: "I have been told by a man—I will not mention his name—of an organization called the Claw, headed by a man named Grimshaw."

There was no reaction in Mordred's face. "So?"

Inspector Dickson felt painfully frustrated. "Have you heard of it?"

Mordred's lip twitched up in a mocking smile. "I am sorry to disappoint you; I have not. Now that you are finished trying to incriminate me, will you leave?"

Inspector Dickson, striving fiercely to contain his mounting anger, looked to Fred and Jared. "Neither of you have heard of this?"

He scarcely waited for the nods he knew were coming. Quivering with a fury that he did not try to curb, he rose to his feet and stormed from the room.

Wretched with his failure, he remained in his chamber the rest of the day. It was no use. Every time he thought he had found the trail, it petered out into nothing. Because someone was lying. Someone was lying. Who? Could he ever find out?

He was shaken awake in the morning. "Sir, sir! Inspector Dickson."

He opened his eyes groggily, staring at a bleary mess that slowly resolved itself into young Selwyn's anxious brown eyes and rumpled dark hair. "Will? What is it, lad?"

Selwyn relaxed his hold on him, his brow furrowed in a dubious, worried look. "It's that Corian, sir. He's back again."

CHAPTER 12

HE WAS VAGUELY AWARE OF starting up, yanking on his boots and shirt, dashing to the pitcher to fling a handful of cold water in his face, waving to dismiss Selwyn from the room.

"Wait, sir!"

He pulled himself together—perhaps the water had helped—and stared critically at Selwyn. "What is it?"

"I just wanted to say to you that Fred Thorne asked permission to go into the town because a relative of his late uncle requested to see him—concerning some matters of inheritance, he said. I gave it to him."

Inspector Dickson nodded. "Yes, yes, that is all right. Now, where is Corian?"

"Waiting below. I'll send him up as soon as you're ready, sir."

"I am ready. Send him."

Inspector Dickson found himself once again pacing up and down the length of his room like a prisoner in a cell, and stopped with an irritated grunt. He must not hang so much on this. Likely enough, whatever Corian had to say, it was something completely unimportant.

It was less than a minute before Corian's light, nervous step sounded in the hall. He entered the room with an air of timidity, glancing over his shoulder.

"Yes?" Inspector Dickson could not help himself; he tapped his boot impatiently against the floor. Corian's dawdling grew more and more unbearable.

With one final peer in both directions Corian backed into the room and shut the door. "I noticed two men as I was leaving the other night," he whispered. "And it came to me of a sudden, right on the stoop of my friend's house, that I've seen them before."

"Two nights ago?" Inspector Dickson could have shaken him. "Why did you not come back sooner?"

Corian stuttered and backed away. "I was—afraid to! I was afraid to come back at all! They might recognize *me*. But sir, I've come now—I've come—you asked me to come, and so," he panted nervously, "so I have."

Inspector Dickson's frustration ebbed swiftly. After all, the man was a terrified, even cowardly creature; and yet he had dared at last to come with the truth. "You saw them where?"

He already knew the answer.

"In—in the company of Grimshaw," Corian hissed, gnawing fearfully on his lower lip. "Among the men of the Claw."

"And who were they?" His heart was reeling at a pace quicker than the wind, quicker than light. The answer he needed was so, so near.

"I don't know their names. The one was a tall young fellow with a proud way of walking and dark hair. The other one looked some older, a real close-trimmed beard, brown eyes and hair, nothing particular about him. If they're inn guests here, I assure you, sir, I could point them out at once."

But Inspector Dickson knew.

He reached out and gripped Corian's wrist in a fierce hold. "When did you see them?"

Corian stammered worse still. "Some—sometime—year past—not longer ago than a year."

"Was anything said about killing someone?"

Corian blinked at him, showing one of his startling moments of shrewdness. "They would never have talked about killing my brother where I or he could hear, sir."

"Of course." Inspector Dickson released Corian and turned to lean his head against the wall, thinking. Eventually he turned to him again. "But they were definitely part of the group?"

"Without a doubt, sir."

Inspector Dickson strode to the door and shouted for Selwyn. The young man was running to his side in moments. "You will take your men and come with me," he ordered crisply. To Corian: "You will come and see this man—just to be sure. Say nothing; I will do what talking must be done."

Of all the days for Fred to request to leave, thought Inspector Dickson grimly as he headed the cavalcade down the hall. It was very fortunate for him that he had an uncle down here!

Or did he?

Speculations passed rapidly through his head. But time enough to dwell on those later, he told himself,. He did not bother to knock this time but slammed the door open.

Mordred was alone, his back to them as he stood staring out the window. Slowly wheeling, he met Inspector Dickson's gaze and his eyes traveled over the men arrayed behind him.

"Your repetitious invasions of privacy grow ever more bold, Inspector," he remarked, his cool tone managing to transform the statement into a piece of brass insolence. But under his careless bravado there was the barest hint of apprehension.

Inspector Dickson shot a glance at Corian and saw his head dip down in a nod.

"Mordred Kenhelm," he said curtly, "you are accused by this man of submitting to the man called Grimshaw and following his designs in the ring of men called the Claw." He went on to outline briefly, partly for the benefit of the other listeners and partly because he liked to do things in completeness, the nature of the Claw, their telltale mark, and the various mercenary crimes its members committed. "Among other things," he ended, "the men of this band are known to have arranged and carried out the death of one Claude of Croth Dale, and afterwards Gregory Wilson." He fell silent.

Mordred's face was white like a man who looks on death. Inspector Dickson waited for a frantic cry of denial, but whether in pride or the realization that it would gain him no credence, he spoke nothing.

"What have you to say concerning these charges, Mordred Kenhelm?"

"I am innocent of them," Mordred answered coldly. His voice was little beyond a whisper.

"Then have you proof that this man Corian is lying? Do not try to deny your culpability to me without evidence of your own."

A scornful look lifted Mordred's lip. "I do deny it," he said in that soft, haughty way.

Let him, thought Inspector Dickson. *The rags of his hauteur are all he has left.* "Will Selwyn," he said. "You, and Oth, and Rodyn, and Holt, and Handra; stay in this room and keep a close watch on him. Do not let him leave."

He waited a moment, to see whether Mordred's quiet would break now, whether he would at last crumble and cry mercy. But Mordred never stirred; he held himself in almost an alarming stillness, his lips pressed together in that arrogance that would not shatter.

Inspector Dickson looked deliberately away and turned to the innkeeper, who had come up on them a short while ago. "I should still like to be sure that he and Fred were the ones who carried out the killings," he said. "You will not object if they remain under guard a few days?"

"No—no, sir." Galesper's eyes darted uneasily to Mordred, and he crossed his arms with a frown.

"Tell me when Fred returns. See to it he does not return here. I want them kept separate from each other."

"An' what of Jared, sir?"

"Where is he?"

Selwyn spoke up. "Down in the common room, sir."

"There is no indication of his involvement so far. He may take another room for his own use, but he need not be guarded."

At last, he thought, descending the steps and hurrying out to the stable, things began to come together. The picture was growing clear.

~

Selwyn looked silently at Mordred as the door shut behind Inspector Dickson. The young man was shaking, and he was white around the lips.

Above the betrayal and distrust growing in him, he could not help a sense of pity and even concern all the same. He went forward to Mordred's side and carefully put out a hand, asking, "Are you all right?"

Mordred jerked violently away as the hand touched his shoulder, and Selwyn started back a little. "Leave me *alone,*" he said roughly. Pulling away from Selwyn, he clenched his hands in an effort to stop their trembling and walked to the little table, where a folded paper was lying. He sat down and took a pen, and began to write rapidly.

He had not been at it long when Oth, who had never learned to control his curiosity—and it was the size of Arahad—approached him and jerked the letter out from under his hands, saying, "Let me see that," before Selwyn could say a word to halt him.

"Oth," he said, warningly, but Oth was already lumbering over to him, not listening.

"Ay! Selwyn! What's he up to? Writing at letters to somebody."

"Well, I doubt they will be sent," said Will sharply, snatching the paper from Oth's grasp. "But that doesn't mean you need look at them."

He refolded the paper and handed it to Mordred, avoiding his gaze. Their fingers brushed; Mordred's were ice-cold. Then Mordred let the paper fall to the table as though it were the least of matters, and sat again with a small, shuddering sigh, burying his head in his arms.

~

By the time Fred returned to the inn, Inspector Dickson was back from a brief excursion on horseback over the hill country. The ride had cleared his head, and he had spent much time thinking back over his first few days here, the murders, and every action of both Fred and Mordred that he could recall.

Corian was staying, he had seen to that—at least until Fred arrived and he could give sure recognition on him as well.

Inspector Dickson was dining in the common room when Fred entered, his bearing as quiet and unhurried as it ever was. He took no notice of Inspector Dickson, and would have gone on up the stairs if Inspector Dickson had not swiftly come forward and barred his way.

He listened silently to the accusations, a dazed look slowly overspreading his face. He was quite still, but a different stillness from Mordred's iron control. It was like a bird dashed against a tree, as if of all the things he had ever expected this one was furthest from his mind and he could not yet believe it. But when Inspector Dickson mentioned that Mordred had been accused as well, a horror sprang into his face.

"Sir, not Mordred! It could not be!"

"He has ever been more likely in my eyes than you," Inspector Dickson returned dryly.

Fred drew in a shaken breath, the dazed look seeping back. "Sir, there must be a mistake—"

"Enough." Inspector Dickson set his jaw hard. As easy as Mordred's disdainful cool had been to face, Fred's courtesy and concern was by comparison that much harder. "Do you acknowledge these charges?"

Fred's eyes widened. "Acknowledge them? I cannot, sir. They are not true!"

"Mr. Thorne, should you choose to confess your wrongs now, it may go easier with you later."

The gentle face before him wavered. "Sir, they are not true."

Inspector Dickson said no more. Faced with that steady denial, he felt he could not. He turned and walked back to his meal, leaving the other men to escort Fred Thorne to his new confinement.

~

"Why aren't you arresting them *now*?"

The incredulity reverberated off the walls.

Inspector Dickson sighed. "Murcod," he said slowly, "it's only one man's testimony. I believe him, but something in me just wants a little more certainty. Whatever happens, they can't do any harm; I am having them watched day and night. Seven days I'll take, to search into the details of the matter, and at the end of that time I shall arrest them, further proof or no."

He waited for Murcod's laugh, for his retort about a "proof-mongering" friend. But Murcod only nodded. There was an odd gravity in his manner that Inspector Dickson had not noticed before.

"Is everything all right, Murcod?" he asked.

Murcod glanced at him, and after a minute his lips twitched up in a wry grin. "I'm quite all right, Dickson. I've just been thinking about things lately. Possibly doing too much thinking."

"About what?"

Murcod stretched. "Mostly about how I could have turned out different," he answered casually. "Worse."

Inspector Dickson guessed there was something behind those distracted eyes, something Murcod did not plan to share. "Well, you didn't," he returned with a familiar slap to Murcod's shoulder. "I don't think I would worry on it too much."

Murcod replied with another grin. "I shan't. But it's something I think I shall remember all the same."

CHAPTER 13

INSPECTOR DICKSON HAD LEFT IT up to Selwyn to decide how he was to manage the guarding system for the night hours. In the end, Will ordered Oth and Handra to split the watch; he himself was a light sleeper, and trusted that he would wake should any danger present. "Stand in front of the door," he instructed them, "so that if you do doze off you'll at least be blocking the way out."

Now, as the dawn arrayed herself in rose-golden splendor, Will watched the shifting colors through the window and wondered why anyone would kill in the face of beauty like this.

But beauty had never been the answer, he reasoned with a cool, hard common sense. The world was full of beauty, and men thieved and raped and killed just the same. Mordred had the keenest appreciation for beauty of anyone he knew, and yet he—

Selwyn's brow darkened, and conflicted feelings teetered in him—affection and hurt, pity and resentment. He turned away from the window and found himself facing Mordred, who was sitting on his bed with hands clasped over one knee. The other young man's face was hard and distant, locked in a mask of stony indifference, and he stared flatly back at Selwyn until Selwyn turned his face away.

How many days of this? Seven?

Or until Inspector Dickson found more proof.

Selwyn heaved a long, tired sigh and shot a glance around the room to see that all his men were accounted for. Rodyn, the local inspector-in-training, met his gaze with a small salute. Funny how in a few years, the red-faced, sheepish fellow would be just like Inspector Dickson and taking more salutes than he gave. Not much an Inspector of the Peace could answer to besides the king.

Oth *was* asleep, he noticed with a dry humor. He considered rebuking him for it, but shook his head; the man could not help himself. He would fall asleep just the same. Selwyn would have a different guard take his place. At least Mordred had not attempted flight, he thought, his gaze flickering back to his charge. He wondered if Mordred had slept at all.

As he had done yesterday, he sent Rodyn down to the common room to bring a meal up for all of them. The men shared the food with noisy relish, making a mess of their corner that Selwyn told them sharply they had to clean, and Will himself ate heartily. But Mordred, alone at the little table, ignored the plate that Selwyn had set before him, as he had twice yesterday.

"Mordred," he said, standing directly in front of him. Mordred had not slept, he was sure, looking at the gray eyes—shadowed and listless, dark as burned spots in his white face. "Mordred, you ought to eat."

Mordred's shoulders went back and his eyes sharpened on Selwyn. "What do you care about it?" he demanded harshly.

Selwyn drew back slightly, offended at the tone. "I do not want you to starve."

Mordred's lip curled a little. "I wonder that it matters to you what happens to a *murderer.* Oh, he said he wanted to be more certain, but he still believes it was I—they all do—you do, do you not?" He threw the last words passionately at Selwyn.

Selwyn could not answer. He did think it, and yet he could not bear to admit the cruel answer.

Mordred's face grew whiter, harder, colder. He tossed his head contemptuously. "I expected no better."

Words trembled on Selwyn's lips, angry words. But Mordred's eyes fell, his face turned away, and so Selwyn never spoke them.

Whether Selwyn's persuasion had done it, or whether hunger finally touched him, Mordred did eat his breakfast before noon came. It was some time after he had finished it that he came up behind Selwyn and spoke his name, startling him.

"Aye?" Will asked quickly, trying to cover his nervous shy. But it had not been lost on Mordred, whose mouth tightened into a yet thinner line. When he spoke, however, it was not with insolence, only a stiff cool.

"You said that my letter would not be sent."

Selwyn's eyes traveled down to the paper held lightly between Mordred's fingers. "It would most likely not," he answered quietly.

"May one ask why?"

"You might be sending a letter to your friends in the Claw, asking for help in an escape. Such a thing would only bring on us more danger and death."

"It is to my family." Mordred's chin lifted in an even more painful stiffness.

"Maybe, but it's not for me to say. You can show it to Inspector Dickson and see what his judgment is, but I would not expect him to give his approval." It cut Selwyn to speak so bluntly, but he knew he must be honest. There was little reason for Inspector Dickson to grant such a request when it could turn on all of them later on.

Mordred gave a little tight nod. "Thank you," he said and turned away, and carefully he set the folded letter on the table.

Selwyn wondered briefly if he would choose to ask Inspector Dickson. But then he realized that Mordred would never bend his neck to such humiliation. No, Mordred would not ask. And that was doubtlessly for the best.

~

The cloud cover hung low and soft gray, broken by glimpses of sun and a skylark that dipped and shot upwards, out of sight. Distant creaking and clopping, a barrow of uncarded sheep's wool hauled by a bristly mule, sounded from the crook in the road. The front door of the *Fisherman* hummed with commotion, patrons drifting in and out while urchins congregated by the eaves, but there was never much going on behind the inn. Only the open swath of patchy snow and soil, and a whistle of birdsong, and a glimpse of the fishers' inlet between the dotted houses on the downs.

Jared let the wind that whispered of coming spring beat irregularly against his face, snapping against his clothing, and was grateful for its cold, clean touch. He was trying to think things over, in his quiet way. Everything had come about so bewilderingly yesterday morning. Without a second's warning he was forbidden to return to his room. Mordred was accused of conspiring with a criminal organization called the Claw, suspected of perpetrating the murders. Fred was likewise denounced. All of it had happened with a blinding speed, which left Jared's careful, logical mind scrambling for a foothold like a fish for the water.

It was not two days ago that he had released the bitter poison of his anger and despair, and this put him further at a loss, for he was still climbing up out of that, adjusting to the feel of level ground after the long months of a sheer tumbling slope. He was not ready to be confronted with a new trouble.

But confronted he had been. Now he bent himself to ponder what had happened, and see whether it could be made clear.

They had been accused, aye, but by whom? One man alone. Suppose that man were lying, thought Jared.

Then the other side presented itself to his grave consideration: why would he lie?

He decided that, at least, Mordred ought to give his own explanation; for that he had not heard. Certainly it looked bad against him, but ought he not to give his own defense? And Fred—Jared could not believe this of Fred. Not yet at any rate.

But after all, he reflected as he turned to enter the inn again, what did he know of Fred? He had only seen him at the castle work, and once or twice else. He did not know whom Fred might have been acquainted with, what sort of life he might have led before he arrived in Ceristen. Yet could that gentle man he had seen kill mercilessly? Would he not have been living an utter lie all this time?

Jared, a line of perplexity biting deep between his eyes, stopped at the door of his old room and knocked hesitantly.

It was the gaoler's son, Will Selwyn, who opened it for him. "What do you want?" he asked curtly, blocking the aperture.

"May I come in?"

"What do you want in here?" repeated Selwyn.

"To speak with Mordred. Is that a forbidden thing?"

Selwyn looked shamefaced at the reproof veiled in Jared's brief words. "Come in," he said, extending the door wide to the familiar, squarely constructed room. It smelled more than it had when Jared had slept in it.

The curtainless window in the wall was wide open and swinging, the way Mordred always kept it, but one bed was gone and the other in disarray.

Selwyn motioned Jared toward the little table on the left, nodded, and drew back to the window.

Mordred sprang to his feet upon seeing Jared. He was either very glad or very alarmed, and Jared could not tell which, for he said nothing but merely nodded in greeting.

"Mordred," said Jared, and frowned slowly, determining how to say what he wanted. In the end, he asked directly, "Is it true?"

Mordred gave a bitter half-smile. "Why do you not ask Inspector Dickson? *He* knows everything."

"Mordred." Jared frowned deeper and folded his arms. "Are you saying it is true, then?"

"It hardly matters whether it is true, does it, since no one has asked my opinion?"

"But I have asked it, Mordred," Jared pointed out simply.

Mordred let out a breath that caught oddly in the middle and his eyes sank from Jared's. "Of course it is not true," he muttered wearily. "I knew nothing of this Claw thing before he spoke of it—but why should he believe me? He believes me in no word I have ever said. I told him of Claude and he would not believe me. I told him of Ahearn and he would not—"

It was as if by a great effort that he ceased his incoherent rush. He lifted a pleading face to Jared's. "But you trust me?"

Jared hesitated. For the first time in his life he wished to utter a lie. "I do not know yet," he admitted quietly.

And he would have taken back the words in the next moment if he could have done it, for Mordred flinched away like he had struck him in the face. With a blind step backwards he dropped into the chair, his head falling forward, his shoulders high and rigid.

Suddenly he jolted himself up and cast a glance toward the other side of the room. Selwyn was with his back to them, speaking to Handra. Mordred snatched something up from the table and thrust it toward Jared. "Send it," he whispered brokenly, his eyes burning in a frantic plea. "Please, send it. Whether you think me a murderer—or no—send it for me."

Jared knew what he was about to do. That Mordred could send this by no other way than him meant that Inspector Dickson and Selwyn were not permitting him to do so.

He looked at that desperate countenance, taut with agony, and his resolve formed in a quiet, steady way.

If this is to help a murderer, so be it.

He silently reached out and took the letter from Mordred's hand. Slipping it into his jerkin, he turned around and left the room.

~

"Not wrong today, am I?"

Inspector Dickson wheeled. "Not wrong about what, Murcod?"

"Your birthday! Today is the twenty-first of February."

Inspector Dickson shrugged. "So? I am one day older than I was yesterday, one year older than this time last year."

"You're a killjoy, Dickson."

The killjoy bent over his notes in an effort to hide a smile. He had no enthusiasm for birthdays to begin with, but his utter lack of interest had been deliberately contrived to get a rise from Murcod. "Thirty-one is nothing to prance about," he replied indifferently. "I shall be sprouting gray hairs soon, I expect."

"Killjoy," reiterated Murcod.

A companionable silence thrummed pleasantly between them for a little.

"How goes the search?" Murcod asked at last.

"You mean the search for further proof? It has only been a day."

"I take that as no."

Inspector Dickson stood up. "I am going to talk to them both, and see whether I can get them to tell me anything. Wish me well, Murcod, at least with Mordred. I do not look forward to that conversation."

Murcod nodded. There was a pensive look in his eyes as he said, "It's rather terrible to think of that young man—who was so kind to me that first day—with blood on his hands."

"Murder is a terrible thing," returned Inspector Dickson. He set his pen in the inkwell and strode for the door.

Fred Thorne greeted him in the same courteous manner he always did, which irked Inspector Dickson in a way. He did not understand why, and he held the feeling back and returned the bow.

"What is it, sir?" Fred asked.

"It is that I wish to ask you some questions," answered Inspector Dickson. "When did you join with the Claw?"

"I was never with them, sir."

Inspector Dickson bit his lip. He had hoped he might trip him up with that question. "You insist on that, then."

"Sir, I could not have been with them, I assure you. Please believe me. I lived in Harotha my whole life until this past autumn, and I have never so much as heard of the Claw."

"Harotha is a far distance away; yet how am I to know that the extent of the Claw does not reach even there?"

"Perhaps it does, sir," Fred acknowledged softly. There was a weary set to his shoulders.

"Mr. Thorne, heed me. If you will tell me what you know of the men you worked with, if you come clear with all your doings, your involvement with Claude's death, and anything you may have been pressed unwillingly into performing, it is possible the law will offer a degree of clemency. Sometimes a man is caught between two hard places; and I am willing to believe that taking up this life was not a ready choice."

If the words had any effect upon Fred at all, Inspector Dickson could not see it. "Sir, I am not with them."

"Denial will not serve you and your friend in the courts."

Fred's gaze seemed to withdraw in on itself; he said nothing, and Inspector Dickson, wishing more than ever that he could reach behind that persistent barrier of quietness, rose with a stifled, irritated sigh. He bade Fred a perfunctory farewell and turned to go to Mordred.

The young man was staring out the open window, and he turned to stare at Inspector Dickson as though he found him a curiosity of little value. "Aye?" he said, his tones bleeding with derision.

"Selwyn," said Inspector Dickson shortly, "why do you let him stand by that window? He could climb out of it any moment."

Mordred slowly stepped aside with a gesture of derisive politeness as Selwyn came to shut the window. "I would not want to inconvenience the sagacious Inspector Dickson," he remarked scathingly.

"Enough of this," Inspector Dickson snapped. "I am not here to be insulted."

"No?" Mordred cut in. "How shocking."

"I am here"—Inspector Dickson struggled with the desire to knock Mordred into the wall—"to ask you about the Claw."

Mordred raised his eyebrows as though in astonishment. "I only wish I could help you."

"I am quite convinced you *could* help me, if you would."

"Oh, I had forgotten . . . I am supposed to know of this Claw. How could I think otherwise, when Inspector Dickson himself told me that I know of it?" Mordred's tone dripped with sarcastic homage. "And we know that Inspector Dickson is never wrong."

Anger seethed hotly in Inspector Dickson; he dared not answer for the fear of losing his temper completely.

He found himself suddenly tired of this whole affair. Two people who would admit to nothing, a single witness with no further evidence in sight, and a foul criminal ring threatening on the horizon.

Had he really set himself to endure six more days of this?

CHAPTER 14

INSPECTOR DICKSON STEPPED OUT OF the inn into the rainwashed air. It smelled of freshness and wet earth and spring. *I wonder how the crocuses back in Bulca are doing,* he thought and felt for the first time a pang of homesickness for the small, cramped cottage on the banks of Rale Creek and the occasionally exasperating Harris.

Seven days. Seven days it had been of waiting, wondering, rereading notes; of questioning a quiet Fred, an insultingly sarcastic Mordred, and a whining Corian.

All Corian wanted to do was return to his own town and his own house, but Inspector Dickson had told him he must stay until the trial was over and done with, so that he could witness against the accused. Since that time, Corian had met him with a resentful attitude, and had been very little help in determining further ground with either the Claw in general or Fred and Mordred in particular.

Seven wasted days was what it felt like; for he had discovered nothing new as he had hoped. But they were over, coming now into the morning of the eighth, and it was no use to dwell on the infertility of those wasted days. Ahead was a final end to the long labor and a return to Bulca.

Something twitched unpleasantly in him. Was it the end? The Claw band was still at large, and he had maimed it by arresting two of its members. Would the rest retaliate? The serpent would be outraged, if hardly much harmed, and they had not cut off its head.

Dickson, get this out of your head. These are things beyond your capability, beyond your control. If they come after you, they come after you, and you can avoid them; there is no need to embroil yourself further into the meshes of this web.

Nonetheless, why did they let such a band roam freely? The Claw ought to be routed out, or an attempt should be made. The law should not let such danger lie.

Dickson, have you an army at your back? No. This is madness.

The king does. I can send a petition to him when the trial is over. The menace must be stopped!

He leaned one hand against the corner post of the inn, eyes narrowed into the rising sun. Words out of years ago spoke through his head. *". . . You'll never leave a task half-done, Dickson."*

"And I won't," he muttered aloud.

Yet maybe there would be a short rest for him when this immediate business was finished, a reprieve of sorts. There would be an inevitable wait, indeed, as soon as he turned any written request over to the legislative system, through whom it must pass before it ever saw the king's seal, and for once he did not chafe at the thought. His mind ached to be free of the constant, tense drain that this problem demanded from him.

It was over, he thought with relief. All but over.

Again that faint, pestering twitch, though from a different quarter. Suppose he were mistaken?

For, truly, he had only Corian's word against the two . . .

Inspector Dickson entered the stables and began to curry his mare in a slow, brooding way. Two halves inside him slowly tore apart from one another, one keeping his hands moving along the mare's flanks and belly, saying silently, *Go . . . you have done all you can, it is time to go . . .* The other replied, *You need a surety—do not shirk—stay.*

He found the saddle, heaved it up to settle it on the horse's back.

"Inspector, sir! Inspector Dickson!"

He turned and set the saddle back down. Galesper was beckoning to him rapidly. "What is it?"

"Sir, the dog was frettin' to go out, so I took him out and let him run about on the yard, and he—well, sir, I think you ought to come see it."

Inspector Dickson followed him swiftly out into the piercing sunlight and across the yard, to a place where the ground was torn up and clods were glistening sodden and muddy. There was something dark tangled among them, a mess of soaking cloth, and he bent and picked it up, brows veering down in a dubious look. It was a shirt.

He lifted questioning eyes to the innkeeper.

"I saw a bit of it sticking out of the ground, Inspector sir, 'twas the cuff of the sleeve, I think, and the dog, he ran over and started worrying it and clawing away the earth before I called him off. It's been buried there, sir, who knows how long, and I s'pose the rains washed away the soil an' all that was covering it up. But it ain't a normal thing to do, bury shirts, so I thought . . . "

The rest of the innkeeper's words faded out of Inspector Dickson's hearing. He gripped the shirt in his fingers, water squeezing out between them, and stared at the buttons that marked a row down its front.

Green-black obsidian buttons, thick and as large as his nail, a raised design glinting on each of a mountain surmounted by a circlet of stars. There were six altogether, with a wide gap and an empty buttonhole between the fifth and sixth where one more was missing.

As he ripped one of the buttons off, examined it disbelievingly, something slipped out of an inner pocket and splattered soft in the mud at his feet. He bent and snatched it up at once—a crumpled piece of vellum, half-protected by the lining of the shirt, barely legible now that the ink had run.

Fred Thorne, . . . are to accompany Mordred Kenhelm to Cobren . . . trusted by Grimshaw . . . orders concerning Claude of Croth Dale. . . . the Fisherman; kill him directly and report . . .

Inspector Dickson's hands were cold, his heart burning. *This* was what he had needed all this time. And it established the truth at last beyond doubt.

~

The door to Jared's new room opened and swung shut like a clap of thunder behind Inspector Dickson. Jared rose instantly, puzzled; he had scarcely seen the lawman for days. "Good—"

"You were in the hostel, with your two companions, the night Claude Simon's son was murdered."

"Aye, sir?"

"Tell me what happened the morning that his body was found."

The Inspector's eyes were bright with a strange excitement that vibrated in his whole stance and mien. Jared almost did not understand it, and yet it frightened something in him. "When do you mean, sir?"

"From the moment you woke up."

Jared hesitated. In a moment he sat down again, to think better, and Inspector Dickson did not ask him to rise. "Mordred left the room early before dawn, sir, and that was when I first woke. I dozed a little after that, but I woke again when Fred left."

"And when was that, that Fred Thorne left?"

"It must have been sunrise then. The light was making shadows on the floor. I got up and waited in the room until they returned."

Seconds of silence passed in the morning-lit room, pulling Jared's memories back and forth between that sunrise and this. What had happened in those few hours? What had Mordred said—going out for a walk to quiet his thoughts?

Inspector Dickson nodded abruptly. "It is clear enough."

Jared stood up again. "Sir. What is clear?"

Inspector Dickson took a breath, and looked at him. "The truth."

~

"Dickson? Dickson. What are you in a frenzy about? The innkeeper thinks you've gone mad."

"Mad?" Inspector Dickson checked, whirling on Murcod, and gave a short laugh. "Satisfied, maybe."

He flung the ragged bundle he had been holding at Murcod's feet. "Fred killed Gregory Wilson."

Murcod stared at the filthy tatters. "How do . . . how does this prove anything of the sort?"

"It was his shirt. This letter is to him." Inspector Dickson handed the wad of thick parchment to Murcod. "And the buttons—"

Murcod looked a little befuddled by the sweeping blur of information. He held the letter blankly in his hand. "Do you mean Mordred is cleared?"

"No. The letter incriminates him as well. In fact, he is likely the one who killed Claude, unless Jared's account is mistaken; Fred left the room too late." Inspector Dickson fell silent as fragments whirred through his head. *". . . I saw a friend of mine entering behind me. We spoke a while, discussing what to do . . . "* Mordred's aloof, defensive face and clipped words . . . Fred's reserved, quiet manner—his quick, alarmed glance from Mordred to Inspector Dickson . . . "*. . . came to the common room just after he found the man . . .*

"What did you speak of?"

"It was naught to concern you . . . "

"Murcod," said Inspector Dickson suddenly, though he turned towards the door as he spoke, "I think I shall be staying in Cobren one last night. The journey to the gaol will take some time, as I have not mounts for everyone, and 'twould be a long way back to Bulca from there. Tell Galesper that for me."

"All right, Dickson. I must go now—but say, I think I shall come back this evening if you need company."

A day there and back, another to summon the justices and jury and arrange the trial; three at the most. Inspector Dickson glanced up, Murcod's words coming through. "I hardly think I shall need company, but you are welcome to come."

Murcod tsked. "A trip to the gaol; you'll need cheering up, I warrant it." He hurried out with a wave.

Inspector Dickson dallied for a moment after he had gone. At last, with a swift, hard movement, he strode forward.

~

"Frederick Thorne."

For once Fred did not stand, did not acknowledge him; he remained with his head bowed, seeming afraid to look up. It was as if he sensed what Inspector Dickson was here to say.

"Frederick Thorne," repeated Inspector Dickson quietly. "I arrest you for murder done in a willful and malicious spirit. For this you will stand trial in three days' time."

The man so accused raised his head, and his face was tired, immensely tired, a deep anguish in his eyes. It ought to have been guilt, yet any guilt was gone, rooted out by suffering. And such suffering that Inspector Dickson felt a deep pity overtake him. What had driven this man, after all, to such a pass? His hand was gentle as he touched Fred's shoulder and said, "We will take you to the prison. You understand it will be no use to struggle."

Fred Thorne's head dropped in a nod as he got slowly to his feet.

"Bring him along," Inspector Dickson ordered, indicating two of Selwyn's men. "Wait outside for me," he continued as they approached Mordred's room.

Mordred was sitting half-turned away from the door, one foot perched on the rung of the chair and his hands locked about his knee, his eyes trained on the window in an absent reverie. The only indication he gave that he heard their entrance was a slight tightening of his shoulders, and other than that he did not turn or stir.

Inspector Dickson cleared his throat, began to speak, but Mordred altered in neither expression or position; he continued to gaze away in a statement of complete ignoral.

"—trial in three days' time," finished Inspector Dickson between his teeth. As Mordred's face remained in that cold, indifferent mask, all the anger of the past month surged up and his forced calm snapped.

He kicked the small table viciously, sending the dishes on it skating forward. One wooden mug tipped over and rolled off to land on its handle, which split in two with a loud crack.

Mordred glanced toward him with a feigned interest. "Good morning, Inspector Dickson," he said cuttingly. "I trust that you, as a law officer, have a very good reason for throwing my cup on the floor."

Inspector Dickson closed his lips until he thought his teeth would draw blood. Giving a sharp nod to Selwyn's men, he said, "Take his arms."

Mordred rose slowly to his feet, with an air of insolent leisure, and allowed the guards to march him from the room.

Inspector Dickson led the way, and they left the inn.

The gaol was seven miles away, in Caleham. It had been built during the institution of Inspectors centuries ago and kept up well, a low structure of quarried granite, darkened with age and isolated from the streets with a perimeter and two heavy gates. As they went a small crowd gathered, trailing behind at a little distance, not willing to miss the break from a daily monotony.

Mordred held his scornful calm all the way to the prison, his dark head carried high and arrogant, his lips closed in a thin, rigid line. No man looked more the part of the young, reckless criminal than he that morning, and he attracted far more attention than Fred, who walked with a weary step and his head bent a little. Then, as they entered the gaol and the doors crashed shut behind them, something seemed to break inside him. He began to struggle violently in his guards' grasp, writhing like a cat, sheer and unreasoning panic in his eyes. His breath came in choking, frantic gasps.

"Mordred!" Fred cried, stretching out a hand.

The men maintained their grip on him, but with difficulty; he had nearly torn loose in his first plunge. Tight-lipped, they held his arms as his lunges became more wild and his sobbing pants quick and erratic.

Inspector Dickson approached them and stared at the thrashing, desperate young man. Never had he despised him more than at this moment. His hand lifted, swept forward, and struck him across the face; he spoke, his voice hard and level. "You will behave yourself."

Mordred's struggles came to an instant, quivering halt. In his eyes flashed a second of searing hatred, and then the proud calm returned. He turned away a face as white as death, and he did not look at Inspector Dickson again.

They reached the short hall with the separate cells, those for dangerous prisoners and the ones condemned to death. At the first empty one, Inspector Dickson directed Fred's guards to it. A few yards further on there was another.

Someone opened the door and the guardsmen pushed their burden in. He swayed, every trace of stiffness crushed, the fight gone from his frame, and crumpled to the floor. There he lay, unmoving.

Inspector Dickson looked at him a moment, and coldly turned away.

End Part One

PART TWO

The Blade Falls

CHAPTER 15

MOONLIGHT SHONE DOWN ON DELGRASS, through the small window of a gaol cell, over the young man facedown on the cold stone floor. There was a straw pallet in the corner, but he scarcely recognized its existence and could care even less. He lay where he had fallen when the guards shoved him in, motionless as a dead man. Torment whelmed within him, higher and higher, like a cruelly raging ocean, waxing to the very peak of agony, until it seemed to his tortured soul that there must be a waning—but there was never a waning.

"See—" The voices would speak, the fingers would point. "See him, the murderer."

"Murderer . . . "

He drew in a harsh, shuddering breath and sank again to the stone. Cold it was, and he knew it not; he was cold and hot, hot with anger, cold with grief. Hours passed over him and more hours would pass yet that night, but he neither stirred nor slept. Thoughts and memories spiraled about him, taunting him, passing through the doors of his mind. Faces he saw, face after face, all in the light of a bitter despair. *Inspector Dickson's face as it was when he had struck him, the contempt in his eyes and the hardened set of his mouth . . . the young officer Selwyn's, hostile, bewildered . . . he saw Jared Earle's, filled with doubt and distrust . . .*

He saw Braegon's, puzzled . . . Therelane's, shaken, betrayed . . .

He saw Fenris, grief-stricken . . .

He would have wept aloud then, but he could not even weep. A seal was on his lips; he made no sound.

"Whence came you?" Faintly came the words, borne into the stillness of his despair, yet scarcely distinguishable into speech. Only the light breeze of night carried them to his ear.

"From the tunnels, my lord. Hopheg reported you were by the gaol."

"What needed you with me, then? Speak! We are alone."

"Only to hear how the plan shapes, my lord. Has it gone well?"

"It has come more swiftly even then I intended; aye, it has gone very well. They were arrested this morn."

"Ah! And what next?"

"What follows now? We are done; there is no more need for interference on our part . . . "

The wind died, the words fading with it to a garbled oblivion. Mordred did not stir, did not breathe.

" . . . shall rid myself yet of that Inspector. Too moral, I find him. He may cause trouble later on, and he discovered far more concerning us than I should have preferred. The trial is in three days. After that is over I shall slay him, that he may know before he dies what an injustice he has carried out." A cruel, vindictive triumph breathed in the speaker's barely audible voice, and he slipped into a tongue full of such hissing and muttering that even the wind could not bear it into the prison cell.

"My lord, far be it from me to brazen you, but the night has ears—"

"I tell you, we are alone. But search the area, lest any followed you, and return to your quarters."

The voices came no more.

Mordred rose trembling to his feet, and sank down against the wall below the window. His hands shook; he felt a sickness almost to the point of fainting. Sickness from the words he had heard, and the danger over his head, and the thing he realized he must do.

CHAPTER 16

THE DAWN HAD COME WITH a tang of cold. Inspector Dickson gradually woke and rose from bed, moving softly around the room, straightening the chair and table, pulling on his boots.

Languorous stirring came from the makeshift pallet on the floor. "Where . . . " the sleepy voice of Murcod slurred. "What time?"

"Barely sunrise," answered Inspector Dickson.

Murcod shoved himself up on an elbow, blinking and yawning like a disturbed owl. "Where are you going now? Back to Bulca?"

He did not answer at first. "To the prison first; to see if they will confess."

"Do you think they will?" Murcod rested his hands on his knees, the doubt plain on his face.

Inspector Dickson thrust his knife heavily into its sheath, buckled it around his waist. "No," he replied. "But it's my duty to ask."

~

Fred was sitting when the door swung open, but he rose and nodded his head to Inspector Dickson.

Must he always be so courteous? "Frederick Thorne," he said curtly. He paused, studying Fred's appearance. The man looked worse—almost ill. "Do you want a physician? You seem unwell."

Those steady brown eyes looked as though they could have laughed if they had not been so dulled with weariness and grief. "No," he said softly. "That won't be necessary."

Inspector Dickson's lips thinned at something in the tone the words were uttered. "Are you considering suicide, Mr. Thorne?" he demanded.

The accusatory words seemed to strike Fred like a blow. Inspector Dickson had never seen him flinch—only the smallest start when he charged him with Corian's damning witness. But now, whether broken down under weariness, guilt, or something else, the quiet image slipped. Pain poured across his face, puzzlement, recoil, and ebbed away as the surface calm closed back. "Sir, I had not . . . "

Reeling from the glimpse beneath, feeling as though he had seen not a killer but a martyr, Inspector Dickson shut his teeth against a crashing wave of doubt and with a wave dismissed the subject. "I am here to put a simple request to you, no more. You have heard it before, and answered often, but I beg you to reconsider. Earlier, you might have escaped the charge of murder through lack of definite proof, if not that of membership in Grimshaw's band; but now nothing will spare you the gallows save perhaps your own confession and plea for mercy. Will you admit to me what you have done? It may be a relief to your own heart as well."

Fred's eyes were fixed on the ground a little while. At last he lifted them to Inspector Dickson, and his tone was quiet and sad, but without regret. "I have never killed a man."

"Mr. Thorne, the evidence is against you."

Fred held his gaze steadily, and he shook his head. "I have only one confession to make, and that is that I have never, with or without intent, directly or by another's hand, taken the life of any man. Must you press me? I fear it will become a relief to confess—I know not how I can go on, I . . . " His eyes were glazed, his face too pale.

"Sit down," Inspector Dickson ordered him brusquely. He whirled and left the cell, struggling to control his emotion—not the compassion, for he had never shunned compassion to a criminal, but the dread doubt that this man was not and never had been a murderer.

But it must be so. He could not execute an innocent man. It must be so.

~

Outside Mordred's door, he steeled himself and resolved to keep his temper. "How has he been?" he asked the guards standing by.

"Quiet, sir," answered the elder. "Never a sound out of him—not a word, not a cry. I've had the ones that fling themselves around and cause a ruckus that way, but he didn't do that either. Just lay on the stones where he fell first, didn't move, never touched his food though I brought it to him twice yesterday. Was he still like that when you went in this morning?" he asked his companion.

The other shook his head. "He was by the wall, lookin' most burned out. Hadn't eaten anything though. Asked me where the Inspector was, all quiet-like; I said I didn't know, but that you'd most likely be around later. He kind of shuddered and turned his face to the wall, and I left."

"He asked for me?" repeated Inspector Dickson, not a little incredulous. Maybe, after all—

He nodded for them to unlock the door, and walked eagerly in.

A day's interval had wrought at least as much change in Mordred as Fred, if not more. He stood by the narrow window, his lean frame supported against the wall. At the sound of the hinges squealing he whirled, and Inspector Dickson saw a thin, exhausted face, hollow-eyed with sleeplessness, rough locks of hair clinging damply to a pale forehead. He had no impudent words of greeting for Inspector Dickson, nor indeed any words at all; he stared at him, not speaking, anger and something else striving for supremacy in his eyes. Could it be remorse?

"Have you considered confessing?" Inspector Dickson asked as gently as he could. He knew it was a mistake as soon as the words left his mouth.

Mordred's chin flew up; his arms folded stubbornly, scornful anger suffusing his face. "I see you have come to do naught but mock and torment me," he returned.

Inspector Dickson clenched his teeth. "Have it as you will," he snapped. "You know very well that I came only to fulfill my own duties. I would have persuaded you to take the course suited for your own good, but you will have none of that. So be it."

"I am not a murderer," said Mordred in a low, passionate voice.

"There you lie, murderer," replied Inspector Dickson, furious beyond the point of reason and no longer caring what he did.

Mordred's lips turned white. "A child are you, then?" he said, mockery whispering in his stifled voice. "To call names is no better than an infant. I thought you a man, but maybe you are a brat."

"And now you have done it yourself, in naming me a babe," retorted Inspector Dickson. "Aye, the only difference is that I am not a child, but you are still a murderer."

"I am not a murderer," Mordred choked, but as though to himself. He seemed strangely agitated.

Inspector Dickson looked at him a moment, and made a move as though to turn. "I think I may as well—"

"No!" Mordred cried. He took a painful, shaking breath. "Laugh at me as you will. Last night I could not sleep, and I heard men speaking, two men's voices. They plotted the death of Inspector Dickson. They seek—your death." He ended in a gasp and looked away.

Silence hissed around them.

"Also they spoke of—"

"Yes? What else?" Inspector Dickson prompted.

"Never mind," said Mordred, softly, with a strange hint of pride. "It was nothing."

Inspector Dickson scanned his features slowly. "How do I know you heard anything last night?"

It was not simply a doubter's question, though there was doubt in it. But, Inspector Dickson realized, there was no way for Mordred to know that. No way for him to tell it apart from the last insulting remarks he had hurled at the young man's face.

Hurt and betrayal rose up in the gray eyes so near his own. "Leave me," he whispered hoarsely, and then cried out, *"Leave me!"* He whirled away and flung himself down onto the cold stones.

"Mordred—" Inspector Dickson began, attempting to mend his words, to at least explain them.

"I am done with you!" came the bitter answer. "Would that I had never said it. I only hope you die knowing what you have done."

Mayhap he should have pressed him. But he did not. He left the room, and locked the door behind him, and there he stood, lost in thought, perplexity on his face.

~

The small cottage on the banks of Rale Creek seemed empty when he returned to it, too empty, too silent. He thought of Murcod rambling on and on last night about their childhood days, the girls they had chased, the brooks they had set fish-traps in, rambling until they both could no longer keep their eyes open, and wished selfishly that Murcod were here to obliterate the silence again . . .

Then it seemed too loud.

"Back at last, Dickson?" Harris strolled cheerily into the room and poked up the fire with a great deal of clattering. "Heard tidbits on it now and again from local gossip. Something of a tough problem, wasn't it?

"Been pretty quiet here while you were gone, really; a chicken thief, but that was about it until this morning. Funny chap called, not from around here, and he didn't want me, he wanted you. He's waiting in the other room, in fact. You'd best go take care of it."

As Inspector Dickson wheeled sharply, Harris called after him, "Hope you haven't been badmouthing Dirion's top man, Dickson!"

"Tough problem . . . "

"Yes," he whispered aloud, his hand on the doorknob. "And what's worse, I'm not sure I've solved it any more."

The man was half-turned, pacing rapidly to and fro; he did not immediately see Inspector Dickson. In his erect bearing was authority, and in his face compassion. Some instinctive part of Inspector Dickson reached out, saying that this was no ordinary man.

"Who are you?" he asked, and the figure turned to fix him with a pair of gentle, penetrating dark eyes. He did not smile.

"I am Derek Winston. Most know me as the General of Orden."

"The General of Orden!" Inspector Dickson echoed in astonishment. "What do you want *here*?"

He heard the temerity of his question, and flushed. "Forgive me, sir. I am very much—out of sorts this morning."

"Unwell?"

"Nay, only troubled; it is a problem that recurs whenever I think I have quenched it."

"And this problem, what does it deal with?"

Inspector Dickson was bewildered by the general's apparent interest in this problem, rather than his own. "Murderers, sir," he said softly, and saw Fred's gentle, tired face and Mordred's proud, angry one before his mind's eye.

"Explain it to me," came the quietly commanding voice.

"I—sir—do you not want me to tend to your own—"

"Explain it to me."

Inspector Dickson gave up. *Do not the great men of the world do as they wish?*

So he told him briefly of the murders, and of the arrest the day before, ending with Mordred's words to him that morning. "I know not what to do . . . " he murmured. "Whether he spoke truth or lies, how can I tell? And it does not clear him—does it?" He raised his eyes to the dark, stern pair opposite him. "In any case, let us now attend to your business."

The general held up his hand. "Give me leave, Inspector Dickson, to fetch certain people whom you must meet." And with those cryptic words he turned and left.

Inspector Dickson was trying to make sense out of his statement when the door reopened to admit the general, and not the general only, but two others following him. It was the girl that made Inspector Dickson start and nearly cry aloud.

He could not have mistaken that broad, low forehead anywhere, those expressive brows, that wide mouth and stubborn chin. She could scarcely have been more alike had she been a man; and yet the femininity itself enhanced the resemblance. He almost expected her to grow dark hair instead of bright, and those green eyes to change to gray.

Kenhelm.

The boy beside her was less like in some ways, more in others. He was straight but slightly built, slim as a lath, with a thin, sensitive face and wide-set gray eyes that were fastened on him with an almost despairing anxiety. The harsh line of a newly healed scar ran up his forehead until a forelock of dark hair hid it from view.

The intensity of the boy's pleading gaze faltered as he sensed what Inspector Dickson was looking at. He flinched and turned his face away.

"Kenhelm—" Inspector Dickson uttered aloud softly, disbelievingly.

The general looked keenly at him a moment in silence. "Fenris and Laufeia Kenhelm," he said. "They accompanied me from their own village of Ceristen."

"But," began Inspector Dickson, wildly flustered and confused.

"I doubt not you are wondering why they are here," the general said, "and why I, of all people, am with them. It is not such a long story; but—if you do not object—we might sit down for it."

Ceristen, Orden - Three days prior

A bright sun spilled through the window where Laufeia sat, feeling the heat on her hands and head as she bent over the shirt of Fenris' she was mending. But as her fingers moved deftly in and out, her brows were puckered in a worried frown.

It was well into the last week of February. Surely Mordred would not have stayed so long if all had gone well. Nay, perhaps he had meant to return with Fred and Jared. But they had expected Fred to return by now as well . . .

But plans often went awry. The boat could have been delayed or caught in a storm.

Or wrecked.

Laufeia shook her head angrily and jerked the innocent cloth in frustration. Oh, how she wished Fiona would visit, or Mirda, and then she would have something to do besides turn her worries inside out.

Besides, Mordred had promised he would return as soon as possible, and he would not have readily changed his mind. What had they wanted him for? Suppose—suppose her fear had been right, and someone had sent that letter who knew . . .

But what could they want him for then? A kidnapping—a ransom?

"Ai!" she exclaimed, springing to her feet. What one's mind could think of when left to itself! Her mind was made up; she was not staying in this house a moment longer.

But she had not yet taken one step before a knock sounded and her thoughts flew a'tumble. A visitor, and no one she knew, of that she was sure. The knock was a resounding blow, cold and officious. She darted into the kitchen and sent the door swinging open.

There she stood, breathless and conscious of her bare feet as she stared up at the imposing figure of a mail courier. He stared back down at her.

She lifted a questioning brow. "Sir?"

"I seek the house of a"—he glanced down at a letter in his hand—"a Kenhelm."

Laufeia's eyes widened, and her heart began a painful racing. "You have found it, sir."

He handed her the letter; she held it closely against her chest as his hoofbeats faded away, and she slowly turned into the house again, opening it at last with quivering fingers. The date written at the top was that of two weeks ago. The clear, flowing hand was unmistakably her brother's.

February 11

My dear brother and sister,

I write to you from a small inn in the village of Cobren. The men I came to treat with, though I sent them a letter, have not answered it or come to me, nor do I think they ever mean to. I would come back directly but for an unpleasant occurrence which keeps myself, Fred, and Jared here.

The morning after we arrived a man was found dead in the hostel's common room—murdered, quite plainly, and since that time the police of the place have endeavored to find the culprit among us inn guests. The Inspector in charge seems to make very little headway, and is a most trying skeptic who will not accept on faith that his morning bread is made with flour and water. I fear we do not care for one another's company in the least.

Do not worry about me; now that you have received this letter you will understand why I am gone. When the matter is cleared up, I and the others will return straightaway.

Fenris and Laufeia,

'Tis but a few days since the above. I may not be returning home for a long time, I fear—why, why does he suspect me? Do not fret overmuch for me, my sister and brother—it is only suspect yet. But how he persists in these hateful questions and looks . . .

February 21

I do not understand what madness this is. I can scarcely think. He says that I have done this, and not only that but Fred as well is suspected.

If you hear from me again, you will know we have been acquitted. I do not believe we will be.

Horror smothered the breath in Laufeia's chest, making her lightheaded as she reread the last lines of the letter. There was a jerky, blotted line of ink after the last word and no signature.

Suspect—accusation—murder—arrest—*death*—

Mordred! her heart cried. And "Mordred" slipped in a faint, pleading whisper from her lips. Her hands were trembling, the tears were falling from her eyes, she scarcely knew what she did as she donned her shoes and stumbled out the door. She walked blind over paths and lost them, fell into wet snowdrifts, wandering she knew not where; all she knew was the letter in her hand, hot like a branding iron against her fingers with its dreadful message. No—no—no—

Her shoulder drove into a surface that gave a little, and her face was suddenly hard against something alive and throbbing. She went staggering backwards, blinked away the tears, and in front of her she saw a horse—a very beautiful horse. Nay, the horse was not more beautiful than any other; it was its careful grooming and fine, expensive harness. A rich man's horse.

Her eyes flew up to the stern, dark-eyed rider. "My lord," she stammered. "Forgive me!"

"What is this?" he asked gently. His face was not angry or disdainful, but filled with compassion. He dismounted and reached out a hand towards her. "You have been weeping."

"I—it is my brother, sir—" The tears spilled out again, and she struggled in vain to check them under his quiet gaze.

"What is amiss, young maid?"

How could he help? she wondered wearily, but quelled her sobs enough to hand him the letter. He read through it swiftly and returned it to her, and did not speak directly.

"Oh, sir, he is my brother!" she burst out, begging, she hardly knew why. "And he went to Delgrass—now he is accused of this—my brother is angry at times, even very angry, but he never had cause to commit a murder. My lord, it cannot be true! They will arrest him and kill him unjustly, and one other, one other as well, who is well known to all of us and betrothed to my own dear friend—he is a courageous and loving man, who could never harm another. And oh, sir, I have a second brother, and I—I could bear Mordred's death, maybe. But his life is bound in Mordred's—and if Mordred is killed, I dare not think how he will suffer. My lord, I do not stretch the truth when I say that he would die of grief."

She broke off, aghast at all she had said, yet she was unable to let go the growing hope inside her.

The man spoke at last, slowly. "It grieves me to see any man condemned unjustly. I very much would desire to help this brother of yours. But he is not in Orden now?"

"Nay, in Delgrass, a week's journey south." Her heart sank.

"That is far . . . nonetheless, you are of Orden. I will bring the matter before the king. What is your name, child?"

"I am Laufeia Kenhelm, sir."

Something in the man's face changed subtly. "Have you other sisters?" he asked in a moment.

"No, no other sisters."

"Brothers?"

"The two I spoke of, sir."

"No others?"

"I—" She stopped. "I cannot tell you, sir. You would laugh."

"I will not laugh."

She saw the intense gravity of those tender eyes, and she knew he would not laugh.

"My other brother—he is called Ahearn. He does not live here."

"Aye, that I know well. He resides in Dirion, in the palaces of Ederan and of the king."

"You know, sir!"

"I know, young maid. Your brother is the King of Dirion." He smiled down at her. "I have seen him, your brother; and you are like him, a little. You have his firmness of mouth. He is young, and inexperienced; but he is firm. He rules well.

"But that is all neither here nor there. That you are kin to Dirion's ruler throws the matter in a new light. I am free to help you as I could not have otherwise; indeed, with such a question at stake, I may be able to accompany you to Delgrass itself!" Again he smiled, a light, laughing smile, and touched her shoulder. "For a poor peasant, alas, the General of Orden can do little. Would that it were not so! But for a prince of Dirion he may do much, and that with great swiftness."

"Sir, we cast aside the status we could have had. He is not a prince."

"Child. Shall I leave you in distress, when I could aid you? He is brother to a king. We may leave it at that."

Laufeia dared at last to smile back at him.

Then words that he had spoken returned and smote her, and she reeled inwardly at their impact. "My lord, you are . . . the General of Orden?"

"Aye, and I was journeying up the mountainside to view the castle's progress. It is well indeed for you that I did so."

~

"How we came so swiftly, you may wonder," said the General of Orden. "But we were granted the use of two dragons from Mitheren, and thus came as far as Addis Muard before we left them with the proper housing and proceeded to Bulca by horse."

"So they truly are," Inspector Dickson began bemusedly. "Mordred Kenhelm is—"

"It is the truth, though hardly known, that Ahearn King of Dirion had brothers and a sister who refused to remain with him but journeyed on to Orden," said the general. "I was there with a delegation from Orden not two months past, and held discourse with him; and he spoke to me the name of Mordred."

"But why did they—" *Why did they refuse,* he had been about to ask. But something in the general's eyes warned him that this was not the time or place to speak of that.

"Where is Mordred now?" demanded Laufeia, stepping forward. "Is he well?"

Inspector Dickson forced himself to meet her eyes. "He is in the prison."

Laufeia's hands flew to her white face. "Then you—" she whispered.

"I arrested them. I am sorry."

"But now—will you not relent? You will release them?"

"My lady," Inspector Dickson stammered, hating the look of distress on her face, "I have no proof to counteract that which I have now. Until I have that, I can do nothing."

"Let them see him," the General of Orden intervened, "and this Fred Thorne as well if they wish it. But you, Inspector Dickson, I wish to ask certain questions regarding the young Kenhelm's words to you this morning."

"Well?" Inspector Dickson asked when they were alone in the room.

"The young man . . . when he told you that men were plotting your death, did he say the reason they desired it?"

"I think . . . " Inspector Dickson cast his mind back to the conversation. "No, as far as I can recall, he never mentioned that."

"Repeat your exchange, if you will, as nearly as you can."

Inspector Dickson obeyed, and with no difficulty; every word of it was painfully fresh in his mind.

"So," the general said when he was finished. "There was something more, that he would not tell you."

"Aye, that is so, it seems."

"Why would he have done that?"

"I do not know." Inspector Dickson envisioned that hard young face, shuddering with the effort of having warned the man he hated so; and then that unusual, uplifted look and the faint pride in his voice.

"Maybe," the general offered, "he believed it would lessen the credibility of his story."

Inspector Dickson frowned sharply and contemplated the suggestion.

The general's voice broke in again on his thoughts. "You must find it out from him. All that he remembers."

He will never tell me, thought Inspector Dickson. But he nodded and followed the General of Orden out of the room.

CHAPTER 17

"MORDRED!" LAUFEIA LET OUT A cry and ran through the opened door. Inspector Dickson, about to follow, felt the general's restraining hand across his chest and halted. This was not the place for his intrusion.

He watched Mordred's head lift sharply, his eyes widen in disbelief. He watched him gather Laufeia tiredly into his arms, and press his head against her hair. He saw him release her and catch his breath a little as he caught sight of Fenris. A deep, nameless emotion tremored in his eyes.

The younger brother walked forward and put his arms wordlessly about him, and Mordred held onto him as though he would never let him go.

Laufeia began to speak at last, but Inspector Dickson had seen enough. He walked a little away and sat down against the corridor wall, trying to shut out the hushed babblings—a question in Laufeia's light, anxious tone, Mordred's deeper answer, the hesitant murmur of Fenris. He hated their reunion.

He hated himself.

~

"Are you all right? Are you sick? Mordred, you look terrible. Are they feeding you? Why did they imprison you? We shall make certain you are freed. Mordred, do you not believe that you will be acquitted?"

Mordred brushed off Laufeia's queries tiredly with muttered answers. At her last one, he looked up, his eyes hardening. "No. I have no hope of it."

Nay, he had not meant to say it like that. It hurt them, hurt them both—Fenris especially. They would mistake it for an unreasoning despair, they did not know and he could not tell them of the dread words he had heard last night . . .

"Mordred," Laufeia protested, recovering herself, "you do not understand. We have the general with us, the General of Orden, and he means to aid us for Ahearn's sake. 'Tis but a mistake, and we shall set it all to rights."

"Forgive me, Laufeia."

She smiled gladly. "I forgive you, Mordred. Then you do believe—"

"No! I do not. Forgive me, my sister, but even the General of Orden can do nothing for me, not unless he can show Inspector Dickson another murderer. Do not try to make me hope, Laufeia. I can see none."

She was silent and lowered her eyes, tears glistening threateningly in their lashes. Then she lifted them again.

"Mordred . . . " There was a question in her eyes, a fear. "Promise me you did not do it."

He placed his hands fiercely on her shoulders. "I promise you, Laufeia." He sighed and relaxed his hold, raising his eyes to steadily meet Fenris' gaze. "I promise."

~

Inspector Dickson felt someone touch him.

"It is time," said the general.

They entered the stone cell, startling the three within.

"We have words to speak to your brother," the general said to Fenris and Laufeia, motioning them from the room.

With their going the gentle side of Mordred vanished, sucking away inside of him. He turned a rigid face to them and waited.

The general was the one who stepped forward. "Well met, Mordred Kenhelm. I am Derek Winston, General of Orden; your sister and brother have told you of my presence here?"

Mordred looked at him, an almost questioning look it was, as though he sought to read the other man. Inspector Dickson moved to the side so as to glimpse the general's face himself, instinctively gauging the firmness there, the power in his gaze. A forthright bearing that reminded him of Fred Thorne, but deeper, and a kindness that he, the would-be cynic, found himself failing to question. For the first time Inspector Dickson guessed why Ordenians spoke with such fervor of their general.

Perhaps Mordred saw the same. At any rate, he bent his head with the greatest deference Inspector Dickson had ever seen in him. "My lord," he murmured.

"You know I shall do all I can to see you cleared. However, we are not here to discuss that this morning."

Mordred tensed, wary confusion flashing through his eyes. "What then?"

General Winston nodded to Inspector Dickson and stepped aside.

Inspector Dickson walked slowly forward. "You concealed something of what you heard last night, Mordred. I must know what."

Mordred clenched his jaw visibly. "Why should I tell you?" he demanded harshly.

"You must. If it is of importance, if especially it is tied in with those men who desire to kill me, you have no right to keep it hidden."

"Why should I tell you? You will mock me, you will deride me, you will call me a spinner of lies to save my own skin, all of which I am *not*."

"So this thing may weaken the suspicion on you, if it is true?" Inspector Dickson returned.

Mordred remained silent.

"Might it then weaken that on Fred Thorne as well?" He saw the start, the comprehension dawning in Mordred's face. "Can you keep from him the chance to go free?"

"If you scorn me, I know not what I shall do," said Mordred in quivering tones. He halted, and forced himself on at last.

"Two men spoke—a leader and a subordinate. They said that the plan had gone well. That 'they' had been arrested that morn, and the trial was in three days. That they feared lest you cause trouble for them later on. That after the trial they would slay you, and tell you what an injustice you had carried out." The words did not make sense for a moment. They repeated themselves louder and louder in his head, banging into one another and muddling, but over and over again he heard one phrase, loudest of all.

"What an injustice you carried out . . . "

He put a hand to his head, staggered.

"What an injustice you carried out . . . "

Maybe he is lying. Maybe—

Enough prejudice, he thought grimly. Maybe he was lying. But the shattered face before him could not easily be that of one who had lied.

"What an injustice you carried out . . . "

What have I been playing into? What have I done? What can I do now?

~

"We are dealing with a dark thing," said General Winston gravely.

They were alone in the gaoler's quarters. Inspector Dickson nodded, scarcely taking in the general's words, and leaned his head against the back of the chair. He was sick inside, sick, dead, shamed.

"What have I done?" he muttered.

It would have been bad enough to arrest one innocent man. But *two*—two who had not deserved the stone walls that enclosed them, two whose names were already scarred—

The thought of Fred pained him the most. The brown eyes rising up before his mind reproached him because there was no reproach in them, and had never been. It had been that, in a way, that had made it easier to believe the deed of him: Fred was never angry nor resentful like one would think of a man wrongfully accused. But then, Mordred had been all the latter, and had he listened to such behavior? he thought drearily. Now the realization that all the gentleness, all the courtesy, had been inherent and genuine, cut him to the quick, and guilt tightened in his heart.

So Fred tormented him the more; and yet when he thought of Mordred there was a sick, knotted feeling in his stomach like dread and a host of other things that he did not try to name. Perhaps it was because the one who had hated him so bitterly had been the one in the end to warn him—and had refused to tell the words that might save himself because he knew he would not be believed. He shrank from the sensation, tried to shut it out, but he kept seeing Mordred's dreadful, stricken face at the words he wished he had never uttered, *"There you lie, murderer."*

He leaned forward and dropped his head in his hands, shaking it as though that could erase the image.

"Inspector." The clear voice rang on his ears, urgent and almost rebuking. "There will be time later on to dwell on grievances and errors, but we must discuss what is immediately afoot. If the young Kenhelm spoke truth, and it seems apparent that he has, then he is cleared, and the true killer is not yet found. And when he knows that we have anticipated his plan, what then? He is a ruthless man, not given to leaving things to chance."

"You mean he will retaliate."

"Without a doubt."

"But how can we stop him? We know nothing of where or who he might be."

"I think that perhaps it would not be wise to stop him."

Inspector Dickson gaped at him. And then all at once he saw a flash of where the general was leading.

"Guard, yes, keep watchful," continued General Winston, "but this man is undoubtedly as cunning as a shapeshifter. The only way for us to know anything of him is if we wait for him to strike again. And furthermore, if he does, Mordred Kenhelm's words will be borne out beyond question and you may know surely he and the other are innocent."

Inspector Dickson nodded heavily.

"To win," said the general, "we must expose ourselves to him."

~

"Reprieve, Mordred!" Laufeia took his hands, clasped them tightly, joy on her face. "It is reprieve for the present."

"Reprieve?" he repeated cynically. "What of it? That Inspector wants only to see me convicted, and I do not doubt he will do all in his power to see it done yet." But he did not speak with the same despair that he had before.

"You do him an injustice, Mordred," Laufeia remonstrated. "He is doing all he can to help us."

"I don't care! I don't want to hear a word of it. Be quiet, Laufeia. You do not know what it is—*you* were never—"

He stopped himself with an effort. To take out his bitterness on Laufeia, to burden her with it, that was something he could not do. She must not hear how Inspector Dickson had mocked him—how he had struck him—all the innumerable ways he had succeeded in making Mordred hate him more. How he had pried his most painful secrets out only to scorn them.

"Leave me, Laufeia, please," he said softly, afraid he could control himself no longer, and she left him alone with his raging anger.

~

Harris looked askance when Inspector Dickson returned late in the evening with five companions.

"I saw those three earlier," he said, referring to the general and the younger Kenhelms, "but where did these others come from? Did you tell them they could sleep here? Where do you think we have the room?"

"We'll bed up in the kitchen for now," Inspector Dickson told him. "General Winston, you may use the bedroom."

"Unless it is a very small room," the general said, "I do not need to keep it to myself."

"There are two beds," Inspector Dickson admitted. "And one of them could fit two people on it. As for the others, there is a little room to the side where we can fit you in."

"I do not need the bedroom," said Mordred in a flat sort of way. He had not looked at Inspector Dickson once.

"Let Laufeia and Fenris take it," said Fred generously. "I am tired enough that it will certainly not matter where I sleep."

They ate a largely silent supper and sat for a little, while a rainless wind moaned softly outside.

"Have you and your partner worked together long?" General Winston asked.

"Six years," answered Inspector Dickson.

"Is it mostly quiet, or do you often have such strange events?"

"None so bad as this."

There seemed to be a quiet menace under every word they spoke, hovering in the air around them, a tenseness in the dark beyond the fire. The general's stern dark eyes were veiled; the flickering light tore groping fingers of shadow over his face, wreaths like smoke and legend. He looked like a seer out of the ages, old and fell. Fenris' head was drooping and Mordred put out an arm and drew him against his shoulder in a silently swift, watchful movement, his eyes glimmering and alert.

The general stood, quietly enough, and yet Inspector Dickson started. "It is time we slept," he said. "The night is already wearing."

~

So Mordred and Fred did not sleep in the prison that night. And the plan, which had been falling into pieces, lay once again wide open . . .

CHAPTER 18

MORNING CAME WITH CLOUDS LOW in the west, dark as soot and moving in quickly.

"We shall have a rainstorm before nightfall," Inspector Dickson murmured to himself, opening the door for a better look. "Or maybe a blizzard," he added as the wind knifed coldly into him, battering against the sturdy frame of the cottage. He slammed the door again and set about preparing breakfast; thinking he felt a draft, he went back to close it a second time.

He still felt the draft.

It was probably that the door needed mending. Had Harris never taken care of that?

He heard stirring, doors opening. General Winston appeared in the aperture to the bedroom.

Inspector Dickson took no notice of him at first, but very soon he realized that the general was watching him, and he turned to see a strange expression on his face. It struck a reaction from Inspector Dickson, because it was like an echo of the way he had felt the day he found Mr. Wilson dead.

General Winston beckoned to him. "Come," he said. And Inspector Dickson followed him, past the sleeping forms of Fenris and Laufeia, into the adjoining close where Mordred and Fred had stayed.

There was no one in the room.

Inspector Dickson stared.

The blankets lay tangled and discarded. The window was ajar, the shutters flapping, banging intermittently in the vengeful wind.

They ran . . .

He felt angry, betrayed, furious with himself and them all at once. *Why did I let them sleep together? Why did I let them sleep alone? Why did I let them trick me into freeing them for one instant?*

"Dickson!" Someone ran into the room.

He spun around. "Murcod?"

"Dickson, I know you're wondering why I'm up here, but listen. Corian is dead. The word was all over Cobren this morning."

"Corian is *dead*?" Inspector Dickson broke Murcod's gaze after one stunned second and stared at the twisted, empty blankets. He picked them up in a sudden swoop and hurled them against the wall. Their soft thump did nothing to dissipate his anger.

"They are gone!" he cried, whirling accusatorily on the general. "Gone! I let down my guard for one day and they turn into the monsters they were before. How much more death is to happen now? How long before we can find them again?"

General Winston gave no answer at first to Inspector Dickson's angry castigation. At last he said, simply, "But Corian is dead."

Inspector Dickson looked bewildered at him. As if Corian's death did not prove it beyond a doubt!

"It all but disproves it," said the general in answer to his incredulous stare. He paused. "Because of Corian's death," he said deliberately. "And because this is exactly what we should have expected. They were meant to be blamed; they were cleared. Now the retaliation. Our enemy redeems his plan by incriminating them again."

Inspector Dickson saw at last what he meant by Corian's death. "You are saying that if they were guilty, they would surely attempt to preserve their innocence by avoiding another murder? Well, I can see how it is possible. But can we be sure? Maybe they had a reason for needing to kill him, despite the blot on their name."

"And because," said the general softly, as though Inspector Dickson had not even spoken, "of this."

He stooped and picked up one of the blankets fallen by the wall, and turned it to reveal a jagged rip in the cloth, where a whole corner had been torn entirely away.

"Where is the rest?" asked Inspector Dickson, frowning. His eyes scanned the whole bare, little room, and nowhere was the missing scrap of cloth.

"That is what I asked myself," said General Winston.

Inspector Dickson shook his head. "I know it was not cut like that last night. Why would anyone tear off the corner and hide it?"

"Buried under the ashes of the fire," said the general quietly, "I found this." He unfolded his hand and let the dusty strip of cloth flutter free.

Inspector Dickson took the fragment.

It was bloodstained.

Danger rolled in his ears, the silence lengthened, and he held the piece of wool between his fingers like a serpent that might strike. Excuse after excuse bobbed up like hollow casks, but none of them would serve. No one would waste time to hide a bloody rag but someone who wanted it to appear a bloodless flight. This had not been a rescue, or an escape. It was a capture.

"Where is Mordred?"

They had not heard the light footsteps coming up behind them. The three men turned to see Laufeia in the doorway, her fingers holding a half-plaited braid in place while her eyes searched slowly over the room.

Inspector Dickson made a guilty move to slip the cloth into his pocket, too late.

"What happened?" she asked very steadily and sensibly.

"We hardly know yet," Inspector Dickson faltered. "They are both missing."

"Aye," she said, nodding; and then, "I will go tell Fenris."

"Brave little woman," said Murcod, staring after her. "Is she Mordred's sister?"

"Aye," said Inspector Dickson dully.

"Do you think she is all right?"

"I think she is not going to faint, if that is what you mean," Inspector Dickson answered with a dry laugh. "As for all right, we are none of us that."

"No," said Murcod, "maybe not. I think you are not, anyway. Do you mind explaining what has happened and who are all these people?"

"Another time, Murcod." Inspector Dickson started for the door. "I need to see whether I can find anything about Corian's death."

He yanked the door open and the wind tore it from his hand, smashing it against the outside wall with an ire that made the house shiver. The skies drooped low and ominous, the dark gray furrowed with black, and the first snowflakes began to fall hard and fast.

Murcod shoved him back into the house and tugged the door closed with a violent effort. "Never mind that, Dickson," he said. "No one's going anywhere today."

~

It had been a long day.

The snowstorm had continued unabating, the muffled drone of the wind such a constant noise that they almost forgot it was there until it rose in a shriek like the cry from a human throat. And then they would start, and cease what they were doing, and it would slowly fall to the old low moan and they would forget again.

Inspector Dickson had seen little of Fenris and Laufeia. They had both appeared for breakfast, dinner, and supper, but Fenris had soon retreated to the bedroom and Laufeia followed him at once.

Harris was curled up comfortably near the fire with a blanket draped over himself, a book in his hand and a stack of them beside him. He said a peddler had stopped by two days ago and offered him five old books for a real bargain. What kind of bargain was it, Inspector Dickson wanted to know, when the binding was coming off, the pages falling out, and how much money had he spent on them anyway?

Harris, as usual, ignored him.

Inspector Dickson leaned back in the slatted, straw-bottomed chair and closed his eyes, questions pounding painfully in his skull.

"Dickson," said Murcod, musingly.

"Aye."

"If they didn't do it—like you said—then who did?"

Murcod had echoed his own thoughts so exactly that he sat up with a start.

"It must've been one of the other two guests," Murcod went on. "Right?"

"Houk and Syrinna! And I let them leave, days ago. They're far down the river by now, impossible to find—"

"No, wait, Dickson! We're looking at it the wrong way." Murcod suddenly looked very excited. "Listen, if it was not Fred and Mordred, then Corian *lied*. And—oh, my thoughts are all confused. I don't know where they went."

"Wait!" Inspector Dickson clenched his hands around the seat of the chair, inside desperately, grimly quiet. "I begin to see. If the killer were either of them, Houk or Syrinna, then they cannot have left the area for good, because they had to have killed Corian last night."

"No, Dickson." Murcod was shaking his head. "No, that's not right either. We keep forgetting that this is not confined to one person—this is a ring of many. If Houk or Syrinna did the killing, they could have left as soon as they were free to go, and one of their companions could have traveled here later to finish Corian off." He frowned, broke off, and started slowly again.

"Remember how you told me of the conversation that Mordred Kenhelm heard?"

"We are assuming it was true."

"Of course. At any rate, he heard people speaking of their plan—a plan that got Mordred and Fred blamed for the murders. And you said to me, when you relayed the tale, that it seemed likely the speakers had been members of the Claw."

"Yes, I said that."

"Maybe the leader he heard was even Grimshaw. Now, if Houk or Syrinna were among this group, Grimshaw wouldn't need to keep them near at hand in order to carry out his bidding. He has enough other men, and he could surely let Houk or Syrinna go to keep suspicion off them."

"All right." Inspector Dickson shut his eyes again. "So it could have been Houk or Syrinna, but it may have not been. It really doesn't matter, does it? Because we need to strike at the root of the problem, and that is neither of them."

"Unless one of them is Grimshaw," said Murcod wryly.

"Houk could be, I suppose, but Syrinna?" Inspector Dickson laughed.

"She was a flirtatious little creature," said Murcod seriously, "and a good actor, I daresay. Who knows what she might have been capable of?"

Inspector Dickson shook his head. "Grimshaw was a man, by Corian's account; and a burly one, too."

"No matter," said Murcod with a wave. "We are straying from the point. Dickson, back to Corian's lying. He lied about seeing Fred and Mordred with the Claw. Who told him to lie?"

"I . . . don't know," said Inspector Dickson slowly. And then he started. "Sam! Sam sent him! Have I been playing into the hands of—"

Murcod shook his head fiercely. "Not Sam."

"But—?"

"How could it have been Sam? Sam *sent* Corian, yes, to tell you about the Claw, because he wouldn't himself, for whatever reason. But when Corian arrived, it was two entire days before he came to tell you lies about Fred and Mordred. A person who wanted lies spread would make sure they were uttered as soon as possible! Someone else told Corian to lie in those few days."

"Yes," Inspector Dickson said softly. "Yes, you are right. But who told him to? Houk or Syrinna? Or someone else altogether?"

Murcod shook his head, as though he were not listening. "Dickson, there's something I don't like about all this."

"That being, Murcod?"

"It took too long."

"What did?"

"The whole affair! If someone were aiming to get them incriminated, get suspicion off himself, why did he take weeks about it? Surely, if he were an inn guest, he would have been trying to speed matters up a little bit, to make sure that nothing was uncovered against himself. Why, it all seems to have been planned out as coolly and unconcernedly as though he were watching and orchestrating the whole thing from the outside."

"A plan," murmured Inspector Dickson. "'The plan has gone well.' You are right; it is as though the whole thing centered around their ultimate accusation and arrest." He rose. "Not the murder."

Why did he think of King Andra just now?

The call of the wind rose up, thin-throated, twisted and wild, and echoed another cry in Inspector Dickson's memory. Suddenly his thoughts were flooded with the recollection of a thin cold morning, of the soldiers in his bedroom and Getta's warning at the gate and a shrill scream behind a gold-plated door. *"I never want to see you again, Inspector!"* Connections clicked uneasily in his head.

Someone had coerced Corian to lie.

Had that same someone threatened King Andra to let him go?

He had never told Murcod of that thin cold morning and his strange departure from Balhorde, dismissing it in all its inexplicability and seeming irrelevance. He told him now.

"It fits," said Murcod. "It does fit. An inspector languishing in a Mattadonnish dungeon or spiked headless on the gate couldn't carry out an investigation and arrest—and without you on the job, it's doubtful anybody else would have picked it up. But Dickson, you realize what I'm saying: that in the case of an outside plan, the murderer would not be one of the inn guests."

Inspector Dickson nodded.

Murcod flung up his hands. "And yet he must have been!"

"There are too many pieces to this," said Inspector Dickson helplessly. "Too many shards in a windowpane. We are missing something, something crucial that draws it all together. How could it have been anyone but an inn guest? I was over the events of that night a dozen times with Galesper; there is no loophole for someone to have left—not by ordinary means, at any rate."

"I suppose he flew out the window!" said Murcod wearily.

He had not said it in a jesting way, but Inspector Dickson laughed all the same.

Movement gathered in the corner, and the general got up and walked out of the room.

"Did I offend him?" asked Murcod, startled.

"I should hardly think so. Murcod, let us leave the matter for tonight. My head is spinning and I am too tired to think any longer."

Murcod nodded. The gale beat the snow against the wall.

Inspector Dickson leaned down and picked up one of the books that Harris had nestled against him. Harris mumbled and his head lifted to sink sleepily down again on the pages of his own; Inspector Dickson settled the musty tome on his lap and riffled through the contents.

> *Being a Lengthy Treatise on the Creatures which Inhabit this World and the Nature of Them.*
>
> *"... And the thindran, reputed to be a fable and no more, are yet regarded as truth in old legends and histories, which gives rise to the idea, that unless the men of long ago were so much less intelligent than we ourselves, they must have been speaking the truth concerning these things, like wingéd horses in appearance but with a luster on their coats like the stars and the light of truth in their eyes ... "*

". . . but Veno Thir, in disputation, writes in his Challenge to Ahlus a'Hohlin: 'And he, that is, the Ruler, sent the legaeësser among us to give counsel, that they in their fairness and power might give us a picture of how much more is the one who sent them . . . '"

". . . And to Man was given the worlds, that he might flourish, and the thindran were said to be near to him in those days, and manifold, and they walked near with men and did not shun them . . . "

". . . For to the shapeshifters are the lust of blood, and they walk best in the shape of a wildcat; and one may know a shapeshifter in his human form by this, that he will have skin that is paler than the whitest snow, paler than a corpse or any man, though his hair be dark, and his teeth, though not filed, are sharp like an animal's . . . "

Inspector Dickson's head jerked up. He had been drowsing. He searched in vain for his place, unable to remember what he had last read. His gaze trailed down to the end of the page.

"On the Creature that is Commonly called Werevultures. These are a creature that take two forms, that of man and that of vulture; and they are of a dark and vindictive nature, for they desired from the beginning that the world might be given to them, whereas it was given to be stewarded by man and the werevultures were to be his helpers.

"Werevultures are exceedingly dangerous, possessing strength slightly beyond that of a man and vast agility in both their forms, and furthermore their minds are devious, ever plotting out the hurt of others.

"But in these days werevultures, or ugthoda, as the Rodronians call them, have no ruler, but they wander alone, striking in dark and

secret ways, gathering about themselves small groups of men like Glumintorians and thieves and murderers that they might strive for dominion as best they can. They often name these silent societies in a clever play such as the Beak, or the Talon. However, rarely do they proclaim themselves openly as the leader of these bands, but work behind another guise or lieutenant, for they are the more dangerous while they lurk in secret.

"The language of werevultures is full of such noises as may be uttered by the throats of birds, and it is—

Inspector Dickson read no more. The words were blurring as his heart quavered sick and terrified in his breast. *The Claw . . .*

That crucial thing had come, was drawing everything together, pulling the cords tight into a noose for his neck. He had been blind, blind all along.

"It is as if the whole thing centered around their incrimination, not the murder."

Were not werevultures known for their cunning, revengeful spirit? Tale after tale lay submerged in history of the torturous lengths they took to wreak vengeance on men who wronged them.

"How did the man leave? I suppose he flew out the window?"

Maybe he did just that.

Inspector Dickson shuddered involuntarily, stumbling to his feet. He entered the bedroom, where the general was standing quietly, staring out into the white, swirling night.

"My lord," he whispered. "It is not a man we have to fear."

General Winston turned. "I, too, have dreaded that," he said.

CHAPTER 19

MORDRED PASSED OUT OF SLEEP'S weakening clasp with the keen, penetrating touch of fear.

Heat was radiating on him from some near source, and the smell in his nostrils was dry and earthy. He could feel a presence very close to him; for some reason every iota of his body shrank from it in terror. As he opened his eyes he saw a face above him, cadaverous, narrow in plane, thin-lipped, its black eyes glittering bird-like in deep-set caverns below the brow.

"You were long in sleeping, *ihssa-moz*."

"What are you?" His words were a gasp in his own ears.

"Ah . . . you are afraid, little son of men. You are very young, and yet you know there is something wrong." His lips pulled back in a cold smile. "Shall I tell you what? Nay, let you tell me that. Do you not recognize my voice? For I know you have heard it, *ihssa-moz*."

And he was very aware that the thin, almost raspy timbre struck familiarly on his ears. Memories touched him—moonlight, a stone floor, soft voices on the night wind. "I . . . I have heard it. Are you this Grimshaw?"

The man lifted his right hand and behold, it was not a hand. The dim yellowed firelight shone on a hard, leathery sole and three curving talons, black as dread and death, their tips winking bright and sharp as arrows. "I am the Claw."

"*What are you?*" His voice shook like aspen leaves in a tempest.

"Do you not know? I am a werevulture, O son of the weaker race. Or so your kind named us, in arrogant ignorance. We are no mere shape-changers, nor man, nor yet vulture; we are the *Kakirkiss,* we are a race apart."

"But"—his breath came in quick, heaving gasps—"I do not understand. I have not heard that any werevultures bore a bird-hand in human form."

"No, you know little of the kakirkiss. Shall I tell you, *ihssa-moz,* whence came we of the maimed hand—we, the House of Grey, which is named in the foul Thiredanian tongue *Ithera*? We the *kakirkiss* call it Hirghuiss."

He was silent a moment, holding out his claw-hand and watching the light play over it.

"Long years past, when your kind were coming out of the Dark Years, the thing came to pass, that a werevulture did an unspeakable deed. He took to himself as wife one of your kind, the *nikorss*. She was an Ordenian woman—Ridith of the House of Ithera was her name. Among your kind, naturally, this was considered a scandal, an evil of the highest order; but we, we the *kakirkiss* hate him more, for we hate *you,* and the thought that any *kakirkiss* should join himself to *nikorss* is abhorrent beyond telling. Curses have been heaped upon him more than any other *kakirkiss*." A hissing noise escaped his mouth.

"Children should never have been born of that union. And yet Ridith bore twins. One of them was feathered, and beaked, and was a werevulture: yet he was tall for his kind, and when he changed to human form, one of his hands did not change, but remained as a claw. The other child was *nikorss*. He was human. But he was stricken with various disabilities, and infirmities of the mind, and these things he passed on to his descendants, even as the werevulture did the claw-hand to his. And so the House of Ithera, or Grey, both *nikorss* and *kakirkiss,* is afflicted with the curse of the mingled blood."

"Not the Greys—the Greys—" Mordred could not speak for astonishment.

"Yes, those Greys. Those that dwell in your little village of Ceristen." The werevulture looked down at him, a kind of mocking laughter in his face. "The blood works strange things upon them, does it not?"

"I do not understand." Mordred flinched away from the thin, cruel face as it lowered near to him. "What does this have to do with me? Why am I here? What have I ever done against a werevulture? You—you sought to make me a murderer in the eyes of men!"

"Yes, now comes the question." He laughed drily. "You shall know the whole tale yet, *ihssa-moz*. It begins a long time ago; for it is tied into all the history of the *kakirkiss.*

"We, the werevultures, we work alone. To no man or other creature do we answer, not even of ourselves. Gone are the days when we could gather under a single ruler. Yet still do we seek to cause what destruction we can among the race of men. Some work among them, sowing discord, stirring up disputes and wars; some of us, like we the Hirghuiss, we cannot walk openly among you, and so we remain in secret, plotting what our servants can carry out. We gather to ourselves those who will serve us; men of depraved mind, those who know the truth: that the werevultures are the only ones worth serving."

"What kind of truth is that?" Mordred demanded, anger conquering his faintheartedness for a moment at the cruel, pompous assertion. "The world was not made for the werevultures."

"So you say, you little *eglikha egiss zahruniz,*" snarled the werevulture, his face darkening. He reached out and wrapped his claw-hand around Mordred's throat. "You, parroting words spoken by other men as if you understood them. Not made for us? Not if we can take it by force. In the end, we will triumph."

Mordred lay rigid, fighting back the nausea at the touch of the cold, sharp claws against his skin. As the werevulture released him, he sagged trembling and turned his face away.

"Now, to return. You know of dreamers, surely?"

Mordred, still sick and sweating with horror, could not answer.

"Speak, you whimpering son of men." A hand—it was a hand this time—wrenched his face back to look at the werevulture. "You know of the ones who have visions in their sleep?"

He nodded.

"So. It is my design to kill all such bloodlines, for their endowment is no aid to the *kakirkiss* but great harm." He paused and looked down at Mordred, his curved nose outlined like a hooking beak. "Three houses I have obliterated in the four-score years I have pursued the dreamers, and as I thought to commence a fourth, I heard to my surprise of a Kenhelm . . . which I had thought already a dead line, needing no interference by my hand. Perhaps you, little ignorant *moz,* did not know the heritage of your own house?"

He must have seen Mordred's start of confusion. "Long in your line have been the dreamers. Yea, and why you were found in Orden I know not, for the Kenhelms are a Dirionian house, but so it came by a certain servant of mine to my ear."

"Who—who told you of this?"

"One of my servants, as I said. Hadana, daughter of Ruil Marhadith; or the Silent Woman, as she is named among my ring, for hers is the stealthy work of searching out dreamers, and she passes ever unnoticed. She wrote me a letter concerning the presence of a dreamer-family, a Kenhelm, in the Ordenian village of Ceristen."

"Hadana," repeated Mordred brokenly, the name strange on his lips. "No; she let me go."

"She played the traitor, yes. I have sent one after her to slay her for my recompense. But in seeking to kill you she also acted in haste, against my wishes, and in her treachery she served my ends; for I wished to do away with you myself, and thus I contrived without a falter to bring the house of dreamers to me."

"But I am no dreamer!"

"Nay? It matters not, for it is your line. Should you take a wife and she bear you sons or daughters, your children might inherit it, or your children's children. As long as your house exists, so does the possibility."

Mordred started to ask why only he had been selected, and not Fenris and Laufeia as well, yet snapped his mouth shut at once. If the werevulture knew nothing of his family, then let it remain so!

"I was surprised to learn of your kin; the Silent Woman did not write of him."

He was silent, terrified that the werevulture had somehow laid bare his thought.

"But," the raspy voice continued into his bewilderment, "it was a simple matter to widen my plan and include him as well. Indeed, framing two men together was almost a simpler task than one."

The realization crashed on him, but it was a realization that made no sense. "Fred—you think that Fred Thorne—is my *kinsman*?"

"And should he not be?"

"He is not! You are wrong!" He threw the words at the thing, seized in the midst of his shaking, swarming thoughts with a bitter passion to make him know that, for once, his clever rightness had been wrong.

The dark, glittering eyes narrowed at him. "You speak with the ring of truth. It is possible that the information-gatherer I sent to the hostel mislaid or misheard the words in his report."

"Fred traveled to see his own kinsman. His family dwells at home. They come from Harotha—they were nothing to me before this past month. You were wrong!"

The werevulture's brow furrowed, and he tilted his head back. "Perhaps you are lying. But after all, I think I like it the better if you are not." He began to laugh, a dry, rustling laughter. "To think, I have caught a completely hapless and innocent man in my nets as well, not to mention the one for whom they were meant!"

The laughter made Mordred sick, sicker than anything else. Fred was innocent—innocent not only of the deaths, but of this strange accusation of a dreamer's heritage—and the werevulture was *glad* that he had inflicted this pain, this horrific pain, on a mere bystander.

"Where is my friend now?" he asked hoarsely. "Is—is he here?"

"He is not too far," said the werevulture dismissively. "You may see him sometime soon, perhaps, if I see fit."

"But where are we, and why did you bring us here?"

"We are in a certain working of tunnels in the sandhills on the eastern side of the Dirion River; it is not far from Delgrass." He snorted. "Why, you ask? *Ihssa-moz, you broke my plan.*" He seized Mordred's neck again. "You cleared yourself by spying on me, hearing my words, when I thought there were none to hear. So I had to mend my plan again.

And I have done it. Do you know how I have mended it? I spirited you away from that Inspector's house in the night, so he will think you have escaped, and I killed Corian and left the claw mark across his face."

He flung Mordred backwards. "And I will not return you to them again, to face the trial and judgment. I will keep you and kill you in my own time, and let them think you roam Legea at large. That way, you have failed, he has failed, and I have won."

"I still do not understand," whispered Mordred. "I do not understand."

"What do you not understand, *ihssa-moz*?" There was contempt in his voice.

"Why?" Mordred said softly, heatedly, his dizziness fading against the one question not yet answered. He reared up all at once. "Why did you do *this* to me? Why not kill me and be done? Why was it so cruel, so elaborate? My name is defiled! All men will speak of me with the name 'murderer' on their lips!" He choked on his own vehemence and desperation. "Why? Was there no other reason?"

The taut, thin profile above him scarcely stirred. "Yes, you speak well, Mordred Kenhelm. If I had simply wished the death of a dreamer, I could have done it with something as swift as a poison in your drink. And I would have been angry that my Silent Woman had not killed you, instead of glad that she left you to my hand. But I did not only wish the death of a dreamer. I wished the destruction and defamation of a house whose presence is to me rage and humiliation and utter abhorrence.

"There is blood between my family and thine, Mordred Kenhelm. Thedral Kenhelm, brother to Lord Carras of Kenhelm, slew my cousin."

"Lord Carras of Kenhelm." The words fell, half-familiar, almost inaudible, from his lips. "My father."

"Thedral was your uncle." The werevulture spat on the floor, hatred glaring from his features. "It is a fine, brave story among the *nikorss*, how he slew a werevulture and freed Dirion from a scourge, but he lived a short enough time to rejoice in his victory. The family of Hirghuiss rose up and lay in wait for him, and he died but a year later. Who regretted his passing? None of the *kakirkiss*. Who was satisfied at his death alone? None of us. To visit his death on others, that is something I have long yearned to do."

Mordred turned his face away again, shuddering, strangely numb inside. "Why on me? Why not on this man's children?"

"I would still have slain you, for the eradication of the dreamer's house." He laughed scornfully. "But Thedral left no descendants, and at first I knew not where any of his near kin might be. And then—ah! you were delivered into my hand, as it were, and by a happy chance indeed."

He stood, as Mordred made no reply. "Farewell for now, or fare ill, young Kenhelm," he remarked. "I make a guess that you will not sleep much this night."

His footsteps passed away, faint, echo-less thuds, and Mordred was left alone in the dying torchlight, to abandon himself to a despair darker than the night, more painful than death.

Still he could not weep. His shoulders shook; his head he buried in the dirt of the floor; but no sound came.

CHAPTER 20

TIME PASSED SLOWLY, MINUTE AFTER minute without ending, while Mordred lay in the piercing silence on the ground. He thought suddenly to see if there was a way to escape, but he could not summon the mind to move. The torch guttered and burned out.

He thought of Fred, somewhere near, suffering with him. He thought of Fenris and Laufeia, who would be missing him by now, worrying for him. He thought of the general, who had promised with such certitude to clear his name and return him home. He thought of Inspector Dickson and his mouth hardened in a dry, bitter anger. Inspector Dickson who must be smiling now, believing that he was right, all along. And from there, somehow, his thoughts jumped to Ahearn.

Ahearn . . .

Memories flooded relentlessly into his head, and he was too tired to stop them. He relived each insignificant detail, each spoken word.

Ahearn . . .

Dirion, Two and a half months prior: December 21, 2909

The group of four paused on the rise. The biting-cold wind whipped at them; there was a light dusting of snow on the ground, less than an inch, and their footprints trailed a muddy brown behind them, away over the gentle hills and the southward-winding road.

"'Tis a city," said Laufeia, her tired, pinched face lighting with interest as she lifted a quick finger.

"Aye," murmured Ahearn, the oldest of the young men—at least twenty by his beard, which was old enough to have lost the softness of youth. "And a large one."

There was relief in all their faces.

"How many days has it been, Mordred? Four?"

"Five since we last saw a village," said Mordred. "Then there was the steading that gave us a night's shelter."

Ahearn nodded. "They were good folk."

"Good folk or no, I do not mean to take food by charity like that again," said Mordred stiffly. "We can earn our bread."

"Mordred," Laufeia interposed quite sharply, "do not fault Ahearn for that. He offered again and again for us to work, but they would not accept."

"I am not faulting him any more than I am them. I do not want to be looked at as though I am a pauper to be showered with beneficence," Mordred snapped back.

"You cannot help it if there are kind people in the world, Mordred."

"They were just pitying us. I cannot stand that kind of sick pity."

"Both of you, enough," said Ahearn wearily. "Is it not sufficient that we have at last reached a town, and can seek out labor that we may eat tonight?"

They walked on in silence. Fenris lagged behind.

"Fenris, is it well enough?" Mordred asked anxiously, holding back to let his younger brother catch up.

Fenris nodded, his breath panting a little. "It is well enough, Mordred." He gave a soft half-smile.

Four days without food was hard enough on all of them, but Fenris—Mordred dreaded the day when Fenris could go no further.

How much longer would this uncertain journeying take them? They had been making their slow way north for months now; few and far between the villages, few and far between the meals. Orden, some kind of golden promise, lay to the north—but where?

But in the city, maybe there would be some certain word. Some direction. Mordred jerked at his belt to tighten it against his fluttering stomach, put an arm around Fenris' thin, valiantly squared shoulders, and walked on.

It was some hours after noon when they passed under the heavy, honey-brown wall and mingled with the milling people in the streets. A fuzz of noise was all around them, and Mordred kept an arm on Fenris, who looked dazed.

Someone snatched Ahearn's arm. "Did you hear? The king is dead!"

Ahearn shook away with a shrug and continued leading them on through the streets.

After a while he accosted a gray-haired woman with a slatted basket of chickens in her arms, and asked, "Old mother, if you please, what is this city?"

"Why," she answered, seeming surprised at his ignorance, "this is Ederan, lad. Where have you come from, that you do not know the capital of Dirion?"

"Rehirne, Mother," said Ahearn apologetically. "And we have been traveling for many days without sight of a village or other person. Thank you for your assistance."

She smiled, her faded eyes peering inquisitively over them. "There, I take no harm. Where are you bound for?"

"For Orden, and we must be near it now, are we not?"

"Aye, the West Gate is but a few days' ride from here."

"That is good to hear," said Ahearn gratefully. "Rest and good health to you, mother."

"The same to you, and may it be a safe journey for you young folk," she answered with another winsome smile, and went her way, the chickens clucking on her arm.

It was an awkward thing asking for work in a city, more awkward than in a little village where men walked through life simply and travelers were a rarity. Here there were already so many seeking to earn their keep, and beggars trickling throughout the streets as well. Their requests met with indifference, or even suspicion. After a few of these unsuccessful tries, Ahearn suggested that they try the inns—"A tavern keeper is generally in need of help."

The first that they came to turned them away at once, indeed nearly threw them out, but that they made a quick enough retreat onto the road again. They approached a second, and entered warily; but this one was better lit than the first, tidy and quiet, with a more wholesome bustle about its tables. The younger two waited by the door while Ahearn and Mordred went forward to the owner. "We will do any work you ask," Ahearn assured him. "You may pay us however you see fit."

The tall, broad man looked toward the doorway. "And those two? Are they doing any of this work?" He asked the question in a not unkind but meaningful way. Fenris was nearly spent.

"Sir," said Ahearn, flushing just the slightest, "it is not customary to pay before the work is done, but if you would give us—him food now, he can do his share."

The man looked at him and Mordred and Fenris in turn, in a quick, appraising way. "No, 'tis not customary, but I am not a hard man and if you should turn thieves there is little you can do against me. The lad is beyond standing, and you are little better; sit a while in the back there, and my Kirre will bring all of you sustenance. Afterwards we may discuss what is payment."

Ahearn hesitated for a moment. Then, gathering his dignity, he made a bow and said, "Thank you, sir."

They sat together in the far back of the room, and the keeper's wife brought them meat, bread, and cow's milk. Her watchful eyes showed that she did not accept them yet; perhaps she was wary of her husband's big heart. When they were done, however, she did offer to let Fenris lie down "in the kitchen."

"You needn't trouble," protested Laufeia.

"Oh, come, lass," retorted Kirre. "Whatever may come of the rest of you, he shall not be causing any trouble. 'Twill do no harm to let him rest on a sheepskin in front of the fire for a little."

Mordred started to rise to his feet, knowing that Fenris would not be easy letting any stranger lead him somewhere, but he was more tired than he knew and it was Laufeia who took Fenris' hand and followed Kirre out of the room.

The innkeeper came by shortly and told them that they might as well bed in the stables tonight—that Kirre would get them some blankets—and tomorrow they could spend the day helping with the animal care and the kitchen and asked if that seemed fair enough.

Ahearn affirmed that this seemed fair, and so the bargain was made.

The food, the shelter and the warmth were good for them; they all were better in the morning. Even Fenris rallied in a surprisingly swift way, his eyes bright and vigorous and the blood back in his face as they broke their fast.

"He has strength and pluck in him," said Ahearn to Mordred. "You should not fuss over him so like an old woman."

Where had *that* come from? Mordred's jaw went taut and he glared at Ahearn. "I know he is strong! When did I ever deny that?"

"Every time you bristle because someone seems to think him weak," Ahearn muttered in a low voice, "you admit that you believe that in your heart. You want to protect him, I know, but you must stop treating him like a piece of porcelain on the shelf."

Mordred struggled to control his breath. "If you were not my brother, I would not let you say that."

"Is it not true?"

"What do you know about Fenris?" Mordred hissed. "You scarcely ever saw him. I never saw you trying to shield him from taunts, from blows, from all the undeserved beatings. Was that your way of trying to prove his strength? A loving way, that!"

"Mordred, stop! Why are you so angry? It is true, I scarcely ever saw him, or any of you. It is not my fault that I was older and put to older persons' work. But I do not like to see you mothering him with the constant eye of a nervous hen. He will never grow into a man that way."

"You . . . know . . . nothing of Fenris," said Mordred, spacing each word with furious care. "He is strong, and he has yet to grow into that strength, but he will, and it will not be because I left him to fend for himself in the brutal indifference of the world." He sprang to his feet and walked off to a different corner of the common room.

The argument tingled between them all morning. By noon Ahearn appeared to have all but forgotten it and wanted to let it go, but Mordred had not forgotten, and he was still angry. Laufeia came between them, pleaded with Mordred, and at last he gave Ahearn a grudging peace; though his manner threatened Ahearn not to broach the subject again.

Ahearn did not.

There was a quiet space in the middle of the afternoon; few people were about, and Kirre told them to rest a little and gave them fresh milk to sup on while they sat.

Mordred, lost in a mere of thoughts, observed in a half-conscious way that someone had come in and begun talking to Ahearn. Suddenly aware that Ahearn was conversing with the man, not serving him, he grew wary and began to listen.

"Kenhelm, eh? I knew a Kenhelm once, but he's long dead. Do you live near here?"

"Nay, not at all. We come from Rehirne."

"How strange! Have you never lived in Dirion?"

Ahearn laughed. "Is the name Kenhelm, then, so attached to Dirion that its proprietor must be from there?"

"I never heard of one that wasn't," returned the man. "Come here, I like a game. I'll try and guess your father's name."

"Guess away," said Ahearn, laughing again.

"Is it Thedral?" asked the man, his black eyes sharp as daggers.

"No," said Ahearn.

"Doelthe? Cevra? Driun?" And he fired off barrages of them, a storm of bewildering, foreign-sounding names, while Ahearn shook his head, continuing to look mildly entertained.

What a stupid game. Mordred lost interest and stared out into nothing again, shuffling his cup back and forth between his hands. Then one last name struck on his ears, startling and sharp with familiarity. "Carras?"

"Yes, as a matter of fact," said Ahearn. "Though I don't wonder that you finally found it, having said so many already."

There was a dead, strange silence, and then the man asked, with a tense softness: "What was your mother's name?"

"Filiga," answered Ahearn. "What? What is the matter?"

"You must come with me—in haste," said the man, and Mordred's eyes snapped open just in time to see the figure dragging Ahearn across the room and out the door.

He leaped up, knocking the table clear over, and tripping on it sprawled winded to the floor.

"Mordred!"

Laufeia's alarmed voice came from some direction, and she was helping him up to his feet. He pushed her hand away and sucked in a quick breath. "Ahearn."

"Where is he?" Her eyes were wide, dark with fear.

"I—I do not know. Someone took him away."

"Did he hurt you?"

"No," said Mordred, annoyed. "I pushed the table over without meaning to. But I must go after him—"

Laufeia seized his arm. "No," she said firmly. "Wait. Did he seem like he meant harm to Ahearn?"

Mordred hesitated.

"Just tell me what happened."

He told her, and she asserted that they should wait and see what came of all this. If Ahearn did not return shortly, then maybe it would be time to start searching. Mordred consented with great reluctance, and Laufeia said, "Besides, we must explain what has happened to

Kirre and Ilvad; it would look very bad if the two of you appeared to flee with no warning."

Ilvad heard them out and was disturbed. He would not say what bothered him, and insisted that he was "not even sure" whether he was right, but he did not accuse them of anything and said that if Ahearn was not back by evening then he would send out for the Watch to go look for him.

And so, his worry little allayed, Mordred waited.

Sunset had passed and twilight was darkening the world when a man dressed in richer finery that Mordred had ever seen entered the inn and spoke words that branded themselves one by one upon Mordred's memory.

"King Ahearn of Dirion, son of Lord Carras of Kenhelm, desires to see his brothers and sister."

Laufeia reeled against Mordred.

He spoke, holding her tight and upright with one arm, sure that the voice must not be his own because he was beyond speaking. "Where is he?"

"In the palace. You must come at once."

~

"It is a wonder," said Ahearn, pacing back and forth in an excited manner.

A domed alcove of pillars framed him, dim and austere; over his shoulder, dimmer still, Mordred glimpsed a dais all hung with damask draperies for the mourning of the dead king. Draperies dark and mothy gray, and still worth a fortune.

"A wonder," Ahearn repeated. "A wonder that they found us. Did you know that our father was the brother-in-law of King Hiartho—that they would not let him wed and so he eloped with our mother Filiga, and never came back—never! No one knew where he had gone till today." He swept a hand across his hair, knocking the silvery circlet askew. "The king died just yesterday, and his only successor was a fifth cousin of ill repute, they had despaired of finding any nearer relations, and then—us!"

"And I see you are very pleased about it," said Mordred in a tight, hard voice.

Ahearn whipped around and faced him, his gray eyes narrowing in confusion. "Mordred?"

"What about us?" Mordred demanded. "We were traveling to Orden, we were going to live together and work together, and you would betray us for this?"

Ahearn's mouth dropped open. "I am not asking you to leave, Mordred!"

"I am asking *you* to leave! What put this stupid idea in your head? You are not a king!"

Ahearn snorted a little. "Hardly, but they will teach me."

"'They will teach me,'" Mordred mocked in falsetto tones. "You mean they will feed you."

"Mordred, I do not understand. If I were to give this up they would be condemned to the rule of a worthless, unkind man. How could you ask me to do that to them?"

"What does it matter? Let them have him. But all *you* want is the comfort of a fat, rich life, slaves fawning over you and your feet shod in silk every day. Anyway, who says that this other relative is so bad? They are probably lying to you. They jumped for you because you are ignorant of politics, easily manipulated—they will wield you like a puppet, and you will not care because all *you* want is the juices dribbling down your chin and a full, round stomach—a greedy, selfish, stupid puppet—"

"Mordred, enough—" Ahearn's voice was as hard as Mordred's own.

Mordred tossed his head. "Oh, you already fit your role so well. You can order me—do this, do that."

"Mordred!" shouted Ahearn, frustrated. "I am not trying to be your king. I am your brother!"

"You may as well disown me; you clearly care more about your kingship than any other connections you ever had."

"Mordred, stop!" Ahearn cried, his teeth clenched with anger. "It is you who are being stupid."

"You are in this for your stomach. You, always hiding under the guise of politeness, pretending that you want to be *nice*, when all the while you crave only the satisfaction of your whining innards."

"And you—" choked Ahearn, eyes snapping, "you crave the satisfaction of your pride! Your stupid, stupid pride that will be the death of you!"

"You have no honor."

"Honor!" Ahearn flared contemptuously. "What do you know of honor? Your honor that would have you starve in the streets rather than accept a gift! Your honor that thinks your own brother should be babied like a girl!"

Cold, blinding anger formed a rod of steel in Mordred's center. "And your honor is so much better," he shot back, his voice shaking with passion, "your honor that will crawl to the dictates of whoever can dangle a spitted pig in front of your nose. What right do you think to have to accept a kingship that you do not deserve? You will not be a king for them, you will be a lazy, worthless dog slavering for your next meal—"

Ahearn stamped his foot against the floor. "Will you see sense? Stop insulting me and listen!"

"And apparently you have no more control over yourself than a child—"

"Mordred—stop!"

Ahearn's voice rose to such a level that both of them fell silent, staring at one another in the dim stone room, panting for breath.

Mordred spoke, his voice set and cold. "I am leaving."

"Leave then," said Ahearn, still angrily. "You are not my brother."

Mordred lifted his chin with delicate scorn. His anger was ebbing, leaving a dark, hard resentment in its place. "Thank you; I do not think I want to be your brother." He turned away.

Ahearn made a move suddenly. "Mordred, take something. For pity's sake, take a little money with you—"

Mordred whirled. "Pity?" he spat scathingly. "So I am not your brother any more, and yet you would give me your condescension? Keep your gold, lest I throw it in your face. I will never ask you for anything again."

He stormed to the door, flung it open, fled the room and the palace until he was at last out in the dark, whispering streets. He leaned his shaking body against one of the pillars that formed the gateway and did not know how long he stood there, but it did not seem to be very long before he felt a light hand on his arm and knew that Laufeia stood beside him.

"You think I was wrong," he said, half-defiantly, daring her to speak.

Her face was pale and sober in the dimness, some distant fire-glow lighting her green eyes like a cat's. "Wrong or no," she said softly, "I want no high life if you are not in it, Mordred."

She laid her other hand on his arm, and they rested there warm and reassuring. "We are coming with you."

~

The memories spun themselves out. Mordred shut his eyes against them, but sleep refused to come.

The resentment was still there, dark and hot, but an aching sorrow had begun to accompany it as well. *Would I have done that if I knew? If I had known then what lay ahead of me?*

He did not want to see him, not ever again. But the knowledge came suddenly that he *could* not see him, and that somehow was worse. *Whether I wanted it or not, it would never happen; not if I am to die here.*

And the tears fell then, burning, unstoppable, a river of agony that gave no release, only further pain.

CHAPTER 21

"GENERAL, HOW LONG HAVE YOU suspected it?"

A chill dawn had lit on three feet of snow and an air of hopelessness among those in the Inspector's little house, dwellers and guests alike. Even Murcod, absent from yesterday's work and now today's, could go nowhere until the roads cleared. But uppermost in Inspector Dickson's mind was the terrible discovery of last night that had both answered all his questions and slashed his confidence apart.

"Not long," responded the general. "I feared that first day, when the young Kenhelm told me in greater depth of what he had heard. He said that the man had spoken in a strange language, all hissing and clicking on his ears, and I feared. Yet it was only a small thought of many in my mind until your friend uttered those words, 'He flew out the window.'"

Inspector Dickson turned his gaze to the floor, shuddering. "A werevulture. What have I done—what have I done . . . What we now face!"

"Dickson, easy." Murcod came to him and set a hand on his shoulder. "You couldn't have known. You did what you thought was right."

"I know." He pushed Murcod away and got up, shaking his head. "I know."

"And he knows, too, that to go against a *thangrisser,* and one of such a cunning mind, is a greater danger than you ever feared." The general had stood as well. "The creature must be dealt with, and yet to attempt that now may mean your life."

He came forward and faced Inspector Dickson. "It is yours to go on or turn back."

Inspector Dickson could barely meet his gaze. "You will not turn back," he said softly.

General Winston looked back at him with grave eyes. "I gave my word that I would return Mordred Kenhelm to his family."

Inspector Dickson stared again at the ground, ashamed of his weakness, his teeth shut hard. "You know my answer," he said at last, not lifting his head. "You know I could give no other. But I am afraid."

"We are all afraid," returned the general.

~

Inspector Dickson started as the footsteps came behind him, quick and loud. He turned to face Laufeia Kenhelm, her green eyes staring levelly at him and her mouth set in that taut, flint-like way he had seen so often on Mordred.

"What are you going to do about my brother?"

Her voice snapped with surprising accusation. He gasped speechless at her.

"It is the second day since my brother and Fred have disappeared, and no one has so much as spoken of searching for them." Her eyes flicked very quickly back towards Fenris, who was standing by the window, and to him again. "Well?"

"My lady, we will search for them, most certainly," said Inspector Dickson hastily. She had not been in the room earlier to hear their discourse; of course she was anxious. "Yesterday it was storming. As soon as I can, I shall make plans to look about . . . "

"Not that it'll be easy," said Murcod bluntly, coming in at the most inopportune of moments. "They have a day's head start, and of course they were captured by a werevulture."

Inspector Dickson kicked him none too lightly. Murcod's eyes flashed cluelessly from him to Laufeia and he gave Inspector Dickson a look of exasperation.

"Yes, I know," said Laufeia, her tightly upheld courage faltering a little; she looked pale, weary. "General Winston told us last night."

The defeated look cut Inspector Dickson keenly, and he made an awkward gesture as though to mend the thing that could not be mended. His own shoulders slumped as he turned to leave the room.

"See," Murcod's voice rose in annoyance behind him, "now you've made him upset . . . "

Inspector Dickson wheeled. "Murcod, leave her alone," he barked. "If I'm upset, it's my fault!"

He stared at the both of them.

Murcod took a step towards him. "Dickson, I'm serious, stop tearing yourself apart—"

"I am *not* tearing myself apart!" shouted Inspector Dickson furiously. "I—" He broke himself off. "I—Murcod, I don't know what's wrong with me. Just leave me alone."

He walked away, knowing and hating that Murcod's eyes were on him.

"Some argument you were having in there," said Harris observantly as he entered the kitchen.

Inspector Dickson bristled.

"Want to talk about it?"

He wanted to pick up the blithely whistling kettle and fling it into the wall or Harris' stomach. Instead he sat down and said, "No."

~

"Where shall we search?" Inspector Dickson asked insistently. "Did Mordred tell you any further information that might help us?"

The general shook his head. "We will simply have to cast a wide net, and hope that we come upon traces."

"Hope," muttered Inspector Dickson, a little derisively. "Much of that we have."

The general was silent. "No," he said at last. "Little hope."

And, oddly, Inspector Dickson felt the calmer to hear such a steady declaration of the truth. But he guessed that Laufeia and Fenris would not feel the same way.

"The sun is up and hot," said the general, glancing out the window. "For now we are snowbound, but if the weather holds thus, the traveling should be easier tomorrow. Your friend may return to his own village, and we may also ride to Cobren to see what we may find in the place of Corian's death."

"Yes," said Inspector Dickson. He nodded. "We may start with Corian."

~

"So, will you not be leaving soon, now that you are free to go?" asked Aunt Flira inquiringly. It had been five days since her nephew Jared's two traveling companions were accused of murder and imprisoned, and Jared, no longer under remotest suspicion, had come with his few belongings to their house. In all this time he had made no mention of departure, although there was surely no need for him to stay.

Of course, he could not have left the past two days, not with the blizzard. But the snowstorms of Delgrass, so fickle, usually melted within the week, and already little more than six inches remained upon the ground. Jared was not restrained any longer, if he should want to go.

Jared stood soberly by the table, not appearing to have heard above the rest of the clamor in the room—two dogs, four small children, and the clatter of earthenware where the oldest girl was scrubbing pots in the corner. Aunt Flira edged around his tall form, stacking the bowls from breakfast on her arm, and repeated the question. "Will you not be leaving soon, Jared?"

He looked down at her. "Do you not wish to have me, Aunt?"

"Oh, no!" she exclaimed, setting the bowls by her daughter and tucking back a strand of black hair. She was a short, round little woman much like her sister Aliria Earle, pretty still and very quick on her feet. "Why, no, my dear lad, we are most happy to have you here while you wish to stay. But I expect that you are longing to return to your own home again, and you must not feel compelled to remain here."

He said nothing for a little, turning over what he must say in his mind as he usually did before speaking. "Aunt, they will want news of the Thorne and the Kenhelm when I return, and who will bring it if not I? I must wait until the end of the matter is settled. After the trial, I shall depart. Until then, if it pleases you and Hanerd, I will remain under your roof and be a son to you."

Hanerd looked up from where he sat by the fire, and nodded. "That is right," he said. "It is not an easy thing, I think, for you to see your companions so impugned; yet you do well in desiring to bring the full tale back to their family."

Jared bent his head in acknowledgment.

It was not easy. Not easy to see Mordred's strained face, crushed in betrayal, Fred's quiet in despair. And the longer time carried on, the less he could think them murderers.

Yet none of his aunt's family truly knew the struggle and the sadness within him, for it lay beneath his unchanging manner and silent face. Only Hanerd seemed to guess, with sure, canny guesses.

And Jared was glad when Hanerd bade him take out Rivra, the temperamental mare, and work out her paces.

Rivra had not been ridden in three days; Jared had taken her out that time, too. She flung up her head as he approached, snorting and whinnying and kicking at her stall with a vigor to raise the dead. He saddled her with difficulty, for she was so restive that the least touch made her shy and snap, and with no urging she bolted out of the stable at a canter, breaking into a gallop even as she passed the door.

He rode her a long while, letting her have her head as long as she pleased, only checking her speed once in a while to rest her a little, and soon she would be straining at the bit again, eager to run. Morning passed them by, and the noon sun wheeled overhead and sank behind a bank of cloud. The plains, spotted with the remainder of snow, rolled under Rivra's beating hooves, and at last they found themselves in the tall grasses and half-frozen mud of the marsh.

Jared reined her in, ready to turn back, but Rivra snorted and shook her head. She smelled the water, and she wanted to get into it. Jared hesitated; yet the sun behind the clouds was still high, and Rivra was hot and blowing from her morning of exertion. He turned her head aside a little and trotted her northwards around the marsh until the Dirion River glimmered flat and silvery before them.

Rivra pranced in it a little, going in up to her withers and snuffling the water with a foal's excitement, and showed signs of wanting to swim all the way across. Jared would not have let her, but the river was shallow for a long way and not too wide; so he nudged her across, not caring much that the water traveled over his own boots and soaked his legs. He, too, was hot with riding.

After that Rivra wandered mostly where she wanted, now walking, now cantering, and Jared sat her quietly and thought his thoughts.

The snow had not fallen this far east, or else it had melted away altogether by now, for the wide flats were bare and sandy, sometimes thick with last summer's dead long grass, sometimes rising in low, rounded humps of hills. It was at the base of one of these that Rivra slowed and began nosing the base, and Jared, lifting his eyes, caught sight of an odd shadow on another hillock not far away. It looked to him more like a cave than a shadow.

He guided Rivra toward it, and saw to his surprise that indeed it was a hole in the hill, and a large one; much larger than any fox or badger den. Five feet and a half tall at least, he measured with his eyes, and near as wide. As he came closer still, nudging Rivra up the slope, he saw that fallen from it was a wide screen of grasses, as though to conceal the opening.

His light brows knit between his eyes; he scanned the opening, the tunnel within as he drew level with it. It was wide and well-shored, ribbed with wooden beams, the floor trodden smooth. Light peeped out of the thick blackness within, giving form to a curve in the tunnel, coming nearer—

He saw the man, heard a startled gasp, and more gasps echoed behind. He saw the swift movement and felt the blade sing past his face.

Jared wheeled Rivra, spurred her on with heels and quick, low words. More things hissed over his head, arrows maybe. He buried his head in Rivra's neck, shrinking back from the deadly hail, and dug his heels harder into her sides.

The arrows finally ceased, but he did not look back.

CHAPTER 22

THERE WAS A DIFFERENCE IN the room.

Ever since the torch left by the werevulture had burned away, he had been in darkness. How long the time had been, he did not know, but hunger had waxed and waned in him and he had drowsed into ugly, fractured dreams. He wondered if he had been forgotten. Or if the werevulture planned to let him slowly die alone, as had the woman of the black house. That he could not know the passage of hours sent a creeping fear in him, and he would try to count the seconds before his concentration faltered and spun away into other things.

But now there was light, and Mordred, opening his eyes on its yellow-orange gleam, raised himself curiously up on one elbow to look around his prison.

It circled him about, a little earthen cave with fallow walls reddish and downy in the soft torchlight. If he turned his head to the right a tunnel bored itself into the dirt, and almost directly in front of him another did the same.

Suddenly excited with the chance to *get out,* he started to scramble to his feet, but arrested himself at once with the knowledge that if there was light, there must have been someone to bring the light. Swiftly, warily, he swung his head around, looking for the source. The torch was flaming high on the wall, but he saw no one—and yet he knew now that there must be a presence near at hand. And then the shadows in the left-hand tunnel shifted and gathered into a new darkness, and the werevulture stepped into the cave.

He was smiling, and it came over Mordred again, that strange, rooted terror at something foul, something just too intangible to see or smell or grasp, but strong enough to fear. Against man he had defense: he had words, he had a shield of arrogance and mockery; but against this he had nothing. He watched, struggling to hold back the instinct to recoil, as it approached.

The werevulture threw something down in front of him and he shied back, in spite of himself. Mocking laughter hissed out above him and he bit back fiercely the shamed tears that sprang up.

"Eat, *ihssa-moz*," ordered the werevulture, kicking with his toe the food that he had dropped. "I did not come down to watch you flinch like a maiden."

Mordred, through a blinding screen, saw stringy, red-brown dried meat and a thick rind of bread. His hunger, earlier so ravenous, was nothing now, and shaking his head defiantly he turned away.

His face was seized in that horrible pinching claw-hand, and the voice said coldly, "You will eat it, wretched son of men. I shall be keeping you alive much longer than this, and you have supped naught for two days. Eat." And he thrust the bread against Mordred's teeth.

But Mordred could not eat, not with that claw biting into his skin and the cruel mortification still tormenting him; and besides, his instinctive stubbornness had now arisen and he did not want to give in to the will that had crossed his own. He shook his head in defiance again.

The werevulture raged under his breath, glottal sounds of spitting and gurgling that were meaningless to Mordred's ears. With finger and claw he pried Mordred's jaws apart and rammed a portion of the bread into his mouth.

Mordred's stomach revolted, and he gagged; the lump flew out and landed on the ground. The werevulture uttered another outraged exclamation and shook him.

Mordred found his dread, oddly, ebbing in the face of such foolish frustration, and his head seemed to clear. "Well?" he said coolly. "There is little you can do, since it is clear I cannot eat right now. And it is less than useless for you to make such a fuss about it."

His breath left him painfully as the werevulture knocked him backwards and two claws, not one, dug into his chest. Feathered wings beat the air around him where the thin shoulders had been a moment before. A beak snapped venomously shut barely an inch from his nose, and the glittering black eyes glared at him from a wrinkled, hooded head.

"You, hateful, miserable man," snarled the werevulture, the words strangely ululating and distorted. "You *khissta khavfa-moz—*"

The whistling, dissonant words whirled around Mordred; the stench of the thing's breath smote him, his head ached and he was dizzy. Everything grew pale and distant, and when at last he came to himself to find that he could breathe freely again, the werevulture was gone.

He rolled over, weak now with both hunger and lack of air, and with a hand awkwardly shaking managed to bring the bread to his mouth. Tired and faint as he was, he could barely force it down, but he knew that he needed to eat, and he consumed it and the meat. As a whisper of strength returned to him, and with it a sudden surge of thirst, he looked about and saw a small pitcher abandoned nearby, half-filled with water he must have been meant to drink.

A wonder the werevulture had not knocked it over in his plunge, he thought, a half-amused smile moving his lips at the memory of its idiocy. He drained the pitcher, lay back, and closed his eyes.

The claw gripped him again, pulling him up by one shoulder to his feet. Had he slept?

“Move,” the werevulture commanded grimly, shoving him forward. Mordred jerked away, something impelling him to lunge for the other tunnel—to his own surprise he broke free. Stumbling, running—

The claw clamped onto his neck, whipping him backward. His side burned and he choked as the werevulture twisted his head around and pricked a dagger into the side of his neck.

“You poor fool,” he said, his voice filled with contempt. “There is not even any escape for you down that way; it is a dead end.” He let out a scornful cackle. “Come, move.”

Where are we going? Mordred thought, but he was too tired and too proud to ask it of the werevulture. They walked through the dark winding maze, the earth softening their footfalls, the dagger-blade digging warningly against his neck.

At last they came into a small, rounded cave much like the one they had departed, grass-roots dangling bristly and snakelike out of the ceiling, a torch high on the wall. A man was standing at the opening, and he bowed his head as the werevulture walked past.

“Has he caused you any trouble yet?” the werevulture inquired over his shoulder. “Any escape attempts?”

“No, my lord.” The man spoke with a foreign accent that Mordred could not place.

The werevulture laughed. “This one did.” He thrust Mordred into the cave, letting him go suddenly.

Mordred staggered, landing on his knees in front of the other prisoner. “Fred—Fred Thorne.”

~

Fred, roused abruptly from a doze, heard the approaching footsteps and voices; but he did not expect it to be Mordred who, with the tall thin-faced figure of the werevulture, came skidding to a halt before him.

He had never seen Mordred look so young, so vulnerable. It was as if all his hard, carefully retained manliness and pride had been shorn away, and he was only a boy as young as his years, whose gray eyes were wide with aloneness and fear.

"Mordred," he said gently, sitting up.

Mordred stared at him for a little while, blankly, and then he seemed to recollect himself. "Are you all right, Fred? Did they hurt you?"

"Little enough," said Fred reassuringly; and that for its part was true. He had been roughly handled the night they captured him, and he was weary and famished, but he was much more concerned for Mordred now. "And you?"

"I am fine," said Mordred in the ghost of a voice. As though realizing he would be disbelieved, a little stiffness came back into his face, guarding against any show of pain. "I'm fine," he repeated.

"When did that happen?" Fred asked, pointing at Mordred's side.

Mordred glanced down, surprise spilling into his eyes. There was a large rip in the linen of his shirt, blood-stained at the edges; an equally bloody cloth peeped out underneath. "I suppose it was when they took us," he murmured. "Now that I think of it, I remember something scraping along my side while I was struggling. But then they pulled something over my head; I couldn't see or breathe, and I lost my senses after a little. When I woke, I had forgotten."

"It did not stop you from running, *ihssa-moz*," the werevulture remarked from his vantage point by the wall. "Perhaps I should have clawed you harder."

Mordred tensed, glancing back. "He is listening to everything we say," he snapped.

"It does not matter," Fred urged him, fearing for Mordred to incur the creature's anger. "There is nothing we can do for that, is there?"

Mordred shrugged, his body sagging dully again. "So you know about him?" he asked. "He has told you of the Greys, and of his plan?"

Fred nodded. "Aye; he came to me not long after we were brought here. He said that you were unconscious, and I feared for you."

"I'm fine," said Mordred, automatically rather. "How long has it been?"

"Since we were captured? I am not sure. A few days." Fred frowned, seeking to reckon in his head, but nay—it was impossible to tell. "I did not understand, though, and he did not explain to me why I am here. He must think that I am a danger to him, but—"

"He thought you were some relation of mine," said Mordred with a bitter tone. "Some man of his passed along faulty information to him, and like a fool he did not think to check its veracity."

Fred was silent; the words sank into his head, and he both comprehended and did not comprehend them. Such a strange, harsh thing to take in: that all this suffering of his had not been from good, not from evil, not from hate or revenge but simply from nothing. It was almost worse than if there had been a reason, however malignant.

"But you do not care," said Mordred passionately, as he did not speak. "You are at peace—it matters nothing to you—and you do not care that your name is ruined forever, you do not care that all your friends will call you a murderer!"

Fred looked at him, mute with surprise and hurt, not knowing why this storm of grief and anger was directed suddenly at him.

Mordred sucked in a hoarse, gasping breath, and yet he said nothing; for pounding footsteps approached them.

"My lord, my lord Runiz!" Another man rushed into the cave. "Quickly, you must come at once!"

The werevulture whirled at the urgent tone. "Gorstir? Very well, I come." He cast a quick glance at the two of them on the floor. "Watch them carefully, especially the younger," he ordered the guard. "I shall return."

His steps died away.

"You sit there as calmly as if you were still in your house in Ceristen, speaking as if you discussed the doings of the castle work. You are stone, you are silent and stupid as a rock!" Mordred railed at him. "What, do you care nothing for your own? Why does it not cut you? Why must it hurt me, while you sit unmoved as a carven statue? Why must I hurt . . . why must I feel—why—Fenris . . . I cannot—"

Fred reached out and grasped his hand firmly, holding it even as Mordred tried to pull away. And he did try, but his strength crumpled and he fell, his incoherent speech fading into broken, wrenching sobs.

"Mordred," Fred said softly, not holding back the tears that flowed down his own cheeks. "I do care. I hurt. I think of my sisters and my brother, and all that we endured to come to Orden, and wonder: was it all for nothing? I see Fiona, day and night I see her face, and shall I never touch her joyous face again? Shall I not be wedded to her when the springtide comes?"

He could say no more for a moment.

"If I am silent, Mordred, it is because my way is to hide the pain within. I fear that if I speak I will only release a river that will overcome me. I would have died if it would save Fiona, or Daren, or any of them;

instead I must die for nothing—for less than nothing. Mordred, do not think that you are alone in suffering."

Mordred lifted his head. "I know," he answered, his voice exhausted and shaking. "I should not have spoken as I did. I do not know why I shouted at you, what was in me—forgive me." He drew his hand lightly out of Fred's and clasped it around Fred's shoulder.

Fred placed his right hand likewise on Mordred. "I have known despair," he said quietly. "And I will not yet despair again. Strange things have come about, and it may be that we will not die here."

Mordred shook his head and looked away. His breath came in quick, faint pants. "I hoped that I would not be arrested, and where did that get me? I hoped to be cleared, and what gain came of that? I do not care to hope any longer."

"Please, Mordred." Fred took the slender, long-fingered hand between both of his earnestly and held it. "Hope because you are not yet dead. Hope because we have one another to lean on. Hope if nothing else because your brother would not have you die despairing."

Mordred made a small noise that was barely audible, and his head drooped to rest on his arm. A dampness grew on the sleeve, and trickled down to wet the earth below.

Several pairs of swift-striding feet signaled the werevulture's return. He and the man called Gorstir were speaking in sharp low voices.

" . . . so it is clear we must go. All is lost if we remain, but if we hurry away it will be safe. The fools . . . "

The werevulture entered and glanced around the cave. "We shall leave at once. Gorstir, fetch the other prisoner."

"My lord." Gorstir bowed and darted away.

CHAPTER 23

CORIAN WAS DEAD, THE FATEFUL claw-mark across his features and no trace of the murderer to hand. Inspector Dickson rode swiftly home, every beat of the hooves making a desperately resolute chant: *I. Shall. Find. It. I. Shall. Find. It. Shall. Find. It. Shall. Find. It. Shall. Find—It . . .*

His frustration flowed, his resolve intensified, his hope dipped and rose. It was at its low point as he approached the silent and unwelcoming house.

"Where is everyone?" he asked aloud as he entered to a resonant stillness.

"General Winston fellow left for Addis Muard," said Harris, materializing startlingly out of the shadows. "Said he wanted to make sure his dragons were doing all right. The girl took her brother outside. Said *she* wanted to enjoy the sunshine."

"Oh." Inspector Dickson sat down.

"By the way, there's another complaint about chicken thievery, so I'm off to see to that; though if you ask me it's foxes, not men. You're by yourself for a little, Dickson." He walked out the door whistling an old tune.

"Tall trees rising, Many surmising, They will stand fore'er . . . " Inspector Dickson found himself humming the song into the dimness after the door shut. *"At the sun's rising, many surmising naught to fear, naught is near . . . "*

Why was it so dark in here? He got up, half annoyed and half gripped with a slow, slithering fear that had neither name nor substance, to find a window to open.

Fear, what fear? Was he afraid of being alone? He had never dreaded solitude, not he, level-headed Inspector of the Peace. What childishness, he told himself severely. And if it were the dark he disliked, were there not windows in the house?

"Rising eyeless
Captive and mindless
Limbs and garments fast
Waters creeping
Many still sleeping
Tall trees last
Till day is past . . . "

He shook his head as though to drive the words out, vexed that he could let a song rattle him so. But he did not move yet. His hands hung loosely at his sides. The darkness was unpleasantly heavy.

There was a strange wind in the air last night. The words came suddenly to mind, from where he did not know, seeming strangely apt. The general? No, it was not the general's voice he remembered but Getta's, the Mattadonnish guard at the gate of Balhorde. *A strange wind, a dread hanging over us as we stood watch.*

He put his hand on the latch and faltered. He felt the ugly, creeping heaviness again, larger, nearer, and now all his senses were trembling, stiff, because they sensed *danger*—

Danger!

He bolted, and heard the deadly crack in the wood behind him. And all he knew was running, running, and running before he stopped on the edge of Bulca's sleepy market. He looked back; there was no one on the road.

He tried to order his memories and reason it all out clearly, but all that he could remember were the sounds. The sound of a door slamming, despite no recollection of slamming the door. Running footsteps. The click of a windowpane opening. The last thing he knew for certain was his hand on the latch, then a blank of fear and disordered noise, and tearing down the road.

His legs shook under him, and his breath was coming so heavily that he felt faint. He sat slowly against a rail fence, staring at a bruise darkening on his hand. A voice spoke his name, but he did not make sense out of it, and did not look up.

" . . . *please,* Dickson, explain what you're up to here."

It was Harris staring at him, pure bewilderment on his face and a string bag of potatoes on his shoulder. "You look sicker than a horse with worms." He offered Inspector Dickson a hand and pulled him up.

Inspector Dickson leaned his weight on the fence, looking away from Harris. "Someone tried to kill me."

Harris scratched his head. "Dickson, is this the Claw mess you got yourself into?"

"I didn't get myself into it!" Inspector Dickson roared, whirling on him. "I did not ask for any of this!"

Harris took a step back from him. "All right. I didn't ask for it either, in case you cared to know." The words were caustic, but he spoke them quietly. "Don't take it out on me, Dickson."

He hefted the potatoes again and walked away.

Inspector Dickson stood against the fence, not knowing what to do with himself. He felt like he could not go on any more with a pretense of normal existence. The threats were real, someone had tried to kill him, and someone would try again.

"Inspector Dickson." The grave pronouncement of his name lifted his eyes to a well-known face.

"I did not look to see you here," said the general, swinging off his mount and approaching him. "What has happened? There is a horror in your eyes."

He told him, and the general said simply, "Let us return to the house," and Inspector Dickson was almost mortifyingly grateful not to have to go back alone.

But the house was empty when they came to it, though Inspector Dickson searched all the rooms with the general beside him. They found what looked to be the knife-mark in the window-frame, a deep horizontal bite at neck level.

"It was an experienced man to dare such a throw," said the general softly, his fingers tracing the slit. He looked quickly at Inspector Dickson, as though sensing his unease. "Let you not fear much; he is long gone by now, and I daresay he will wait some time before a second attempt."

Inspector Dickson, knowing that the words were given only to comfort him, felt his anxiety little abated.

~

Wind sang over the flatlands. Delgrass was fair in the forerunner of spring, fences spidery and dark sprawling over the stubbled fields; the odd clump of trees huddled in the low places, their bare boughs tossed in a strange tugging, earthy freedom. Patches of snow nested in the crooks of the low slopes.

But Laufeia wandering with her brother down the beck seemed to have little mind for the hints of coming spring-tide and the fresh-smelling muddy banks. Her eyes were tight and dim with pain.

They stopped beside the creek for a moment and Laufeia sat down with a tired little thump, watching the shallow water gurgle by. "Fenris," she murmured, "I cannot be strong any more. I cannot pretend a courage I do not have. *I want my brother back.*"

Her voice gave and the tears spilled out of her eyes, falling onto her hand where they glittered back at her through a blur. Her throat ached with greater sobs, sobs that the nearness of Fenris beside her would not let her utter.

He was quiet. She looked up and saw that he had sat as well, his face turned silently towards the stream. The faintly raised line of the scar was visible on his forehead.

"How do we know he is not dead?" she asked aloud, the words falling flat, thin and empty on the air.

Fenris started and his dark, wide eyes turned to hers. "He is not dead," he said, almost the first words that he had spoken since Mordred and Fred disappeared. Life kindled in his slim face for a moment. "He is not, Laufeia. I know it."

"I do not know it," she said stubbornly, afraid to let herself start hoping. Yet she was ashamed to stamp so readily on his own conviction, and she put a hand on his. "There, Fenris; do not listen to me. I am glad that one of us at least is sure."

They went back towards the house at last, the afternoon sun beating hot and bright against the cool, windy plains. But as they came onto the little beaten path beside the flowing stream that led up to the cottage, there was a rumbling sound of hooves, and Laufeia turned her head.

"There is someone coming up from the east," she remarked.

And they stood and watched while the lathered horse came galloping up over the land and stood blowing to a halt beside the door, and Jared Earle stumbled into the house, saying as Inspector Dickson rose startled to his feet:

"I have found it—I have found the men of the Claw."

~

Inspector Dickson could not move for an instant. And then he sprang across the room and snatched Jared by the shoulder. "You have found the Claw?"

Jared nodded, his usually sober face white and strained, his chest heaving for air. "I found them."

Inspector Dickson began to move away, but checked, looking sharply at him. "What makes you think so, and why did you come tell me?"

Jared seemed briefly at a loss. "It was a secret sort of place," he said at length, "and they shot at me when I saw them; I do not know—it appeared to me that it could only be them. And, sir, why should I not come tell you? To know and hold the secret would have been a base thing." He looked at Inspector Dickson with something like reproach. "Though"—he hesitated—"it is true, I came here in greater haste because I cannot believe that my friends were guilty of the accusations on them, and I hope that by finding and rooting out this band their name may be yet cleared."

"As to that," said Inspector Dickson, "you need not fear for them; they are already proven innocent. Come, there is much you do not know, and you are weary—"

But Jared pushed away the hand offered. "Later I can hear and rest," he said. "I must show you where it is."

"Not now," said Inspector Dickson. "It will take time to muster men, and more time to ride there, and the sun is already setting. Come, Jared, we will go tomorrow. This is a job for the day."

Slowly did Jared yield. "Care for the horse, if you will," he said, turning to the door. "I cannot ride her any more today, but I must be away now to my uncle and aunt, who will be wondering at my long absence."

He turned briefly startled eyes to Fenris and Laufeia, who had entered the house. "Tomorrow I shall come," he said, and left.

~

Hands seized Mordred, yanking him upright. He jerked away, startled, dazed with confusion. Someone was pulling Fred to his feet as well. What had happened?

He twisted around; there were two men holding him, one on each side, and his whole body shrank from the feeling of being handled. He wriggled away, tried to tear out of their hold, but he was exhausted and they handled him with ease.

"My lord Runiz was not lying," observed one, the bigger of the two, whose neck was thick with callouses as from an iron ring. "He fights for freedom like a cat."

"Like a kitten," snorted the other. "And a half-drowned one at that. Look, the babe has been crying."

Mordred trembled, with anger now, and clenched his teeth. Again he lunged against their hard grip.

"Stop it!" said the big man shortly. "We have a piece to go tonight, and you're in no state to break free. You'll only make it harder for us to get you anywhere."

"Is that so? Then I *shall* make it harder," gasped Mordred perversely, flinging himself forward.

A great crack resounded on the side of his head, and he fell, everything blanking and ringing whitely, and after the faintness passed he thought he was going to be sick.

"Move," said a voice, but he did not know it was speaking to him; only after several minutes did he realize that tunnels were passing them by and in front of him Fred was walking between two more men.

They came out to the mouth of the tunnel, and paused there, as though waiting. The night air washed over Mordred's face, and he revived a little in it; he was less suffocated, though his head began to hurt stingingly.

"Ah, there you are." A moving shadow passed out of the still shadows of the cave behind them and the werevulture looked around. "I see not Gorstir," he said.

"Here, my lord," said the man called Gorstir at that moment, and several more shifting blacknesses drew near. Though none of their faces showed clearly under the weak starlight, Mordred could see that the hands of one were bound behind him.

"Very well; we are all here," said the werevulture, raising his voice, and all around them Mordred saw more dark figures stirring and listening. "Come, we must go with speed; the night will not stay young."

Mordred gathered that they were leaving—all leaving; why, he did not know. And he supposed it did not matter to him.

He fell asleep on his feet more than once as they fled that night; once he woke to the moon high and white like a cut coin of radiance above them, and again he woke and it was covered by clouds.

At last they halted. It must have been only a few hours off from dawn. There was bustle all around Mordred as they pitched a camp, and someone lit a fire and flung him down nearby it. He lay there, too weary to so much as inch closer to the heat of the flames. But too tired to shut his eyes, he watched in apathy as Fred was dropped like a sack a foot away from him, and next to Fred a third person: the bound prisoner whom he had seen earlier.

The yellow light leaped across a plain, immobile face and strangely fathomless brown eyes.

Mordred started, his weariness sinking back into some forgotten pit. He had seen that face before, in the common room of The Fisherman. And it was not a face that one could ever forget.

"Sam?"

CHAPTER 24

IF SAM WERE SURPRISED, IMPRESSED, or interested, he did not show it. His brown eyes met Mordred's coolly in the wavering firelight. "Yes, I am Sam," he assented. "You will forgive me if I do not recall your face."

"I am Mordred Kenhelm—one of the inn guests. I saw you a fortnight ago, in the common room asking for the Inspector."

"Ah, yes . . . that," said Sam, in a distant sort of way, as though it were wearisome trying to remember. "It was fifteen days ago," he added, simply.

Mordred said nothing, amazed that someone should care to point out the mere discrepancy of a day at a moment when there were things of far greater import that might be talked about.

"If I may ask," said Sam with that studied, graceful formality of a politician, "why are you prisoners of the werevulture?"

"We were accused of the murders by his design," answered Mordred, "but were reprieved briefly. Rather than get us arrested again, he took us here to await his revenge, I suppose. What is it to you?" he ended rather angrily, for it hurt to speak of, and the thought of Inspector Dickson sent his blood raging like a captive beast; and he did not see why this Sam should care to know, or that he deserved to.

Sam shrugged, indifferent to Mordred's pettish flare. He stared thoughtfully past him, seeming to absorb what he had been told; but no outward sign did he give of what he thought of it.

"Why are *you* his prisoner?" Mordred asked.

Sam focused abruptly on him again. "I was making myself an inconvenience," he returned, very distinctly, and he said no more for a little while.

"To whom?" asked Mordred, perplexed and frustrated by his lack of response. "To the werevulture? Were you working for him?"

Sam raised one eyebrow with an air of greatly tried patience. "Hardly." Then, as one making a concession, he added, "Quite the contrary, in fact."

Mordred frowned a little. "I suppose I see—"

"You don't," said Sam, looking faintly amused.

"But why are you not dead?" Mordred continued. "If you were making trouble for them, somehow or another, I should not think they would hesitate twice about killing you. Are you not more a danger to them alive?"

"Ah!" said Sam, and he gave a very dry, closed smile. "They are afraid. They want to know what I know of them, and what I may have passed on to others. And that I cannot tell them, any more than I can tell you."

Mordred noticed suddenly how gaunt the man's face was, even under the cloaking shadows of the changeful fire. "Have they—hurt you?" he asked, his voice gentler than he knew.

Sam did not deign to answer this one, but rolled over in a smoothly disciplined movement. His poise scarcely relaxed even in sleep.

~

"What do you mean, you're not taking any men with you?" Harris looked at him as though he thought him crazy. "You said last night, I heard you . . . "

"And reconsidering, I decided against it." Inspector Dickson leaned against the mare for a moment, looking into his partner's intent brown eyes. It came to him, oddly, how much he liked Harris. Despite their grating differences—in fact, they lacked almost anything in common—six years had bound them together, and he felt keenly that to lose Harris, while not like the loss of a friend, would be like to lose a brother.

He blinked a little roughly. He was the one going into danger, not Harris. "I have only the vaguest estimate of their numbers," he continued, explaining in quick, clipped words that the urgency of the situation seemed to demand. "An attempt to root them out like this would be to go into battle blind. Instead, I am only taking Jared as my guide, and the general because he wishes to come. We will spy things out first; then we can return with men and a plan."

"I see," said Harris reluctantly. "I don't like that much better. You'd be safer with twenty at least at your back."

"And a lot louder," answered Inspector Dickson shortly. He swung up.

"Do you find your horse all right?" he asked Jared, who was already mounted on the dun mare whom he had arrived with last night. "She was near to foundering when you came."

Jared nodded. "Thank you for your care of her; she looks well. I hope she caused no trouble to you? She is usually difficult, but our run yesterday may have quieted her awhile."

"She was docile enough last night," said Inspector Dickson, clucking briefly to his horse. "This morning she did not want me to come near her."

Jared's gray eyes rippled for a moment in a spark of quiet, dry humor as he touched his heel into Rivra. "I am glad it was no worse, sir. Believe me when I say she is more subdued than usual."

The general came around the stable, leading the dark bay gelding that he had ridden hither with from Addis Muard, and Jared instantly bowed his head, even as the general nodded in a courtesy to them both.

Since Jared had returned at dawn and Inspector Dickson had given him the full of the past week, he had displayed an honest awe at his general's presence here—not in a groveling, obsequious way, but with a complete deference that indicated more fully than anything Inspector Dickson had yet seen what a hold Derek Winston had upon his people.

And was it a wonder, he thought, that he had such a hold? Inspector Dickson himself felt it, the magnetism and the power of this man. It was not any action he performed for them that evoked this adoration; he need say nothing, he need do nothing, and they were still his.

So much power for a man.

It was a dreadful power, a very dreadful one, he mused. So many had only the power that their position gave them, the power to imprison, torture, and enslave as they pleased; but this one could go where they could not; he could take the mind captive. How many in the country of Orden would refuse a command in the face of those dark eyes? Looking at Jared's awe, recalling Mordred's sudden deference, Inspector Dickson knew: if the general chose to, he could seize the rule in a moment.

Yet in eighteen years? He reckoned up the dates in his mind; yes, eighteen since the death of Orden's last general and the ascension of the new. In eighteen years, he had not made a move towards overthrow. What kept him? Was it love for the weak king he served, or moral strength? Or did he feel that, in a sense, he already had the rule of the country?—with his name on every lip, and Conrad the Third's forgotten, cast in shadow. Inspector Dickson wondered how weak King Conrad really was. If he secretly exploited his general's powers to his own advantage, if he walked with the careless overconfidence of

Andra of Mattadon, or were truly so timid, as the reports went, that he could scarcely bear to show his face in public; and again, he wondered at the general's loyalty.

For himself, he repressed a shudder at the thought of bearing such power. If one could be blind to it, maybe—but one could never wield such a power and be fully blind to its potency.

Inspector Dickson's horse balked, pulling him out of his study. "It's only water, lass," he muttered, spurring her into the shallows of the Dirion River. Jared was already half across.

"How much further?" he asked as his mare heaved herself out panting and dripping where Jared waited on the shore.

"Not far, I think," replied Jared. "I will try to remember as best I can; all I am sure of is that it was in those sandhills"—he gestured to the humps rising to the northeast—"but it may come back more when we reach them."

The sun had risen high in the sky by this time; it was two hours or less off from noon. It took them some fifteen minutes to reach the hills, and Jared reined Rivra in to a halt, his young brow gathering in thought, until he led them on slowly.

They had gone only a short way after that, flatlands and river still visible behind, when Jared suddenly slid off Rivra.

"I know where we are," he said. "We had best dismount now."

And they crept behind him, over the shifting ground. On an outthrust spur he leaned against the slope and pointed. "There," he said, very softly. "That is the hill."

"What?" asked Inspector Dickson. "You said there was a tunnel; I see none."

Jared nodded. "They had a screen of sorts that they covered it with, but someone had removed it and failed to replace it by some mischance. I remember how I saw it lying there. But it is the hill. See that black shale jutting halfway on the south side? Rivra almost lost her footing on it when we were going up."

"Very well," said Inspector Dickson with a nod. But as Jared moved out of the shadow of the hill he jerked him back. "Not so fast, lad! They saw you yesterday; they may have set up sentinels to watch the opening. Let us circle around and come to it from the side."

Jared dipped his head with silent assent, biting his lip in a nervous or embarrassed way.

So they worked around the dunes again, and came at their target from the north. No trace of man or beast was on the wind-smoothed sand, and the stringy, dull vegetation hanging from the side of the hill lifted innocently in the breeze. But Jared reached for the grasses, ready to pull them aside.

"Let me." Inspector Dickson again pulled his arm back.

"No," said Jared more quickly than he usually spoke. "That is, if you please, sir, no. If there is something in there that will kill . . . " He did not seem able to go on for a moment. "Then better it takes me than you."

Inspector Dickson stared at him. "Do you know what you are doing?" he asked quietly.

"I do," answered Jared. "But I will be careful."

He lifted the edge and peered inside. For a breath there was silence.

Then a tug from Jared and the whole false screen came tumbling away, to reveal an empty cave whose bony, reddish walls led away to a narrowing tunnel and darkness. Inspector Dickson stepped over the crumpled ferny grasses and entered.

Nothing shot him; nothing struck him. Nothing harmed him in the least as he strode cautiously over the deadening earth.

"They must have thought that they had chased me safely away," said Jared, his even voice echoing in a small and twisted way off the arch of the cave.

The general said nothing; he was busy lighting torches.

They started off down the curving passageway, walking at a slow, careful pace. It was a large labyrinth, but not so extensive as to make them bewildered, and the master tunnel was marked with red-painted pebbles set in the walls.

"A large group might gather here," said Inspector Dickson as he shone a light glancingly into an empty cave that might be a bedchamber. "Not an army."

"It is silent," said the general. "There are no food storages in these caves, no people."

Inspector Dickson nodded. "I wonder—" But he did not say what he wondered, what he feared.

They searched down to the last dead end.

There was no one in the tunnels.

~

Twenty miles to the east, where the trees grew heavy and close, the black, clear-cut figure of a vulture banked and wheeled above the dense forest. There was nothing to show, high as it was with nothing but the blue sky and dark tossing treetops to compare, that it was unusually large for a vulture.

Runiz discovered the gap in the foliage below him, and in a clean, sharp dive he sank toward the small clearing where his followers had halted for a rest.

"How much longer?" he snapped in irritation at Gorstir as he landed. "I could fly to Serin Nadraith and back in the time it takes these worthless *nikorss* to catch their breath."

"They do not have the speed and the wings of a werevulture," answered Gorstir with an ingratiating bow.

"Do not flatter me," the werevulture snapped, but he was pleased. The Glumintorians were a fine nationality, on the whole; they understood what gain it was to serve the *kakirkiss*. They knew how powerful were the *kakirkiss*. If only there were more who were so willing to fall under his kind's rule.

Into Runiz' pleasant reverie broke Gorstir's voice, questioning, "Did you see the assassin?"

"Yes; he is not far behind us, in fact. We shall wait here until he arrives, I think. But he took a fine time in coming, and I shall have words to speak to him. I have great doubt of his success." With an angry snap of his beak he changed to man-form and stalked across the clearing.

"If he did not succeed," said Gorstir, following him, "how then?"

Runiz was silent briefly, staring with eyes glittering and dangerous into the dark forest. "If he did not succeed, then the Inspector is following us. I am sure of it, and I will yet kill him." He turned and stared hard at the three prisoners huddled on the ground a short distance away. "I will make such a killing that all—*all* in this glade may tremble at the name of Runiz."

~

"If he thinks that I shall blench and cry him mercy," said Sam drily, his cool gaze measuring the werevulture, "he is sore mistaken."

Mordred glanced swiftly to the werevulture. He himself, though he had insulted Runiz, did not think he was prepared to do it in a cool head, without any provocation.

The werevulture leapt across to them in a bound, his thin features rigid with a controlled wrath. "Yes, I spoke of you, vile one," he hissed, his claw-hand closing on Sam's neck and shoulder. "And do not think that I will not yet drag from you what you would hide in vain. You will tell me. You shall weep and snivel before me! You will say that I am great, greater than all, greater than yourself—" He shook Sam in his grip, the way a dog would worry a rat between its teeth. Blood dotted the area around each talon, seeping very slowly out into blotches on the shirt.

Stronger than anything else rose up Mordred's highest, most fierce of passions: his rage at anyone that dared to hurt something weaker than itself. It swept him away and he was riding on the crest of its seething wave. "You appear to be making excellent progress in your labors," he observed in his most sarcastic tone to the werevulture.

The guard nearby grabbed his shoulder and hit him—it was the little, wiry one, who had mocked Mordred's tears last night. His fist struck like knobbled rock and whipcord, and Mordred wondered as the blind, sickening pain exploded in his jaw, if he had grown soft since leaving the orphanage. As it ebbed, he gathered command over himself and realized dully that it had not worked. The werevulture, considering him properly punished, had kept his attention all upon Sam.

He took a breath, working his jaw, hoping that he would not start slurring his words. "You are an admirable person, yes," he said distantly. "You are that prim that you dare not even touch me yourself—you let your servant do it. How very *noble*."

"Mordred," whispered Fred urgently—Fred did not understand, did not know what he was doing—

Mordred saw with a surge of pure, intensely sweet satisfaction that the werevulture was dropping Sam, turning with darkening face and white lips.

"Ihssa-moz," said Runiz in a harshly soft tone, coming towards him, "maybe it is you who need to learn what I can do to you."

"Do what you like," said Mordred nonchalantly. The anger was still high and hot in him, giving him a careless bravery like he had faced the woman of the black house with, as well as the pleasure that he had actually lured the foolish creature away with mere word play. How stupid was it? Could it not see that it had obeyed his wish like dog to master? In the exquisite thrill of his victory, he felt no pain as the werevulture flung him backwards, only the passing sorrow that the stupid thing would never know how stupid it really was.

The high foam of the pleasure melted with a catching pain, and Mordred came violently into the moment as the werevulture's claw dug into the scratch along his side. He was ripping it open—it *hurt*—

The werevulture walked away and Mordred lay clenching eyes and mouth shut against the horrible pain, sobbing for every breath. The agony was worse because he did not know what his side looked like, and he could not help but think of great strips of skin mangled and trailing onto the ground, wallowing in pints of blood.

Someone touched him and he flinched away, knowing at once it was not the werevulture, but he was afraid to have anything near his side.

"Mordred, let me." It was Fred's voice. "'Tis going to be all right; only let me bind it up with something."

"Is there very much blood?" He knew he sounded very small and childish, and was ashamed of it, but it was hurting too much not to ask.

"Not much." Fred's low voice was so steady and reassuring that Mordred felt easier, and the pain seemed to lessen.

"Is he—is he still toying with Sam?"

There was silence for a moment, and Mordred did not know what to think.

"Oh, Mordred—" He opened his eyes, and Fred was looking at him with a suddenly understanding expression.

Mordred did not want to be understood. He did not want to be recognized and approved for the thing he had done.

"Nay, he is gone. Oh, Mordred." Fred's hand touched his cheek, cool and welcoming on his hot skin. But Mordred turned away.

He did not want Fred to know. It was like having a part of himself exposed and aired for the world to stare at. It did not matter that he was not ridiculing him; ridicule would be better than pity.

~

"Are you sure that you saw them?"

Inspector Dickson silenced himself at Jared's astonished, even hurt expression. After all, even if there were no people here, the tunnels were here, and someone had been in the tunnels. "Forgive me, Jared," he said. "Yes, I believe you saw them. They were here. But they might not have been the Claw."

"Then who else?" asked the general. "And why did they flee? It is our only lead, Inspector Dickson. We must endeavor to follow it."

"Yes," agreed Inspector Dickson. "General, if you will, and Jared, search for tracks. I am going back to Delgrass. I shall fetch twenty men, and supplies, and return."

CHAPTER 25

FRED WITHDREW HIS HAND FROM Mordred's pale, sweating face, knowing he had said something amiss, but not what. His heart yearned out to the young man, whom he could see so clearly was hurting within, and yet whom he did not understand. Fiona would have understood, if she were here: her swift, bright intuition would see what he could not. And the pain and despair of their lot hit him cruelly as he picked up the linen that he had torn from his shirt and peeled back the stained and soaking cloth from Mordred's side.

It was worse than he had expected, but not so bad as it might have been. He blotted away the best part of the blood with the strip in his hand; as ugly as the wounds looked, they were only surface. Still, the werevulture had badly torn apart the earlier scratch. It would be a long time before it closed again.

Fred tied the bandage as gently as possible around Mordred's ribs: a poor, rough hand of things, but it was all the protection he could offer for the gaping mess.

Mordred was stiffly silent throughout all this, his mouth shut in a narrow, white line, foolishly determined to pretend that he was unaffected and free of pain. Again, anguish lanced Fred's heart. Mordred had said all those goading words and drawn the werevulture's wrath not for a petty reason, not for mere reckless bravado. He had known he would be hurt, had hoped he would be hurt—so that Sam might be left alone.

"Stop looking at me that way!" The words, furious, explosive, flew from Mordred's lips.

"How?" Fred asked in answer, honestly bewildered.

"As though I had done something wonderful, admirable, brave!" He started half up, his face twisted in something too full of pain to be outrage, yet it was unquestionably a kind of fury.

"I do not understand. Did you not? It was a wonderfully sacrificial thing that you did."

Fred could not tell whether Mordred were whiter with wound or anger. "I do not *care*!" he cried, his voice trembling and rising almost to a shout. "What does it matter? I do not want your understanding! I do not want your pity!"

Fred's shoulders slumped in weariness and confoundment. "I do not understand," he said, as gently and as simply as he could, and turned away, almost weeping in his powerlessness to help the proud, bewildering sufferer beside him.

"So, you finally return, Ridgrua," said the voice of the werevulture, thin and forbidding as soft and hesitant footsteps drew nigh. "How went the errand?"

"It failed, my lord Runiz." If the man were afraid, his flat words gave no hint of it.

"Stupid clod of *nikorss*-ridden earth," the werevulture growled. "Have you nothing else to report?"

"Only that I remained near the house for some hours, seeking another opportune moment to kill him. At dusk, however, a rider came to him and brought this word, that he had discovered the men of the Claw. At once I left and made speed to you."

"Worthless *moz*," said the werevulture, ire growing in his tone. "We need him killed! He is what keeps this hunt in motion. If we slay him, the others will fall apart and trouble us no more."

"Perhaps. But, my lord, there is another one you should be concerned about."

"And that is?" demanded Runiz.

"The one who came hither to clear the prisoners, namely, the General of Orden. He has succeeded in convincing the Inspector again that they are innocent, despite your pains to prove the contrary." He added in a lower voice, "And he seems to have discerned by some art the nature of our leader."

"What?" gasped Runiz.

"How they discovered it I know not, but it is common knowledge in the household of the Inspector that you are a werevulture, my lord."

Fred had never seen such terrifying anger on any creature's face.

Even Ridgrua, who had delivered his message with placidity, edged back. "To—to sum up, my lord," he said, clearing his throat, "the general certainly does not intend to rest while you yet live, and therefore any plan of killing should—by my counsel—include him as well."

"Of course it will include him." The werevulture's suppressed voice vibrated discordantly. His hand came up and struck Ridgrua a staggering blow across the face.

"Of course it will include him," he repeated violently, and kicked the sprawled man. "Gorstir! The rest is over. Move eastwards."

Winging up into the air in vulture form, he let out a wordless, grating shriek.

"My lord Runiz!" Gorstir shouted, running forward. "Where are you going?"

The werevulture settled on a branch and thrust its head downwards toward him. “Go and do not wait for me,” he rasped. “I shall return to you when I have killed the wretched *nikorss.*”

And springing into flight again he gained the treetops and disappeared into the pale spring-blue sky.

Gorstir stared after him, the vaguest hint of irritation settling into his face. “So be it, then,” he muttered.

With a few shouting commands the camp was stirring again, ready to move. One of Mordred’s guards, the bigger one, bent over him and cuffed his shoulder. “Wake up, boy.”

Fred was doubtful whether Mordred could walk. But with a resentful twist away from the rough hand, Mordred struggled to his feet and walked, his dark head arrogantly lifted high, refusing to betray a sign of weakness by so much as a stagger or a limp.

“I shall return to you when I have killed the wretched nikorss.”

For a moment the formless hope that Fred had waited on had gained a shape and reality. Now it was gone, or almost gone—as good as gone; for though they yet lived, Fred did not believe the werevulture would fail. And because the hope had been there, and had come alive and breathed, it left the greater void in its going.

~

Will Selwyn sat with his reins loosely on the neck of the horse that he had mounted in dizzying haste moments before, his eyes on Inspector Dickson’s curt, square-jawed face as the man directed and ordered the small cavalcade together.

Mordred was innocent.

He had known of the reprieve, but had attached only doubtful importance to it. After all, the general might want to help Mordred, but how could he nullify the bald proof? And besides, he was a foreigner, and this in Will's mind attached itself to a certain stolid prejudice against, if not virtue, general worthiness.

But now here came Inspector Dickson, in a mad sort of hurry, voice and face grim, men snapping to his orders on the instant, taking Will aside and explaining to him in a low tone the particulars, out of which only one now resounded in Will's head: *Mordred was innocent.*

He felt like a horribly low thing, a sewer rat, when he thought of the moments with Mordred's eyes fixed on him and pleading for trust, and saw himself turning away in answer. Every cold word, though spoken as kindly as possible, took on a painful light, as he fully realized how Mordred must have felt them.

At the same time a second mind of his was glad: glad that Mordred had never been that cold murderer he had thought he must be. Glad for that quick-witted, thoughtful young man so full of life. Glad that he had been right first, and wrong later.

"Oy! Selwyn."

He looked down and saw that it was Murcod, Inspector Dickson's friend, who stood there by his horse, his homely face somber.

"I should like to come with you," he said, "but of course I can't. Dratted smith's job!" He grinned awkwardly. "Anyway, what I mean to say is, well, look after Dickson for me. See that he doesn't make this too much of an obsession. He needs someone to make him laugh once in a while. You're a good lad, Selwyn; you'll do that."

"Yes," said Selwyn. "I'll do that."

He thought that as bad as he was feeling, Inspector Dickson must be feeling ten times worse.

~

Inspector Dickson dismounted, a little stiffly; he had been in the saddle most of the day, and it was mid-afternoon. Hot and panting, he climbed up to the lip of the cave where the general and Jared were waiting.

"We found their trail," said the general, forestalling his very question. "It is hard to pick up, but we followed for about a mile and it seems to be leading roughly east."

"Show me," said Inspector Dickson quickly.

They went through the sandhills, the wind scattering dust into their eyes and mouths, and Inspector Dickson saw what the general and Jared had before him: little fragments of evidence, one here and another there, most long obliterated by the relentless erasure of the wind. Yet a company so great could not pass traceless like smoke, even in the dunes. Flattened grass, collapsed overhangs, spoke silently to their presence.

It led, indeed, in a general eastward direction; and while for some time they watched it closely, looking for any deviation or petering out that might signal a false trail, east it continued. The afternoon was far advanced when they left the hills behind, and came into forest.

Here the ground was low, and mushy with water, and the marks were heavy in it. They were at last able to make a guess at how many and what sort they were following.

"Fifty, maybe," said Inspector Dickson after they had circled the clearest area of prints.

"Forty to fifty," agreed the general, bending down on one knee to look again. "They do not look to have had any horses with them."

"Fifty is much against twenty," said Inspector Dickson softly, but more to himself than the general; he did not want to seem to him a complainer and a prophesier of doom. Murcod would have called him just that, he realized, and a stab of lonesomeness for Murcod's cheerful face smote him in the heart.

They rode on eastwards, the blue, sunless twilight deepening ahead.

~

Fred sank to the damp, loamy soil, his senses dulled with exhaustion. Night air rocked gently over him, a subtle coldness developing in it as the *whoot* of a startled owl rose and faded near at hand. The werevulture had not returned.

Low voices murmured, Gorstir and another man conversing—it might have been Ridgrua. " . . . not waiting . . . werevulture . . . payment . . . "

He dozed off lightly listening to them, and when he roused again it was with an anxious, indecipherable compulsion to see to something—to see to—Mordred!

Fred heaved himself up to his knees and marked Mordred close by, a soft and dim outline under the starlight. His breath came quick, faint and shivering and his forehead was damp to the touch.

"Mordred, are you awake?"

"'m—fine." Mordred forced the words out between teeth that attempted to chatter.

Fred felt the forehead again, an ominous toll striking his fears awake. But though wet, it was cool; the sweat had come from exertion, not from fever.

The fear relaxed, to give rise to more. Fred bowed his head, one tear slipping out unbidden. How could Mordred heal like this? He ought to be resting, but there would be no rest for him tomorrow, only another day of fleeing deeper into the wilderness.

At the least he ought to have a fire. The guards had disregarded this, seemingly, as the night was warmer than the previous one, but that made no difference to Mordred, whose strain and sweat now left him trembling with cold.

One guard remained awake, watching them; the others had gone to sleep. Fred hesitated, afraid to make a request that might be scorned. "Sir," he said softly. "Sir—"

"What?" came the grunting response. It was the big man, with the scarred face and callused neck; his name was Hopheg, a Mesoremnian who had been convicted of murder and sentenced to labor in the silver mines.

"If you would, please, build a fire for him?"

"The night is fair," said Hopheg indifferently, folding his arms and staring up at the quivering stars. "There is no need for a fire."

"Sir, look at him!" Fred pointed at Mordred.

The large man glanced down briefly, took in Mordred's white, shivering form. An unreadable look grew in his eyes, and then he lifted them back to the sky, hefting a little sigh, the indolent look seeping back. "No."

"Sir, can you not see—I beg you—"

"D'ye think I am soft?" asked Hopheg in a hard voice, not looking down again. "Runiz does not take soft men."

An aching pain budded in Fred like a sharp-needled flower, and despite his own words to Mordred the day before, he felt broken despair coming on him. What had they to hope in when the world was so hopelessly vast and cruel? He turned his thoughts to home, to his family, and to Fiona, but they seemed very far away, bitter, tasteless as shells, gray and unbeautiful, filling him not with longing but with a dead darkness. He thought of young Hedron, and the fleeting smile that made the world seem right again, and he began to weep, because now the world seemed to have turned over into endless wrongness, and there was nothing that could make it right.

~

"'Tis pretty country," said Selwyn cheerfully as their horses picked careful footing over the mossy ground.

Inspector Dickson nodded, his gaze passing over the greeneried cliff face and the narrow ridge that made a dubious passage down it. The ridge, dangerous as it looked, they had chosen to take, since there seemed to be no other way down the cliff. "If they made it on foot, we can but try it on horseback," said Inspector Dickson. "We can always lead them if the going is too poor."

But so far the pathway had been wide enough and shallow enough that they could make safe if slow progress. Selwyn, at first seized with nervousness, was now pleasantly confident and remarking on the scenery.

"Look, down there," he said, gesturing to a wide, dark gap in the rock face another quarter of a mile down. "A cave of some sort, I'll warrant—what do you say, sir?"

"I'd agree." Inspector Dickson smiled, in spite of himself; he enjoyed hearing Selwyn's young, eager chatter. He had never seen the lad so bright and animated.

"Wonder what lives in it. Foxes, maybe. It looks quite large. Bears, do you think?"

Inspector Dickson shrugged, managing a grin.

"I should like to go in it and have a look around." Selwyn seemed quite taken with this idea.

"Best not to, I think," said Inspector Dickson mildly. "We need to keep a move on."

Selwyn ceded willingly. "It's probably birds, anyway," he said. "Great, huge unpleasant things that would peck our eyes out." He flushed as Inspector Dickson laughed.

"Nay, lad, you said nothing amiss," Inspector Dickson hastened to assure him. "Say anything you like. I haven't laughed in weeks."

Selwyn flushed even deeper. "Thank you, sir. Do you think we are gaining on them?" he went on with a clumsy subject change.

Inspector Dickson sighed, all the difficulties of the world crashing upon his shoulders again. "I think not. The traces of the camp we came upon this morning were at least a day old."

Selwyn was quiet; and Inspector Dickson found himself wishing that he had said something, even something unbearably trite, to lighten the mood a little.

"Well," he remarked finally, unsure of what he was even going to say.

"Hsst!"

He swung a startled scrutiny on young Selwyn, and saw that he had checked his horse and was tilting his head as though listening. "What," he uttered instantly, straining his own ears. "What?"

"Something is wrong, sir—" And Selwyn lifted his hand backwards toward the height of the cliff, as a dull rumbling noise swelled and crackled, and Inspector Dickson saw what seemed to be the whole precipice rushing towards them.

~

Runiz settled himself in a tall, fringe-leafed tree and polished his beak on his breast feathers as the landslide roared down the narrow chute of the ridge. He waited until the dust had cleared and settled. Great boulders dotted the once-passable slope, and a jumble of rocks, saplings and earth buried the last furlong. Nothing moved.

He winged down, circling over the destruction for several minutes. Then he wheeled about, rising as he caught the current of the air, and hurtled east.

CHAPTER 26

THE NIGHT, AND EVEN THE whole of the next day, seemed strung in a kind of blur for Fred. He did not think much about where he was, or what he was doing, until in the blackening evening, as they made ready to picket camp again, a soft flutter that was more sense than sound came grayly through the trees and Runiz rejoined them.

He looked pleasant and sly, like a dog-fox with an overly large hen in its stomach and her feathers around its muzzle. Fred turned his face away, shuddering, all the hopes that he had raised up for himself even in his despair, without knowing that he raised them, splintering at the base of a long, long fall.

"My lord." Gorstir approached the werevulture, speaking in tones of urgency and poorly hidden annoyance. "The prisoner is ill; he will not be able to go on tomorrow."

"Which one? The *khhavfa-eglik-risshrrith*. Sam?"

"Not that one!" Gorstir snorted aloud. "He is made of cured leather and reforged iron. Nay, your playtoy that you so heartily chastened the other day has taken a turn for worse and not better."

The werevulture accompanied him swiftly, grumbling in his own tongue, to stand over Mordred.

Mordred had gone on all that day by some frantic will. But at the call for halt he had fallen down at once with an incoherent murmur, and did not get up even when the guards fetched them their evening meal. He lay at their feet now, his hair stuck in dark, wet locks on his forehead, shivering and half-delirious.

The werevulture studied him, in his man-form now, but his head cocked in a bird-like way still on one side, as though he had never seen a sick man before.

"It does not matter," he said finally, "for we have flown far enough, now that I have rid us of those *nikorss*. We shall not journey any further tomorrow, only look for a place that will suit us well. If we need to move any distance, the men can carry him."

Gorstir grunted, satisfied.

"It would be a pity if he dies," the werevulture remarked. "I hope he does not die. I have not had half the entertainment that I planned for him yet."

"He will not die," said Gorstir. "I saw the wound, and it is but little inflamed; the fever was brought on more by strain and chill. He is young, and he will heal, only as long as he is given a few days of rest."

"A few days of rest he shall have," said the werevulture with mock magnanimity. "All the better for him to regain his strength a little, while I reorder our camp in this place and meditate on how I may further sate my vengeance with him."

His eye flickered on Fred and Fred drew back from his bright, cold gaze. "Him, too." He took a few strides forward and kicked Fred in the chest, casually and without rancor. "You will like watching your friend scream, yes? I have many ways to make *nikorss* scream. But I wonder if I shall play with you a little first . . . it will hurt him, I think, to see you in pain, more than it would himself."

There was something terribly insensate in the way he spoke of such cruelty, a mercilessness that sickened Fred the way Falgor's callous gibes had cut him once. The nearness of an evil like that suddenly seemed too much to bear. He scrambled backwards, filled with as much horror as fear, and the werevulture laughed.

"Fear, little *moz*. Fear and tremble, and await my pleasure." Runiz left, and the night fell into a heavier silence.

It was broken once, by Sam. "It is a pity that the Inspector Wilhelm Dickson is dead," he said.

And that short, toneless sentence was all the epitaph given to Inspector Dickson that night.

Fred was not sure if he drowsed, but he came suddenly to himself in the silence of the dead hours, the moon high and pure overhead. He shivered with the cold and stood, wrapping his arms about his body, and paced with jerky rapidity. Nothing stirred. The guards were asleep.

It came to him, hit him like a stone hurled from a sling, that they were *all* asleep. They were not all supposed to sleep at once; they took turns watching . . . and yet now every one of them slept, and he was awake, his hands and feet free, the moon up and the quiet forest beckoning. Hope choked him as surely and headily as panic; he stumbled, knelt, and could not quite catch his breath for a second.

There could yet be an end to this nightmare, if he should just get up and run into the trees now. They would not miss him till morning, and he might get far, very far, surely he could make it to people—to help. He did not know where to go, but no matter, he could go . . .

Mordred cannot come with you. The voice spoke for the first time inside him, a quiet, cold check. *You know he cannot.*

His head turned to look at Mordred, who lay under the dispassionate sheen of the moonlight with the sharpness of his hollowing cheeks casting dark shadows on his face. His ribs heaved in quick, feverish pants for breath.

Aye, of course he cannot. But I shall find help and return to save him. It is not as though I leave him to die!

But maybe he will die, before you can return with the help you promise. The werevulture will not wait on you.

I can do nothing for him by staying.

Can you not?

"I do not know," he answered the silent question, half-aloud, bewildered, almost truculent. "I do not know."

You do know. Can you not see that he needs you?

He does not want me. He does not let me help him, and I cannot—

He was unable to finish the thought. Had he not said the same to himself of Sandy—that Sandy would not let him help her, therefore he could not?

But, he argued, *I have truly tried with Mordred, and it avails nothing.*

There was no answer for a little, and he thought that it would not come again, that penetrating voice. Then it came, very quietly, very coldly, as before, in words so defined and plain it was almost disconcerting: *Are you escaping for Mordred, or yourself?*

"I do not know," he admitted honestly, aloud, and it was the hardest thing that he had ever said in his life.

And then he knew that he would not go, not that night. And that there would not be another night.

And he cast himself down on the ground, full of grief and shame and despair; but neither tear dropped, nor sleep came, only dry anguish until the dawn.

~

The grinding of rock on rock, of ripping stone and earth, stopped Inspector Dickson's ears. He flung himself backwards, dust rolling into his eyes and fragments of stone whipping into his face, too quickly to hurt. Then came a great crunching noise, and blackness descended and everything was a great deal more still.

Above the dulled growl and thunder came the general's voice, clear and steady. "Are all here?"

To Inspector Dickson's surprise, his own voice, when he answered, was equally cool and quiet. "I think that all the men made it in. We lost some of the horses."

A short interlude fell. The uproar outside died away to a low grumbling, then sliding and skittering sounds, and then silence.

"Selwyn," said Inspector Dickson.

"Sir?"

"You're all right?"

"Aye, sir."

"Well done in spotting the cave, lad."

"You're the one who remembered it in time to get us all in there, sir."

A different voice spoke, Jared's. "But can we get out now?"

There was shifting, and grunting noises, as the general pushed his way through the twenty-odd people who now filled the small cave. Then more shifting, softer now, and scraping, soughing. "There is a large boulder lodged across the entrance," came his voice again, more faintly. The susurration came again, and Inspector Dickson realized that he was passing his hands over the stone, feeling it. "It is not too firmly settled, though, and I think—"

"No!" Inspector Dickson had sprung forward, shoving his way past elbows and snorting horses' muzzles, before he even knew that he was doing so. He found the general's arm and pulled him back. "My lord, stay a moment! We do not know—we do not know whether anything caused that landslide."

"Yes," said the general after an instant of stillness. "I see what you would say. Thank you; we shall wait."

"In the meantime," said Inspector Dickson, "let us try to get a proper count of who is here. Selwyn, Hiltha, Cander, Lorch—" He rapped out the names, one by one, and each man answered to it until he came to "Rodyn." Then it was Will Selwyn who spoke.

"Rodyn's here, sir, but he's in a bad way. Something fell on his foot and crushed it as we were running for the cave."

"Any others injured?" Inspector Dickson asked to the cave.

Murmuring answers, a bruised arm, a finger sprained, a couple cuts. No one advanced anything of concern; Inspector Dickson was glad of that.

They managed to ascertain that of their twenty-three mounts, eighteen had made it into the cave with them. Which ones, there was no way of knowing for now. Jared had suggested trying to strike a light, but Inspector Dickson was against the idea, even if they could find flint and fuel on them. It was too crowded a place, and hot already.

So they waited in the dark. Minutes dragged away. Rodyn awoke from unconsciousness, moaned in pain several times, and was quiet again. At last, when more than an hour must have elapsed, Inspector Dickson said, "Suppose we try moving that boulder now."

Five of them worked their way up against the slab of rock and set their shoulders against it. One heave—it only rocked, but the general had been right; it was but loosely wedged into the hole. A second push sent it tottering, and then rolling, and it toppled outward with a rumbling screech to pitch a little ways down the ridge and plummet off the other side.

They came out gratefully, gasping in the fresh, cool air, and rested there on the lip of the cave for a little. But Inspector Dickson hurried them on quickly, for no matter what had incited the slide, he did not want to stay on the cliff long. They descended as swiftly and silently as they could manage to the lower ground, and went on until they came to a deep dell, very green and grown over with ferns and soft-leafed shrubs, where they made camp.

"Sir," Will made bold to say to Inspector Dickson as he was getting wearily down from his little brown mare—whom he had been gladder than he had admitted to anyone else to see safe and unhurt. "Sir, if you'd let me see that—"

"See what?" Inspector Dickson was not angry, but he was that tired his tone sounded snappish without him meaning it to.

"Sir, maybe you haven't noticed, but something's sliced your cheek open."

He had not noticed.

Inspector Dickson's hand flew horrified to his face, where he found that while the wind was not yet fluttering around his teeth, there *was* a long scrape of raised skin and crusted blood lengthwise below his cheekbone.

"See to it, by all means," he said, dropping down painfully to rest his back against the withered and split bark of an enormous oak tree. He shut his eyes while Will cleaned out the wound, the smell of evening and green things in his nose. With a sudden ache he wished that none of this had happened, and that he could lie in a place like this forever and feel the grass gently tickling his hand.

The second part of the wish was so unlike him that he recognized how very exhausted he was. "Don't wake me for supper, Selwyn," he found himself mumbling, and let everything glide dimly away on the spring-like dusk.

He did not remember afterwards what he dreamed, only that it was full of green and serenity and low music.

~

Sunrise came with fair fingers of light that worked their misty way even through the tight cover of the forest. Through this or that chink, the golden haze floated oddly against the darkness and the heavy green, as though one could catch it and capture its essence.

Fred saw it with a heart that was beyond delighting in any beauty. He bowed his head, shut his sight away from its mockery. He could not eat or speak; for him there was only the dread of torture and death, if not today, another day; and, far more painful, the hard certitude of his own selfish heart.

It flooded him with hot guilt to think of telling Mordred what he had been about to do. Worse still was the knowledge that he still wanted it—wanted that escape and freedom, even at the cost of deserting Mordred's side. With bitter teeth the pain gnawed at him, chewing a poisonous hole, and it never slackened, for it fed off his guilt and there was always more of that to take.

They moved camp at the werevulture's orders to a grove of spreading pines, where the ground was full of hummocks and mostly bare save for the dead needles. A low rock shelf bounded one edge of the grove, and an ancient, overgrown quarry another. The men began to build temporary shelters.

Fred walked blindly where he was bidden, sat where they shoved him, and suffered under a dark hopelessness too blank and parched for tears.

Mordred's fever left him shortly after sunset. "Where are we?" he asked Fred, not recognizing their surroundings.

Fred told him how the werevulture had moved them here.

"I do not remember coming," said Mordred, still looking bewildered.

"They carried you," Fred answered.

"Oh." Mordred's eyes drifted shut. "Was I ill long?" he asked, propping them open with an effort.

"You took the fever yesterday." It was a strange effort to speak and not to reveal the despair battering at him. His voice was unutterably weary in his ears.

Mordred's eyes wandered absently over the swishing dark branches above them and the fire nearby. "How bright it is," he murmured. "'Tis a strangely fair thing; so many colors, always changing places in a quick-paced dance. There were dances at your sister's wedding," he added inconsequentially.

Fred did not speak immediately, for the words had awoken too many painful things inside him at once.

"Once," he said, softly, no longer holding back the dull misery that edged his words, "once, Mordred, I saw a thindran. It was the fairest thing I ever saw or shall see again. Such light, such glory, such wonder. And afterwards my whole life and the world around me seemed to be filled with light like that, and I thought that it would stay with me forever. Yet my life has shivered apart around me, and the joy and light is gone." His voice broke, and trembled. "There is death everywhere.

I shall never see them again. I tried to hold the light, but it is no use. Where are we, or what have we, that we should hope? There is no more light—not for us."

Mordred had said nothing, all this time; not that Fred had expected him to answer, for his agony held no hope for response or release. Now he said, in great gentleness, "But the light is still there."

His gray eyes were kindled in the tawny fire, and he looked at once older and yet more boyish than Fred had ever seen him. "The light is there, beyond our pain. Even when we cannot see it. It will always be there. Is that not a thing to hold to?"

And Fred answered, saying the thing that was the most foolish thing he had ever uttered, because he was foolish and ashamed. He knew its absurdity even as he said it. "And yet the light does nothing. What if the light is the wrong after all?"

Mordred said steadily, "If it were, it would not be light."

CHAPTER 27

A HORSE'S MUZZLE WAS NOSING lightly at him, lipping at his sleeve and fingers. Inspector Dickson's eyes fluttered open to stare at the wide, dark nostrils of his plucky mare.

"Ger'way, lass," he murmured, twitching his fingers in a vague dismissal that he felt was all he could manage. The tree no longer sat against his back; instead he was lying with his cheek pillowed on the downy undergrowth of the glade. It might have been velvet for all his sleep-drunk body cared, and in the warm golden-green world and the lulling touch of the sun he felt his lids sagging willingly shut again.

A low laugh cut into his fuzzy thoughts, sharpening them against his will. "She'd have a meal off his shirt, eh? Come, lass,"—it was Selwyn, he realized, as the young man came up to lead the horse away—"come now, leave off your gimmicks for attention and eat the grass, if your stomach is gnawing at you so."

Inspector Dickson sat up and rubbed a hand over his tousled hair, finding that bits of leaf sifted down off it. "How do I look?" he asked as Selwyn came back from picketing the mare.

Selwyn hesitated a moment, and grinned stoutly at him. "Like you slept in a forest, sir."

Inspector Dickson grinned back, and regretted it. With a wince of pain, he reached up to examine the injury on his cheek.

Largely, he found by the time they broke camp, the cut was little trouble. But where eating or speaking was involved—and he tried to avoid smiling—it protested with pinching throbs that were painful enough to be just more than a nuisance.

Selwyn must have caught his sour face and awkward chewing as they breakfasted. "Don't worry, sir," he said reassuringly. "It was a shallow thing, scarce broke the skin, and it's closed up already. It should hardly trouble you tomorrow."

"That's small comfort for today," Inspector Dickson grunted. He meant to give Selwyn a smile, to show that he only half meant the ill-tempered response, but it turned into a grimace.

"I fear that the trail is going to serve us ill after this," he said to the general later as they saddled and bridled their horses. "We lost half a day or more with that accident, if accident it were; I suppose we shall never know. And now we must go slower besides, with the loss of the horses."

The general nodded, silent, working the bit into the gelding's mouth with careful touch.

Inspector Dickson watched Jared swing easily up onto Rivra. With a sigh he mounted himself. "Still," he muttered, "we've naught to do but follow it as we may."

~

Evening found them a cross and dispirited group. They had lost the trail more times than Inspector Dickson could number on one hand; once it had died out altogether and they had had to scout the area for a wasted half hour before catching traces again. Rodyn was feverish and irritable with the pain in his foot, and more than one quarrel had arisen between him and the man who had been ordered to give up his horse for Rodyn's sake.

Selwyn, quiet and dependable as he was, could not manage to keep heart and docility in the men forever, and Inspector Dickson felt as he stepped down from his horse that the first person to speak to him would find his ears ringing from a caustic remark that Mordred himself could not have bettered.

His mind shrank from the thought of Mordred. He had barely thought of him as an individual for days; it had simply been Fred-and-Mordred, the two people whom he had failed and who were now suffering because he had been blind and foolish countless times. He had *tried* not to think of them as individuals, because it was far, far more painful. But now he had begun to think of Mordred, and he could not stop.

"I arrest you for murder . . . "

" . . . trial in three days' time . . . "

"There you lie, murderer."

Mocking words flung at him in desperate pride. Eyes filled with hate, pure, raging hate contained under a cold front of arrogant indifference. A voice shaking and broken, goaded beyond all endurance.

Surely Mordred must see sense. Surely he would understand. He would forgive him.

Would he not forgive him?

~

It was plain that the werevulture meant not to return to the tunnels—not for a long while, at least.

"The quarry will serve well enough for now," he said at one juncture to Gorstir, as the two of them stood on a mossy protrusion of rock and looked out over the shadowy depths of their new domain. "I like it; it is dark and full of secrets. We shall be well-hidden here."

While Runiz's men slaved in the abandoned gulch, fashioning a sort of warren out of the caves and the holes and the fragments of rock that remained, the Claw for the present slept and ate in the pine grove, sheltering themselves by makeshift wooden huts.

"Get one for the prisoners, too," Runiz ordered. "I like not how they sleep in the air with a mere distraction on the guards' part between them and freedom."

So a hut was built for the three prisoners as well; and in the meantime, Runiz, seized suddenly with this new concern, commanded that their hands be bound with ropes and the ropes tied to the nearest tree.

Mordred did not care, at least not much; it was just another indignity that had been forced upon him, and he had begun to feel that nothing that happened would ever matter much to him anymore. But it was unpleasant to wake up at night, cold all over, and feel that his hands were not a part of him, and so he was glad when they were moved to the finished hut.

He and Fred spoke little after that one conversation the night they had come to the quarry. Mordred was weak and tired, while Fred never talked readily at the best of times. And there was no heart in either of them for much discourse.

Mordred's weakness weighed bitterly on him in the days after his fever left. He could barely walk on his own. Though little opportunity arose for that helplessness to evidence itself, the helplessness was there, and he felt it with a keen frustration and even shame; and at times he was so tired and thwarted that he would want to weep, which only made him more angry.

But he remained silent; and he was silent for Fred's sake. For he had beheld a part of Fred that he had not known, a Fred who was broken beneath terrible suffering, and he would not burden Fred with his own small griefs. *Does he not bear too much already,* he thought, *without sparing worry for me as well?*

And so Mordred held it all within, resolving to never by so much as one angry word let slip his pain again. Any of his own hurts seemed to pale when he thought of Fred's face distraught and trembling, and the quiet voice dead and empty in absolute despair.

All this while they saw very little of Sam. The werevulture came at odd intervals and took him away, and did not return him for long periods of time. When he came back, he was invariably angry, and Sam was wordless and his clothing bloodstained. He courteously if coolly refused any advances of help.

One night things seemed to come to a head. The werevulture stormed into their hut raging in his glottal language, and flung Sam so that his head knocked against the wall. With a shrieking curse he turned into vulture and flapped out into the night, leaving Sam unconscious on the floor and bleeding from the ears, nose and mouth.

There was a light on the wall, though it was placed out of their reach; sometimes it was lit, sometimes not, but tonight it was and Mordred crawled to Sam's side and pulled his head gently onto his knees, wiping away the blood with his fingers and sleeve.

Sam came back to himself slowly, and seemed slightly put out at the situation in which he found himself, but there was nothing he could do about it; Mordred continued to hold him steady, staunching the blood as best he could and chafing Sam's hands.

Sam submitted as one being put under an irksome trial, though he made one verbal request for Mordred to desist, which Mordred ignored. It was surprisingly easy, he found, to ignore Sam once one put one's mind to it. Besides, his calm, well-modulated voice sounded so very ridiculous when his nose was stopped with blood like any other person's might be.

It might have been hours before the bleeding ceased and Sam could breathe comfortably again. "Thank you," he said, perfunctorily and not at all as though he meant it, but Mordred was startled all the same.

"There was naught else to do," he answered, "and I was tired of being useless."

"Not many would have done it," said Sam. He sounded almost amused, at what, Mordred was at a loss to know.

"Sam," he murmured aloud some time later, exhausted and yet somehow far from sleep, "how did you come to be captured?"

He had wondered it more than once; but this seemed to be a night when Sam might speak of it.

"Sam," he said again, when there was no answer. Perhaps he had gone to sleep.

"Yes?" Sam uttered with martyral patience.

"What happened the day you were captured?"

"It was a night," corrected Sam, and then Mordred knew then that he was going to tell.

He told it, in his dry, passionless way. "I took lodging at a hostel in Rehirne the night after I had spoken to the Inspector. I stabled my horse, and ate. After dinner I was delivered two letters, which I read and then burnt. I had barely finished with that when several of Runiz' men pried my window open and set upon me. One of them was Ridgrua; he is a quite capable assassin, and also does well at taking people alive even when they struggle, which I did not have much of a chance to do. The other was Grimshaw, who incidentally is Gorstir. They overpowered me soon enough, and the rest is plain."

"What was in the letters?" Mordred asked curiously. But Sam was not to be taken in so easily as that.

"One of them was an authorization," he said, "and the other was an admission."

His unremarkable, haggard features were as near to smug as they ever came. "I surmise that you have no more questions, for I am done answering them," he said, and shut his eyes.

~

Inspector Dickson stared into the distance until his eyes ached. They had lost the trail—wholly, finally, lost it—and had not seen it for two days. Such a two days he had never imagined in his life: two days of gloom, of tensity, of strife and sharp words on all sides, of frantic, *frantic* searching and searching until the mind was ten times as weary as the body.

Nothing lay before them but endless woods. One tree looked the same as another, and anyone who cared to tell Inspector Dickson otherwise would find himself facing a biting and none too short reply.

We might be going in circles. Who knows if we can even find our way out again?

He tormented himself with these and like thoughts as he studied the masses of dark trunks rising around them. Twilight was falling, blue and dark and silent.

Tall trees rising . . .

He put the words firmly out of his head. They wormed their way slyly back in.

Many surmising

They will stand fore'er . . .

"Where is Selwyn?"

The general's voice snapped him away from any thoughts of songs and trees. "Selwyn? *Selwyn*?"

His eyes strained into the heavy lusterless shadow. "Selwyn!" he barked.

No answer.

How had he got separated from them? They were too large a group for that to happen, under any ordinary circumstance. He must have ridden off, alone—

Hooves thudded faintly into the silence. Selwyn came trotting towards them, a white blur. His voice shook with excitement. "Sir, I found them."

~

There would be time later for questions, for asking Selwyn what exactly he had done or wrangling out whether it had been right for him to do it. For now, they only followed him.

Inspector Dickson stood leaning out from the flaky bole of a young, straight pine, peering towards the glints of fire in the distance. He turned to Selwyn.

The younger man held a finger to his lips. "I don't know what kind of sentries they have," he whispered. "I didn't dare come much closer than this. But I heard them talking."

And Inspector Dickson heard them, too. Raised, rough voices, speaking of building, of plans, of my lord the werevulture—

"We had best get out of here quickly," he said.

"What are we going to do?" Selwyn asked.

Inspector Dickson looked at the general briefly. "Attack them," he said. "Storm the camp, kill the serpent. What else is there to do?"

Selwyn nodded. "When?"

"Tomorrow. It must be done as soon as possible." Inspector Dickson spoke flatly and quickly, as a man who speaks of getting a tooth pulled. And it was like that for him, in a way; only much worse. For he was not at all certain that he would live through it.

"Maybe it will not be hard," said Selwyn lightly. "He does not seem to have done anything very dangerous after all yet, only flee. Maybe he is not as strong as we feared."

"Nay," said the general. "He flees only because he believes that he has kept his secret safe. That was his main purpose, and far more cunning than making an open fight of things. Once he learns that that has failed, he will turn and he will fight us like a cornered dragon in its lair."

CHAPTER 28

THE GRAY, VAPOROUS HOUR BEFORE dawn was heavy with cold. Ridgrua the assassin wakened Runiz with a soft, urgent cough.

"The men live," he said bluntly with a low bow, as Runiz rose and fixed glittering black eyes upon him. "They are here twenty-odd strong, with horses."

"How did you find this?" asked the werevulture in a quiet, baleful voice. His face did not change, save that it looked strangely fixed and carven as if from stone, every line etched in a wrathful calm.

"I make a point, my lord, of scouting a wider circle about the camp than your sentries are bidden do. I can go silently where most men would draw attention to themselves. I found them not forty minutes since. They speak of making an attack."

"When?" Still the werevulture did not stir, but he was poised and waiting.

"Even as I speak. They were preparing to depart; they must be not more than a quarter-hour away."

The spring snapped, the werevulture wheeled silently in a rapid, fluid motion. "Gorstir."

The Glumintorian who was never far from Runiz entered in a moment, and the werevulture relayed in terse words what Ridgrua had spoken.

"Withdraw all the men into the quarry. Let them find the camp deserted."

"My lord." Gorstir left.

"So, they all live," said the werevulture to Ridgrua. "The Inspector? The Ordenian general?"

"It is even so."

Runiz was silent again, his eyes bitter with a hate of generations. "Let them find that the snake is most dangerous when turned upon," he said venomously. "Ridgrua!"

"My lord."

"The battle will not go ill for us. But if it should, you must do this for me . . . "

~

It had become easy to believe, or half-believe, that their days would go on forever in this hungry, dull, yet bearable existence. But in that gray daybreak, when their guards came swift and wordless into the hut to drag all three of them up and lead them roughly through the whispering, colorless pines, Mordred knew that that in-between time was over and some vast, nameless quake of change was near at hand.

The guards brought them down into the quarry, stumbling over the uncertain, craggy paths formed into the depths, the slubbed mossy surface an unstable and often steep purchase. Beautiful, Mordred thought it, as he looked at the vast, lonely monoliths and lumps and crevasses, cracked walls and tumbled broken slopes, all dark and blue-shadowed and moss-grown. They seemed to him sad and proud and very fair in their forgottenness; and it awoke something freshly living inside of him, that began to hurt.

He lurched on a sudden slippery patch of bare rock, and nearly fell. Geinidh, the smaller, hard-fisted one, yanked him up with a spitting curse and struck him backhanded across the face.

"Save your breath," said Hopheg to him shortly, "and cool your head, or you will be the next one teetering for balance."

"Are you on the boy's side?" jeered Geinidh, failing to take Hopheg's advice.

"I am on the side of us all getting down without any broken necks for which to answer to my lord Runiz," Hopheg retorted, and grimly steered between two squat, misshapen pillars of rock for the sheer-rising side of the quarry.

There was a chink in the wall, an old hole that had been widened recently into a larger cave, and there the guards halted, and Hopheg squinted thoughtfully up into the recess.

"Yes, that will do; put them in there," said the werevulture's voice out of nowhere, and he strode out from the shadow of a tilting slab to join them, Gorstir at his side.

He watched them as they climbed up a narrow sort of catwalk to the cave. Mordred knew he was watching them, for he turned his head once and the thin hook-nosed face was turned up, glimmering in the hint of first light, but at the same time he spoke to Gorstir.

"So, they are all prepared now?"

"Waiting and in readiness, my lord. We watch only for the enemy's arrival and your command."

"You will leave the *hranehka-moz* to me?"

"It is your wish, my lord; I obey. You care nothing for the other?"

"What is he to me? So long as he dies, I am pleased, but the *hranehka, rikiss*! He is mine."

"Wooden-footed fool!" shouted one of Sam's guards angrily as the man staggered without warning and nearly sent both of them toppling off the face.

"Silence up there!" Runiz hissed angrily. "Can one not hold war council in peace? They will be here in minutes, and I want every man of you fighting, so haste your miserable flesh, worthless *nikorss*!"

They had gained the ledge now. Mordred balked at the small mouth of the cave, gripped with a blank aversion to the pitchy dark that was yawning back at him, but Hopheg sent him in with a heavy shove. He skidded onto his knees, small hard things poking at him, and heard the others entering behind him. Then with a grunting, heaving noise, there was a crack of rock on rock, and much of the dim light left all at once; and afterwards many sharp clickings resounded as the remaining cracks were blocked, and the light grew less and less, and finally the sounds came no more and there was absolute blackness.

Mordred tried not to be afraid. He knew that there was nothing to harm him in here, and of course, *of course*, the dark itself could not harm him. But suddenly it came to him that he did *not* know, and he was seized with the idea of soft, creeping things, and what the werevulture might have planned for them in this cave, and the dark was so total and so impenetrable, and he could not see, he could not see, and the dark seemed to be twisting itself into his throat so that he could not breathe—the dark was alive, he had been wrong—

Some sound escaped him, he scarcely heard it, a stifled whimper, and Fred's hand closed suddenly over his. "There you are. Are you all right, Mordred?"

His mind seemed to come back a little, and he was mortified at the terror that had clutched and was still clutching him. He refused to let himself speak, knowing that his voice would shake. What foolishness, that the dark should be alive, he thought fiercely with that small part of him that was not blurred and drowning in panic. But how was it foolishness when the dark was so near—how could the dark be expected to be anything other than alive, no, not when it was strangling him like this—maybe it was not strangling him, but something was—

Nothing is strangling you. Stupid, childish terror. What is wrong with you?

"You are trembling, Mordred."

"I—I'm—not." He stuttered the words, his teeth chattering against one another as though in a winter's storm.

"Mordred, what is it?"

He gave up in a half-sob. "I—I can—not—see."

"I cannot see either. But I am here, Mordred. I am right beside you." Fred's other hand found Mordred's. "Fear not."

He shuddered and found his body quieting. "Fred—I do not want to die in here."

"There is the barest chance that you will not." Sam's voice cut dry through the stillness. "Did you not hear what they were saying as we climbed up here?"

"Who?" Fred asked.

"Our captors seem to be launching an assault upon some unwelcome visitors. Of course I cannot speak to who they are, but the word 'hranehka' does translate to 'general', and there are few enough generals in the north of Legea that Runiz desires to wreak his vindictiveness upon."

He paused, and added, "Not that I recommend hope. It is likely enough that they will die."

"Then why did you choose to tell us?" Fred asked.

"Because," said Sam, "you are the sort that would like to hope all the same."

~

The pine needles were unexpectedly muffling. As many as they were, still there was small sound beyond the whiffling of the horses' breath and the clink of harness. Inspector Dickson watched the carpet pass by underfoot, the drab umber-brown tinged with red as the first filaments of sun reached it.

As he lifted his eyes again to the forest, the general leaned towards him and spoke his name.

Inspector Dickson turned. "Aye?"

"We should have been there by now." His gaze moved from side to side, roving over the trees.

"We are there." Inspector Dickson stretched out a finger sharply to a smoored fire, and more beyond it. Severed stumps thinned the proud forest, a few rude wooden shelters lay under the arching boughs, and a straight face of rock rose up half a furlong away, forcing an abrupt end to the trees. "We are there. They were here last night. Where are they?"

The general slowly dismounted and took a step to the side, his hand still holding the bridle-rein loosely on his horse's neck. An ominous silence vibrated through the grove.

A terrible tension began to build in the back of Inspector Dickson's throat, and he opened his mouth, ready to tell his men to *turn around now*. He knew, as surely as one can know without knowing, that they had walked into a trap, that they were being waited for, that they needed to leap out of it before it closed on them.

But he was too late: only an inarticulate sound left his lips before a dark, winged thing stalked on feathered legs out of the shadow and stood before the cliff, larger than any ordinary vulture, eyes fixed on them and glittering like beads.

"Well met," it hissed, dipping its head in mock courtesy. "*Hranehka*—Dihhkson." The words left the beak strangely, an inhuman note skewing pitch and vowel. Then in an instant the bird was gone, and a thin-faced man stood in his place with dark hair loose upon his shoulders and his eyes gleaming vengefully.

"Well met, I say again," he said, taking one swift stride forward and sliding a sword from the sheath at his belt. "Come forward, little frightened *nikorss*. My thirst for blood is strong this day, and I yearn to cross blades with you."

Where were the thing's other men? Inspector Dickson could see none, though he looked all about the werevulture, and then a horrible thought came to him, the trees—

"Dismount! Duck! Take cover!" he shouted before something knocked him sideways off his horse and he hit the ground head-first. He tasted blood and collapsed senseless.

~

Chaos erupted on all fronts, and man after man met in combat. But the general and the werevulture stood silently looking on one another, and each knew the other, and there was silent, grim hatred between them. And, inevitable and unspoken, there was a death.

They came towards one another in the melee, sword pointed against sword, and halted while the conflict ebbed and flowed about them but did not touch them.

"I thought I would have your blood back at the ridge and the landslide, *hranehka-moz*," said the werevulture softly, "but it is better this way."

The tips of their blades hovered mere inches apart, drawing nearer, but not yet locked; and they wavered and drew back.

"Fearest thou to strike first?" taunted the werevulture.

"This is not the place for empty words," said the general, his face tense and guarded as he watched the werevulture. And strangely, Runiz nodded to his rebuke.

"It is not," he said. "Tell me, why did you come, *hranehka-moz*? What foolish honor of men bound you to seek out one peasant boy at peril of your life?"

The roaring mesh of fighting sounded all around them, and the general's eyes looked keenly into Runiz'. "You know, I think, and I know, that he is not a peasant boy. But that is not why I seek him, *thangrisser*. Tell me, why do you seek to understand the affairs of men? You cannot grasp them, for it is what you cursed yourself unto."

"You men," said the werevulture, and the steely set of anger was in his eye. "Ye think that ye are that much better than the *kakirkiss*, but ye need not even the help of the *kakirkiss* to war against yourselves! There is division among you, discord, abominations; ye hate your own kin. We the *kakirkiss* are the better in this regard. We kill not one another. We were meant to rule this world."

"So you say, and yet it was not given to you, nor did you make it," said the general. "Would you set yourself against the one who did?"

"Words easy for you to parrot," said Runiz harshly, "for they are in your favor."

"Enough," said the general, his eye glinting. "We will get no further with words."

And they met with a clash of swords that rang loud and fell amid the battle-strife.

~

Inspector Dickson blacked out only for an instant. A second more, and he would have been dead. Groggy with returning consciousness, he rolled over by some instinct and heard the *ssst!* of a knife driving into the earth where he had been.

His eyes blinked, and he saw a bearded, snarling face looming up over him, while at the same time his hand fumbled helplessly for his own knife. For sickening seconds he could not seem to grasp the handle. Then he swept it out and swung wildly at his opponent's head. That gave him enough time to scramble up to his feet, and after that he got a level head back and managed well. He had trained well with the knife, and it was a long one with a blade near three feet; with such close fighting as this, he was not disadvantaged.

The bothersome thought remained that someone might stab him in the back at any time, but that was not a matter that one could do anything about.

Inspector Dickson had never spared a moment to attempt commanding his men, save for that one instant before the battle started, and it summed up well anything he would have said afterwards. It was a strange fight. The werevulture's men did not appear to be under structured orders. They behaved as those trained in stealth, not open combat; they fought warily, retreating and slipping away when they were outmatched, leaping out of a shadow to take one by surprise. So it was man against man, each for himself, and Inspector Dickson had not the faintest idea whether it were going well for his side or not. The world was full only of avoiding one enemy, facing down another, darting behind a tree to catch a breather of scarcely a moment before someone found him again.

Then there fell a strange lull in the clamor, as will happen at times. Inspector Dickson, who was not so ignorant as to think that this was the end of it, merely took the moment to catch a gasping breath and wipe his sweating forehead. Through the trees and people he glimpsed two men bent in swift, relentless combat.

They had not halted at the lull. Indeed, Inspector Dickson began to wonder if the quiet had come because of them, because, although the fray began to pick up again, it was not as loud or as fierce as before. As he recognized the two opposing figures, he felt the hand of doom touch his heart, and knew that the outcome depended on them . . .

He watched, and watched, until the fighting caught him and carried him away again, but he could not tell who was nearer, or which fighter had the upper hand.

~

How they fight!

It is like mirrors turned against the sun, and sparks striking on metal. A curious thing to watch.

One of them must die.

Ridgrua surveyed the warring pair, man and werevulture, from where he lay on his unobtrusive tree-limb above the melee.

The werevulture will die. He fights for his life; the Ordenian fights for more lives, and not his own.

Ridgrua nodded, the satisfaction growing in him as his own shrewd guesses proved themselves. Few could have seen how the tide's balance began to shimmer and turn, but it was happening, slowly, it was happening.

Ridgrua cared not; he was an assassin, bound to his master, true, but that might change in a moment and Ridgrua would be none the worse. There was only the last thing that he had bidden him do, and Ridgrua was not averse to carrying that out.

The balance was still shifting, gaining; it might change yet, but the chance was small. It was time to go, if he were to go at all. Ridgrua slipped down from the tree easily and headed for the quarry, turning a knife in his palm.

Only one person saw him go.

CHAPTER 29

THE WIND BREATHED GENTLY THROUGH pinnacles and knobs of rock. Somewhere in the world the sun shone brightly, but it was always dim in the quarry. Shadows thick and sleepy covered Ridgrua's path, and he slunk from one to the other with the keen, cool grace of the assassin on his commission.

"If I should die, the prisoners must not live. Kill them; make it quick or slow, as you please and have the time; only do not let it be too painless . . . "

Ridgrua smiled, and rubbed one hand reflectively over the knife sheathed against his thigh. He could do that.

The cave waited above him, its entrance sealed. He sprang catlike onto the ledge in the wall and began to prise away the stones.

~

They had been in the dark a long time. Two hours? Three?

A low, scraping sound made Fred start. Mordred's hands jumped in his convulsively. It came again, cautious, menacing, and suddenly a chink of dusky light broke the blackness.

More rocks left, seized and torn away by gauntleted hands, but no face ever showed itself in the widening gap. Fred looked at Mordred, saw echoed in his widening gray eyes the hope that he himself could not suppress.

Then a body slid through the opening and landed easily on its feet, the face half in deep shadow, but no longer obscured against the direct light. Something flashed, something that he tossed and caught again, and he was smiling.

"Ridgrua." It was Sam who spoke. "What is the werevulture's pleasure today?"

Ridgrua's smile broadened momentarily, as though he thought that remark one of particular amusement. Then it vanished into a dispassionate calm. "My lord the werevulture orders you all slain."

There was dead silence.

"I do not take kindly to that idea," said Sam.

"Like it or no, it has been ordered," replied Ridgrua with a shrug. "I think I will do you first."

Sam seemed to consider this. "I am of half a mind to deprive you of the pleasure by rolling away and letting you put your blade where I am not."

Ridgrua snorted. "I could pin you against the wall now."

Mordred's hand had gone cold in Fred's when Ridgrua announced his purpose. Now unexpectedly he tore himself loose, staggered to his feet, and lunged across at Ridgrua, bringing them both down in a tangle. A startled grunt burst from the assassin, and he began to curse in a mixture of languages. He wrested Mordred down and rose with a leap, kicking him twice.

"Stupid, hopeless try," he said. "An infant would have known better."

Mordred started to pick himself up painfully, and at the look in his eye Fred knew—

"No, Mordred, please," he whispered.

Mordred threw himself a second time at Ridgrua. This time the man's fist snapped up and struck Mordred on the side of the face;

Mordred lurched sideways with a stifled cry and lay on the stone, swallowing back sobbing breaths.

"That was even worse," said Ridgrua in disgust. "Do you want to die first instead?"

Mordred's jaw locked and he lifted burning, set eyes to Ridgrua's. "I care not what you do to me."

"We will see about that." Ridgrua gave a laugh deep in the throat and traced the edge of his knife.

~

Inspector Dickson's arms shook with weariness. The knife seemed like a king's ransom in his hand. He had driven himself long past the point when he thought he could not go on. Hours of unremitting fighting, real, unbroken, solid hours, had brought him into an exhaustion that he had not known could exist.

Their sides were more evenly matched than he had guessed. If it lasted much more, Inspector Dickson thought drily, they would all simply fall down too drained to swing another stroke.

But he knew that such a humorous situation would not occur. Nay, there were some still who would have strength left, if only to pick off the ones who could fight no more.

For now, he fought on.

His present adversary backed away, dashed behind a tree, and left Inspector Dickson with a moment to breathe. He heaved in a long, shuddering sigh and lowered his burning arm and saw yet another man coming at him, burly and strong of build, with cold eyes as pale as a winter's dawn and hair and beard blown and tousled awry by the long day's struggle.

He pointed his sword-blade at Inspector Dickson. "I am Gorstir of Glumintor, second to the werevulture, Inspector."

"I do not care," returned Inspector Dickson, and it was perfectly true. In that moment he thought of simply dropping his knife and letting the man kill him.

He did not. He brought it up in a ward of defense; his arm felt thick and useless.

"You might as well give up now. You are weary, too weary to fight me off. Put down the weapon and I will make your end quick."

A hot anger that was almost outrage fired unexpectedly in him, waking him a little from the stupor clouding his head. "What nonsense," he growled, clenching his hand tighter around the knife. "Let you kill me? I am not that dim-witted, Gorstir of Glumintor."

"Then you will die by my hand all the same," said Gorstir, and he attacked.

Inspector Dickson was retreating almost at once. Gorstir breathed raggedly and advanced with the ponderous thrusts of an aging bull, but he was fresher or tougher than Inspector Dickson, who found himself able to do little beyond block his cuts. Back he went, back, back, holding him off desperately, and he was afraid; and the fear could make him no weaker, so instead it lent him strength. But it was not enough strength, and he still retreated.

Once he saw, in a brief, vivid flash over Gorstir's shoulder, the werevulture and the general, and they were almost neck to neck, blade striving against blade, and the werevulture was faltering. And then all at once where a man's shape had been there was a blur of gray and black feathers that launched itself at the general, and they fell and disappeared from his sight.

And he felt for the first time a very clear-headed, hard despair.

He looked at Gorstir as the man raised his sword with the glimmer of triumph in his eye. The anger built in him again, now tempered with the despair, channeled and concentrated to a point.

He sprang forward under the cut of the sword and buried his knife in Gorstir's stomach. "He shall not have *everything*," he uttered between his teeth.

He withdrew his bloodied blade, and Gorstir reeled and plunged earthward. Inspector Dickson sank to his knees and bowed his head on the pommel of his knife, beyond caring, pain, or tears.

~

Jared had seen the dark shadow flit away from the tree. It was so silent, so invisible, that he almost might have thought it an animal; but the shape was a man.

He should have thought nothing of it; should have turned back to the battle, but there was something so secretive in that fleeting movement, so peculiarly purposeful.

He did not want to fight; he did not know how, not well anyway. They had only shoved a sword into his hands before the battle lest he find himself defenseless. And so Jared put up the old, notched blade, and followed.

He trailed him up to the cleft where he had seen him disappear, a low gully that broadened out into a huge scoop in the earth dotted with masses of rock. And from there he almost thought he had lost him.

But then he found the black figure again, worming up a rock face and gaining footing on a ledge; and he hurried after him, picking his way with difficulty through the boulders. He disliked the place, feeling as if any moment it would come crashing on him, and so he hurried the quicker; but before he even reached the cliff, the man had disappeared inside a little cave.

Jared was beginning to feel the danger of his situation. He knew neither why the man had gone into the cave nor what might be inside it, and had no surety that he would be able to enter it or even look in without being caught. Yet something impelled him to go on, perhaps a subverted recklessness, perhaps simply a wish to see through what he had started. He walked the little, steep path up to the ledge, and crouched behind the piled rocks, edging his head up until he was looking in.

What he saw froze him where he was.

Fred Thorne—a wasted, dulled Fred, his deep brown eyes hollow, sorrowful, and desolate. Mordred hurling himself against the dark-clothed, armed man and staggering backwards as a ringing slap connected with his face. There was a third man further back that he did not recognize, even more emaciated and ill-looking than they, but he was of little note to Jared.

"Do you want to die first instead?"

Jared did not move. He did not breathe. The first horror had passed, and his steady mind was in control now.

He must not move, not yet. If he were seen, then it was all up. All that Jared had seen of the stranger warned him that if he leaped suddenly onto him, he would not last a second. And yet—and yet he must do something, soon, *now*, for the man was bending over Mordred and his knife was shining and rising high.

Jared had never attempted the thing he did. He never thought his hands would be so steady as he closed them firm around the rock and lifted it gently from the ground. He would not have thought he could heft it so easily, aiming as though he were his twelve-year-old self shying pebbles at the crows.

He let fly, and he knew it would miss before it struck, and so he was already bending down, snatching up another. When he straightened and flung it, the man had already whirled; it caught him in the face.

Jared shut his eyes, but he could not block the crunch.

It echoed hideously in his ears as he climbed in and knelt by Mordred, saying in an almost-steady voice, "I didn't quite mean for it to happen that way."

"Does it matter?" Mordred asked with a small smile, laying a thin, gentle hand on Jared's arm.

"Is he dead?" asked the third man coolly from the corner.

"I do not know," Jared answered.

"Sam," said Mordred softly, "don't bother him."

"He went down without a sound, at any rate," said Sam. "That is something in our favor."

"The fighting is still going on," said Jared. "If he had made a sound, it would have mattered little."

"Jared." It was Fred who spoke. "Whence came you—were you with the fighting then?"

"Aye." Jared stared at his hands, and felt that they ought to be trembling, but they were not.

"Jared." Mordred sounded dazed, or very tired. "Do you think they—your side—will win?"

"That I do not know," said Jared simply.

"What if they do not, and the werevulture returns here?"

"Then when he does, he shall find me with you."

"You . . . cannot do that. He will kill you."

Death seemed to matter very little to Jared right now, in the company of three men who looked like they might be on the brink of death and one close at hand who might have passed already. "I cannot leave you alone now that I have saved you. Is there anything that I can do for you?"

Mordred shook his head. "See that . . . that Fred is all right. Do something for Sam, if you can . . . he's had a cruel time of it." His words were murmuring into one another with drowsiness.

"And you, Mordred?"

"I'm—" He roused himself, and made a valiant attempt at his old, wide smile. "I'm all right. Truly. He never got me with the knife."

Jared lightly touched the bruises, but said nothing.

"Jared," said Mordred.

"Aye?"

"I didn't kill him."

"I know that. We all know it. I am ashamed I ever thought it, Mordred."

Something tight and painful in Mordred's face eased and he lay quiet, his eyes drifting closed. The battle-sound did not reach them here, and the cave was still. Only a robin whistled close by in the trees.

If they did die here, thought Jared, it was not a poor place to do it in.

~

"Inspector Dickson! Look!" One of his men was tugging urgently at him. "Look, sir! It's a wonderful, terrible sight—"

Inspector Dickson lifted his head and rose swaying to his feet. He saw at once what Holt meant—it was wonderful, in the ceaseless, deathlike glory of it, and it was terrible.

The general and the werevulture lay struggling upon the forest floor. The creature was in its bird-form and it emitted sounds of hissing and gurgling, darting with beak, slashing with claws. Feathers were strewn on the ground about. The general had no weapon in his hands; his sword and the werevulture's lay forgotten, useless. A dagger gleamed on the scrabbled earth nearer, but that, too, he had lost.

"When will it end?"

He did not realize he had murmured the words aloud until moments afterwards. Holt did not answer, and they stood silent side by side; the fighting as a whole was not near them.

Then the werevulture arched its head back and with a howling shriek drove downwards; but his aim failed, for the general threw himself to the side and the beak only grazed along his shoulder.

Now he lay flat on his back, his arms outstretched on either side of him, and the werevulture perched itself on his chest with a triumphant cry. To Inspector Dickson's surprise the general made no further attempt to defend himself, and he realized with a sick, shaken horror that he must be dazed or badly wounded.

The werevulture opened its beak wide and lunged down towards the general's throat.

And the general brought up his right hand, the one that Inspector Dickson had not seen, and the dagger glinted bright in it. There was a flash, and a horrible bubbling scream that pierced the length and breadth of the grove.

Then the werevulture ceased to move. And all the fighting ground slowly to a halt.

~

The general rose from the werevulture's body. His hands were bloody; his face was grim and fey, and in his eye a look to quail at. His gaze traveled over the men who had all ceased their struggles at the awful death-cry, and he spoke, his voice like the ring of thunder. "Lay down your arms."

Silence prevailed in the time that it might take a man to count to ten.

Then out of the men stepped Hopheg son of Gethem, and he laid down his sword. "Let you do with me as you will, lord," he said soberly, and he knelt and bowed his head.

At that two men ran; but as for the others, all weapons fell to the ground.

So it ended.

END PART TWO

PART THREE

Wounds Not Mortal Are Still Wounds

CHAPTER 30

INSPECTOR DICKSON SAT ON THE earth floor, watching unseeingly the candle flame's swelling, dancing pattern on the wall. They had taken the wooden huts for shelter that night.

For a few moments he had known the heady, joyous savor of victory—for a few blinding, disbelieving moments there as the werevulture perished and their enemies yielded. But after that came so much else to handle, to learn, and some of it had been very hard to bear . . .

They had found Fred and Mordred easily enough with Jared's help, though when he had found them, Inspector Dickson did not know—and with them, to Inspector Dickson's shock, Sam.

The scenes played themselves out in his head. How Fred had stumbled up, saying in relief, "There you are, Jared." How he had bent his head to Inspector Dickson with a quiet "Sir". Inspector Dickson, ashamed and almost hurt, took his arm at once and told him to sit down.

And how Mordred had met Inspector Dickson's eyes, and jerked them away with a violent tremor, his jaw clenching tight.

Inspector Dickson relived the moment, over and over, and around a little core of hurt he began to feel the slow grate of resentment.

"Sir." It was Holt, the door creaking open for him.

Inspector Dickson looked up. "All the prisoners contained safely and under guard?"

"Aye, sir."

"You think we'll be able to handle them all right?"

"I think so, sir. They seemed mightily terrified by the general and the way he spoke, and to tell the truth, sir, looking at him then, I don't blame them. There was something not to cross in his face. We can't expect that fear to last, of course, but they should stay subdued enough. They're no longer armed, and we're near as many as they."

He nodded. "And what about our prisoners—the ones we rescued?"

"They're sleeping, sir. They look to make it all right."

"Very good; then that's all, Holt. Sleep well."

"Thank you, sir." Holt withdrew and shut the door, leaving Inspector Dickson alone again with his thoughts.

Selwyn was gone. That was perhaps the hardest thing of all—young, quiet Will Selwyn, with his rock-hard sense and unusual maturity, his ready deference and winsome attitude.

Holt had caught him again sometime after everything was over, in the strange muddle of trying to sort friend from foe and get all the Claw men corralled into one place. Everyone, even himself, was moving in a daze, they were all so bone-tired.

"Sir, there's ten of theirs dead, if you count the werevulture. Another couple are wounded bad enough that they're like to die before morning."

"And how did ours fare?"

"Handra's the worst off; he got cut right through the calf, and a spear took him alongside the ribs, but he'll live. Oth and Selwyn are dead . . . "

Inspector Dickson had nodded, taking it quietly, knowing it would hurt much more later.

Now it hit him full-on, and he leaned forward and buried his head in his hands, an empty ache squeezing his heart. Yet he could not weep, only whisper to the silent room, "What shall I tell his father?"

He lay down but could not sleep for the whipping, swaying candle's flame. He pinched it out and gazed up into darkness.

I saw it through to the end.

I did not think the end would be like this.

~

Four days later they reached Bulca.

Inspector Dickson dismounted at the door of the little cottage, having sent Holt on with the prisoners, and knocked.

Harris opened it with a lazy "Yes . . . " that died on his lips as he stared at Inspector Dickson in surprise and some unconcealed relief.

"Dickson!" he exclaimed. "How are you? Look a bit thinner than when you went away. Warrant you haven't been getting your sleep."

He glanced towards the others behind Inspector Dickson. "And you've brought all your friends back. They look as gloomy as you. Come on in, old sourface."

~

Mordred rubbed the reins between his fingers, feeling a complete lack of interest as the two Inspectors talked. He was still tired, even after four days, and the world seemed far more blank and worthless than it had even while he was captured. There was nothing to do, nothing to say, nothing to delight in.

A stir was happening behind Inspector Harris, two figures coming out the door. Mordred's breath caught in a painful whimper, and something awoke sharply inside him. He slipped down from the horse.

Laufeia rushed into his arms, soundlessly weeping, and the pain grew in his chest, swelling higher and higher until it crashed like a wave and left gentle warmth in its place, and he let his tears fall against her hair.

He turned to Fenris, and the pang shot through him again, tearing at him, opening up places long sealed. "*Fenris,*" he uttered and caught his brother fiercely, holding him with all the strength of the love that he had suppressed so long in desperation.

"Fenris," he said again and again, clutching his brother, needing him, the tears flowing endlessly, all the torturous memories finally beginning to fade.

"I'm right here, Mordred."

Laufeia slipped her arm under his and stroked her hand along his back. "We are all here."

~

Inspector Dickson rode to the gaol that day, and came back again in the evening. All that time, he knew what he was going to do. It was the thing that must be done, the thing he had never had a chance to do before Fred had disappeared, and the thing that must now more than ever be said.

He found him sitting alone—he was grateful for that—in the little living room, his hands over one knee and his quiet eyes looking into the fire. He seemed at peace, and in the dim light the remaining traces of his captivity were little apparent.

"Fred Thorne."

Fred looked at him, and made a movement.

"No, please." Inspector Dickson flung up a hand. "Do not get up now. You ought to rest. I merely wished to speak briefly with you."

"Speak on," Fred answered simply.

"The last time we spoke at length, I thought you a murderer and named you such, and I laid harsh and unkind accusations at your door. If you can, tell me that you do not hold these things against me."

Fred rose, and came and placed his hands on Inspector Dickson's shoulders. "You did what you thought right. I have never held it against you and I do not now."

Inspector Dickson's heart bowed, and he was ashamed at such unrestrained generosity. Returning the gesture, he met Fred's eyes. "Sir, I thank you. It is in me that—that I could not have done as much in your place."

"You have never been in it," said Fred. "Be at peace, Inspector Dickson."

~

Mordred, too, had sought solitude. He was in the room where he and Fred had slept that first night, lying among the disarray of a makeshift bed, on his stomach, his eyes open and awake.

Inspector Dickson cleared his throat, and Mordred sprang to his feet as quickly as if an arrow had been fired over him. His face stiffened and grew very cold.

Inspector Dickson did not know what to say, at all. What came out was, "I suppose you will be leaving soon."

Mordred's attitude said, *What is it to you?* Aloud, it was, "Yes. Tomorrow."

He did not know why he had begun this. Fred's answer had given him hope, and he had foolishly thought that, maybe . . .

He made one last try. "I was glad to see you safely reunited with your sister and brother. It is good to see Laufeia smiling."

"Keep your eyes off my sister."

Inspector Dickson stared at him, dumb with shock and outrage. That Mordred would dare pretend he meant—!

"I do not want any woman, least of all any sister of yours," he gritted between his teeth. "But if compassion must be construed as amorous intent—"

"You will pardon me if I have not managed to form a very high opinion of you, baseless, incompetent, prejudiced—"

The color was building in Inspector Dickson's face, fury, contempt, and absolute hatred driving him to the brink. In another moment he would lose control, he *would* strike that foul-mouthed, arrogant face that dared to blame him for everything that was not his fault.

Strike him—suddenly he saw his own hand flashing out in the dark hall of the prison, slapping the thrashing young man out of his wild panic. He took a step back, shaking from all the emotions jarring within him.

"Good night, Inspector Dickson." Mordred's eyes were a cool wall of steel.

Inspector Dickson whirled, torn between mad rage and something else, not quite knowing who he was any more. He wanted to throw things, to shatter things, and at the same time he wanted to break down and weep.

Let them go. Let them leave. Then you can forget about this.

Oh, how he wanted to forget it all.

CHAPTER 31

INSPECTOR DICKSON SAT BACK, IDLY handling his mug. He had had a late breakfast—what came of sleeping four hours past dawn. The front door was open, and the scent of outdoors and of burgeoning spring reached his nose.

"Inspector Wilhelm Dickson," said a calm, carrying, emotionless voice, and Sam stood in the doorway to the next room. He was dressed in nondescript but clean and well-tended attire now; and though he walked stiffly and his lineaments were still worn and fleshless, it was the old Sam, poised and in command, that Inspector Dickson saw.

"I thought," said Sam, leaning slightly against the door-frame, "that you might like to have some answers."

"A-answers?" He stuttered the word, astonished.

"I am a member of the information gatherer's branch of the Rehirnish law enforcement. My acquaintance with Claude of Croth Dale, while he lived, was for the purpose of gleaning information on the Claw. My searching was just beginning to yield fruit when he died, and I had begun to suspect that the band was headed by a werevulture.

"I could not tell you all this before, as I am bound to secrecy in all matters pertaining to my commission; but I told you what I could, and hoped that you would make the best of it. I also sent to my superiors, requesting permission to relay to you what I knew. A letter reached me granting that permission, at the same time as another letter which confirmed my suspicions as to the nature of the Claw's leader, but that very night I was taken captive, and thus had no opportunity to send to you."

Inspector Dickson felt the need to take a deep breath. "I . . . I am more indebted to you than I knew."

Sam shrugged dismissively. "What is done, let it be."

"And what—what, if I may ask, is your full name? Or is Sam your name at all?"

The barest trace of a smile flickered over Sam's face. "I said that I was going to give you some answers, not all answers. Some secrets are my own, sir; and my own secrets, I keep."

With that he turned and walked out the door of the house. Inspector Dickson never saw him again.

~

They were not traveling back with the general.

"I must take the dragons again to Mitheren, and furthermore they have been long without me there." His dark eyes held Mordred's keenly, measuring him. "I will see you again, when you return."

Mordred bent his head, not understanding, yet his heart quickened. "My general."

The general smiled and touched him upon the shoulder; and he mounted and rode away, Inspector Dickson at his side, for Inspector Dickson was traveling with him as far as Addis Muard.

Mordred's chin set hard, and he felt the black anger lapping slowly in him. He pushed it away. They were going home, and he need never see or think of Inspector Dickson again.

But there was so much pain inside him, and he did not know if it would ever heal . . .

No. No. It must heal. There was nothing wrong, not any more. It would be all right.

"Mordred?" Laufeia was looking anxiously at him, a line frowning up between her light, delicate brows.

He steadied his face and smiled. "Ready to go home, little sister?"

Her face relaxed into a glad answering smile. "Yes, Mordred."

~

Inspector Dickson put out a hand and gave the blunt, leathery nose a tentative caress. "So these are Ordenian dragons."

"Not as fair or intelligent as the wild ones, perhaps, the true dragons," said the general with a smile, "but not as dangerous either. These will not kill you if you give them an insult, nor incinerate your house if you give them brass instead of gold."

Inspector Dickson looked at the long, dark-gray lizard-bodies, the lazy tails curving on the grass, the enormous expanse of wing folded snugly against the body. Their necks arched proud as a horse's, and the one beside him puffed lightly. "Do they breathe fire at all?"

"Nay, they are not gifted in that either. Whatever poor man called these things dragons, he must have lived under a rock all his life." The light smile still wormed its way at the edges of his lips, and he gave a loving pat to the neck of the far one. "They are fair creatures in their own way, and they will cover ground seven times faster than an army on the march."

Inspector Dickson was not disagreeing in the least. "As an animal, they are a great sight indeed. I wonder that more countries do not use them."

The general laughed. "Well, that is a long story and full of politicians, but the main fact distilled is this: it is very difficult to maintain a number of dragons. They must have meat, and a great deal of it, and they do poorly in the colder seasons without proper housing; moreover, their breeding age is short. Jealously does Orden guard her dragons. Indeed, if it were noised that I had left mine unattended for three weeks in a Rehirnish town, I think I should find myself facing disapproval from many quarters."

Inspector Dickson found himself laughing in answer. "They shall not hear it from me, my lord!"

The general's eyes were still glimmering with humor as he sprang into the saddle and gathered both bridles, the dragons' wingspans opening dark and broad against the sky with a clap of wind. Against the frayed, sleepless memories of the last two months, that single steady moment seemed to outlast them, a promise of permanence and an end of shadow.

CHAPTER 32

THE DAYS GOING UP THE Dirion River were warm, pleasant, placid. The air began to nip a little after the fourth day, as they drew level with the broad dark feet of the Elerien Mountains, but still the sun shone and the brisk breeze was invigorating rather than chilling.

"Spring is coming up here, too," Laufeia said, leaning on the boat-rail and looking out at the odd patch of snow along the banks.

"Slowly," said Jared, looking ahead to where the drifts were still deep.

Mordred and Fred were quickly regaining their strength; Mordred would not stand to be confined below all day but walked about on deck, resting at intervals and breathing in the clean, wind-blown air. His dark hair, whipped about, grew tangled, and Laufeia secured a pair of scissors, sat him down firmly, and trimmed it close again.

On the sixth day, the boat left the Dirion River for the Zarethir, and sailed between the giant slopes of the mountains into Orden. On the seventh, they docked at the south edge of Orden City and stood on familiar ground, looking at a familiar, flat-topped mountain with broad, still-whitened slopes.

Mordred, looking at it, began to think of all that was waiting for him there: work, the small thatch-roofed house, the old barn nearby it that they might repair when spring came; Therelane, soft-spoken and earnest, and Braegon's bright flashing grin; a whole close-knit village that he realized suddenly was home.

A measure of peace filled him. He had not felt such peace for months.

~

"Is the stew ready yet, Sandy?"

"It won't go any the faster for your asking."

Isabelle spun around crossly, a hand on her hip. "Is it or isn't it?"

"It'll be done by the time Daren gets here, and that should be enough for you."

The air in the little kitchen was dull and ill-tempered. Even Cecelia's quiet, slender fingers, knitting steadily, seemed to pull the yarn more tightly than usual.

Daren felt it as he came in, and his shoulders slumped in a dispirited sigh. Fred would have been able to right things, but Fred was not here. And was that not half the trouble? Since the dreadful word had come from Mordred of the murder accusation, and Laufeia and Fenris had departed, they had waited desperately for more word. But no word came, and the strain gnawed at them until the littlest utterance could spark a quarrel.

The stew was not ready, and this made Sandy more defensive and Isabelle even more angry. Words were flying like hail when the door opened.

Daren, sitting at the table, waiting for the meal to be set with his head in his hands, did not notice. None of them did until Gwenda's small, clear voice said, "Fred."

And Daren spun around and saw his older brother standing in the doorway, visibly thinner than when he had departed, his eyes looking as though he had seen an age of the world and come out of it in peace. Gwenda's head rested against him; his lean, strong-boned hand came up to cradle it.

"You have grown taller, Gwenda," he said affectionately, wonderingly, and his eyes lifted to travel over them all.

Sandy's nose had gotten red, very red, and she was blinking hard, but one tear slid out of her brimming eyes and trailed down her nose. Another followed, and more and more until she gave up trying to stop them and dashed with a sob into Fred's arms.

"I'm sorry, Fred—oh, Fred—I missed you—but I shouldn't have been so horrible to Isabelle, I—oh—"

At that Isabelle dissolved into the rag she had been holding.

Cecelia did not weep; she was never one to weep, but she let her knitting fall from trembling fingers and rose, her hazel eyes grave and wide with fullness. "Welcome," she said in her clear, lilting voice.

"Welcome," repeated Daren. "Welcome, my brother."

Fred looked from one to the other of them with a growing, joyous smile. "It is good to come home," he said. And he stepped over the threshold.

~

Jared walked swiftly; there was much to meet him when he arrived. He knew what he must do, and what he must own, and strangely he felt no fear for it, only a peculiar urgency to have it done.

He met the figure at a crossroads and did not recognize him—it was twilight—but as he passed on the man spoke behind him. "Why, Jared, you're back!"

Jared knew the voice, and the snide, goading tone. He turned, and said gravely, "Well met, Gallert Boccin."

He regarded Gallert with a certain soberness and detachment. He felt no malice toward him, no anger; only indifference, if the quiet disinterest he had could even be called that. As he looked at Gallert and thought of his old taunts and poison, he saw Mordred's anguished, white face, Rivra and the sand dunes and the arrows whistling past his own head, the werevulture and the general circling one another, his friends at the mercy of the armed assassin—the things that mattered. And he saw, clearly, how none of his struggles with Gallert had ever mattered.

"I hope you had a good time while you were away," said Gallert in the sort of tone that was anticipating an opposite answer.

"There were good times," said Jared, thinking of his aunt's brood of small, happy children. "Good night, Gallert Boccin."

The house loomed up at him finally, of a pleasantly familiar shape, welcoming. He reached the door, came in, and shut it behind him. Dinner was over; his mother was darning, nodding her head and murmuring to herself; Lia lay sprawled in front of the fire, blonde hair all tumbled over her shoulders and down her back.

Jared addressed himself to the man who had stood at once, the gentle face lighting in an uncommon show of emotion at his son's return. "Father."

~

A warm wind was coming up from the south and wafting over the slopes of Mount Thiranu. The eaves dripped, and in the clouded afternoon, a dragon banked in the sky and landed before the Kenhelm house.

Laufeia opened the door, and stood quickly aside to let the visitor in. "Mordred!" she called, but the general had already gone into the other room and Mordred had risen to greet him.

"I thought that I might find you returned now," said the general, unclasping his heavy cloak and laying it across his arm. "And that you might not yet have rejoined the castle work as yet."

"That is Laufeia's doing, not mine," said Mordred with a flicker of stubbornness.

"You journeyed safe and well, I trust?" the general said.

"Aye."

And they spoke on little matters, this and that, and eventually Laufeia departed to start supper and they were alone.

The general rose again. "I must be away," he said quietly. "Mordred, will you come out with me?"

Mordred came.

They went out into the clean, enlivened air, and the general turned to study Mordred. "Look at me, Mordred Kenhelm," he said.

Mordred lifted clear eyes to his unafraid. And the general looked at him again long.

"If I said all that is on my heart," he said at last with a sigh, "it would be too much. Know this, Mordred, that this trial has tempered you, and I think that good will yet come of it."

Mordred's gaze faltered. The pain was surfacing.

The general touched his shoulder for an instant. "You are a man of great courage, Mordred Kenhelm," he said gently.

"Thank you, my general." Mordred spoke very softly.

"I say it, and I mean it wholly: understand me so. And yet—" The general in his turn hesitated, his dark eyes probing, deep, sorrowful. "Not all courage is with bodily pain and suffering."

Mordred looked away. "No man ever called you a murderer," he said in a low, hard voice.

Silence touched them.

Then Mordred raised his head and spoke quietly. "Forgive me that I said that, my general."

The general smiled. "We will speak no more of it." He turned to mount, and the dragon lifted its head, eager to fly. "Farewell, Mordred Kenhelm. May we meet again."

~

Memories. He began to think he would never be rid of them.

It had been days. It had been *weeks*. Would he have to wait a year before a day came when Mordred's face did not appear mockingly in his mind?

"Dickson."

"Not right now," he muttered.

"Dickson! The man at the door wants you!"

Inspector Dickson leaped up and headed for Harris' voice. "What do you mean? Who is it who wants me?" He stopped, staring at the owlish-faced man on the door-step who was garbed in the king's colors.

The herald flourished a long parchment and declared, "The King of Delgrass, his Most Gracious Majesty, has summoned Inspector Wilhelm Dickson of the Northern Riverside Precinct to appear before him in one week's time, on April the ninth."

"Why?" asked Inspector Dickson blankly.

The herald shrugged and turned, slamming the door shut.

"One week?" Inspector Dickson repeated, sputtering. "April the ninth—that's barely three days from now!"

"He was reading the paper," Harris pointed out sensibly. "It would have been a week when that was written."

Inspector Dickson heaved a sigh, and headed for the kitchen to pull together a parcel of food. The king had summoned him, and like it or not, he would have to go.

He hoped that it had nothing to do with the Claw.

THE END

TO BE CONCLUDED IN *THE WAR*

GLOSSARY OF WEREVULTURE TERMINOLOGY

moz: man, human

ihssa: derogatory term, implies youth and immaturity

nikorss: humankind, men, the human race

kakirkiss: the werevultures' name for themselves

eglikha egiss zahruniz: idiomatic insult, difficult to render; the closest sense is "grave of graves," i.e. the most rotted, decayed thing that could exist

khissta kkhavfa: hateful and miserable [The werevulture is repeating the same words he had spoken in the common tongue moments before]

khhavfa-eglik-risshrrith: death-house-flesh, or more colloquially, slaughter meat

hranehka: general

rikiss: werevulture expression of greatest hatred

For more information about
Verity A. Buchanan
&
The Claw
please visit:

www.verityabuchanan.com
www.facebook.com/VBuchananWrites
www.instagram.com/verityb.writes

For more information about
AMBASSADOR INTERNATIONAL
please visit:

www.ambassador-international.com
@AmbassadorIntl
www.facebook.com/AmbassadorIntl

If you enjoyed this book, please consider leaving us a review on Amazon, Goodreads, or our website.

www.ingramcontent.com/pod-product-compliance
Lightning Source LLC
LaVergne TN
LVHW020535100826
845148LV00010B/1476

* 9 7 8 1 6 4 9 6 0 2 1 2 1 *